DARKNESS BLOOMS

EDITED BY ALIN WALKER & MONICA LOUZON

FEATURING ORIGINAL FICTION BY

A. Katherine Black

Derrick Boden

Timothy Burkhardt

P.A. Cornell

Kitty-Lydia Dye

Alicia Hilton

A.P. Howell

Andrea Kriz

Nathaniel Lee

Gordon Linzner

Rodrigo Assis Mesquita

Andrew Milne

Marshall J. Moore

Josh Rountree

Denise Tanaka

Rebecca E. Treasure

Brian Trent

PUBLISHED BY THE DREAD MACHINE
www.thedreadmachine.com

ISBN 978-1-957849-10-2 (Hardcover)
ISBN 978-1-957849-01-0 (Paperback)
ISBN 978-1-957849-00-3 (Epub)

Edited by Alin Walker & Monica Louzon
Cover by Yorgos Cotronis

Published by The Dread Machine
https://www.thedreadmachine.com

Printed and bound in the United States of America.

CONTENTS

INTRODUCTION
ALIN WALKER

Welcome to *Darkness Blooms*, a labor of love that took seventeen talented writers and two dedicated editors two years to bring to print. In the spring of 2021, we issued a call for submissions, asking writers to delve into the darker aspects of three intertwined concepts: identity, security, and community. We wanted them to explore the ways darkness—fascism, war, societal collapse—can seep into our lives insidiously, silently stretching its tendrils like creeping vines, or erupt with the sudden violence of a bursting seedpod. We are thrilled to finally present this unforgettable collection, showcasing some of the most talented voices in speculative fiction.

First up, a family copes with a husband and father's temporary revival after a tragic accident, navigating the complexities of grief and the limitations of cutting-edge medical technology in **The Stages of Pre-Bereavement**.

In the walled city of **Boom Town**, citizens have implants at the base of their skulls that cause their heads to explode if they experience sinful thoughts, and sixteen-year-old Mary doesn't think she's going to last much longer.

An estranged son returns home to check on his family, raid their pantry, and confront his past after a contagious freezing virus causes society's collapse in **Thaw**.

In **Old Grief**, almost every human born suffers from hyperalgesia, requiring them to live in tightly controlled padded bunkers deep underground. Erica, a seven on the pain index, risks her marriage to bring joy to her daughters, a three and a six who will never see the sun.

In **The Stains of Now**, two survivors must prove themselves worthy of joining a new "neighborhood," a clan bunker where they can enjoy shelter and protection from the hyperpredatory monsters outside. The discovery of a perfectly preserved hidden room from the past in their personal hab ignites an obsession that threatens everything.

A prisoner sentenced to hard labor on a faraway penal planet chronicles his days by dreaming up messages he can never send to the son he'll never see again in **Hard Time**, a story about parental love that transcends time and space.

In **No More Saudades**, a man learns what he's willing to do to protect his family from a government that doesn't trust its citizens to raise loyal, productive patriots.

A sentient satellite grapples with the devastating loss of its human crew in **Solar Midnight**.

In **Three, Two, One**, an abandoned battleship must contend with a motley crew of intruders who challenge its understanding of purpose. As an unfathomable predator bears down on them all, the ship must decide whether to trust these strangers who lack the proper clearance.

Xu finds herself caught up in a rebellion against the oppressive regime that controls the living walls encircling the last city on Earth in **To Soar, Not Ever Knowing What Took You**, a story about friendship, betrayal, and genesplicing.

Welcome to the Organ Extraction Emporium, where only humans who volunteer to transform their bodies into alien form are treated as equals. You'll have to learn how to become extraterrestrial and lead a better life.

An ambitious professional hires a homeless blind man to pretend to be his dead ancestor and walk for him in a parade among masses of preserved, mechanized corpses in **A New Night Parade**.

On a planet where the **Birds** are not quite birds and the trees are not quite trees, Rennie spends his days on a Tower, scrubbing the creatures' blood off the concrete. When Hardin, one of the scientists, approaches him with a new plan to deter the birds from crashing into the Tower, Rennie agrees to help. But as they work on the machine, Rennie begins to question the morality of their mission.

An island-bound "Crew" welcome their newest recruit—a young girl, orphaned by the shipwreck they caused in **Flotsam**.

In **Correctional Memory**, criminals can have their memories permanently erased as part of their sentences. When a young detective claims Malik was set up for a crime he doesn't remember committing and offers him a chance to clear his name, he has to decide whether it's worth risking everything he has left, including his last remaining memory of his daughter.

In **The Dream and the Weaver**, Ayumi enters a dream world where she must confront her past trauma and grief with the help of Mashoka, a faulty dreamweaver. As they navigate through the twisted dreamscape, they uncover the truth behind Ayumi's pain and the mysterious Dreamer who holds the key to it all. With beautiful prose, vivid imagery, and formatting unique to each character, this story will leave you questioning the boundaries between reality and dreams.

Colonists building a peaceful, compassionate society on a tidally locked planet wracked with vicious electrical storms are afraid there might be traitors on their planet after a bombing nearly kills a recently widowed single father, in **Legacies in Light and Dark**.

Whether you are a seasoned reader of dark fiction or are exploring this genre for the first time, we hope you enjoy glimpsing into the strange worlds our writers have constructed just for you. Delve into the darkness, where the most dreadful stories bloom.

As always, thank you so much for supporting The Dread Machine.

STAGES OF PRE-BEREAVEMENT

A. P. HOWELL

"There was an accident." His eyes are wide, his face pale. You're not used to that; you think of it more as a literary convention than a physiological reaction. Yet here he stands, face pale.

It's a long moment, because the brain is resourceful and cruel. It knows that something is wrong, so very wrong. Your senses are heightened, providing you with more data. Time is, subjectively, moving slowly, providing you with the opportunity to act, to do something to avert the oncoming horror.

But there is nothing you can do.

"I died."

—

You take his hand first, and then you're both crying and hugging, tight and desperate. If you can just hold on long enough, hard enough, you can make yourselves a black hole of despair, a gravitational center of love and need, warping the reality in your vicinity, rewriting the normal laws of time and space, shaping everything around you to your desires.

But that's not how physics works, that's not how any of this works, and amid the real nightmare your brain conjures the potential (smaller) nightmare of the kids seeing you both like this. You look at him, and nod, and walk with him toward the black car parked on the street. The company representative waiting within will explain the details of the situation.

You hold hands, the way you did when you were young—but only sometimes, because when you were young you didn't have this overwhelming need for contact or an appreciation of how limited your time would be.

—

You're not a complete mess when you come back inside. You're the mommy, the strong one. (Or is it, maybe, that when you're not in his presence you have no excuse to be the weak one—no safety net, no partner who will fix everything?) He's outside, and that distance matters more than the fact that his flesh is freshly, imperfectly made. That distance gives you the strength you need to call the kids into the living room and tell them what's happened. The strength to make it through an explanation quickly, clearly, brutally, without your voice breaking too much, without dissolving into tears before they do.

There's a group hug. Three always used to count as a group hug, with no implication of loss. That will never be true again. You find yourself thinking that quite clearly, even as you talk about Daddy outside in his new body, waiting to see them but only if that's what they want. You frame it as their choice, a reflexive parenting habit, but it is not much of a choice. Of course they want their daddy.

—

It's a bonus, a blessing, a chance to wrap up loose ends, a chance to say goodbye. All the things that make sense when it's someone else. All the things that make sense when it's a classmate's grandmother or the nice old guy from down the block. All the things that make great puff pieces on the news.

All those answers make much less sense when it's Daddy (when it's your husband), who wasn't supposed to die until far off in the future. There was supposed to be more time.

There might have been less time. But for the miracle of modern medicine, an insurance program offering a benefit-slash-R&D-program,

and the luck of an intact brain near an appropriate facility, someone else would have been standing on the porch delivering a much more final message.

It's a blessing. Glass half-full.

—

His skin is soft, like the kids' used to be. You remember sitting in the rocking chair, marveling that human skin could ever be so soft, mourning that it would become rougher over time—a metaphor for the entire human condition that seemed an intolerable assault upon the sacred, perfect lives you had brought forth into the world.

You suppose the texture of his skin should be incredibly erotic or a complete turn off. Instead, it's just a thing you notice when you touch him. Like the time he gained weight, or another time he lost weight, you sometimes notice during lovemaking, but on a fundamental level you don't really care.

Have you always been so careless of his form? You suppose it's true. You just hadn't realized before. Maybe it just didn't matter before.

—

The human mind is vast and unknowable. People still talk about uploading their personalities, manufacturing an eternal substrate accessing an infinite power supply. It's a nice dream, if you don't feel too attached to the simple pleasures of the flesh.

But the vastness of the human mind shapes and is shaped by its substrate. Copy it to an artificial substrate and you get...something that is not the person, fit only to be the subject of research papers and case studies of unhappy bioethicists. Copy it into a printed body, cloned from the original, and you get the person, or so close as makes no difference. (You refuse to let it make a difference. He's back, for a little while, if changed—but everyone is changed by their experiences.)

You get the person, just not for long. The processes are new, biology complex. He's probably already got the beginnings of six different types of cancer, and flu season will be terrible. They do their best in the labs, trying to make the clones hardy, but their immune systems are no better than a newborn's.

—

There's not an exact end date. That makes it worse, you think. All the uncertainty of normal life, with the knowledge that there is arbitrarily less.

Many people set an end date. Take control over their second, permanent death.

You talk about it. You even open the calendar—the two of you together, and you alone sometimes, in the dark before bed. You're pretty sure he's thought about it alone, outside your presence, because how could he not? But there's no perfect date.

Never a right time to die.

A fledgling industry is devoted to making it feel like a life event rather than suicide, but that's just not comforting. Whatever date you might choose, there's always something coming later. Another birthday, another holiday, another soccer season, another musical. Something he will miss, because of an irrevocable decision.

You never do get around to picking a date.

—

His freckles are wrong.

You remember a night when you were in your twenties. While he slept, you silently traced the constellations of his freckles. You briefly considered drawing them or taking a photograph, but then decided that would be wrong. It was your duty and privilege to memorize this map of your lover's body.

Now you cannot remember. You stare at his back, moving rhythmically as he breathes. (You try not to think of how he must have looked when he stopped breathing. You try not to think of how it will look when he stops breathing again.) You trace a triangle of dark brown freckles, sure that at least one is missing.

You will never know for certain. His body—his original body, the one that grew in a uterus and was a baby and a child and the young man you fell in love with and the middle-aged man who kissed you goodbye on a comfortably chaotic morning—is gone, cremated, and all its secrets lost forever.

—

He pays a lot of attention to "quality time." It's a thing neither of you have been very good at, in your routine of school and work and weekends, but to a certain extent you've always considered quantity and closeness a type of quality. Fun at home, inside or in the yard, day trips...this was the satisfying rhythm of your life, now rendered hollow.

You force yourself to refrain from documenting everything, because the bike rides and video games and trips to the beach are a part of life that should be normal.

He is painfully diligent about doing these activities at every possible opportunity, and everybody tries to pretend it's not ghoulish. (Do the kids realize it's ghoulish? You could ask, but how could you do that to them, especially if the answer is no and your question disturbs some tiny bit of peace amid impending sorrow?) A dozen times you look out the window, see them in the yard, and think about how you should remember this, all of this, because it might be the last time.

You feel as though you will drown under the weight of potential last times.

———

Should you break the bank and take a trip to Europe? Visit the Pyramids and the Great Wall of China? Trek to Machu Picchu and see a live performance at the Sydney Opera House? These are things that you both had thought you'd like to do, someday, but they don't exactly rise to the level of "dreams." (The dream was living happily, raising kids, growing old together. Oh, well.)

And so you waffle, occasionally compare travel packages, wonder if you should give the kids a New Experience or if it would only be tainted by the oncoming permanent death. (You always think in terms of the kids. It's your job. Mommy has always been your most important job. Sometimes you wonder if you've subsumed your own desires to an unhealthy degree; sometimes you wonder if somehow you don't really have independent desires anymore.)

Just as you never get around to picking a date, you never get around to picking a destination.

———

There are school counselors. You encourage the kids to take advantage of them. You ask the counselors to give you referrals for outside professionals if it seems warranted, but otherwise want to keep their conversations with the kids completely confidential. This is mostly a matter of principle, but if you're honest it's also exhaustion.

You should probably see somebody, too, but just thinking about making an appointment is exhausting. And how could they help? It's not like they'd know anything about your baseline psychological state. (Does that matter anymore? It's not like you'll ever be that person again. You'll always be a widow. You'll always be the person whose family was whole, until it wasn't.)

You consider support groups, but then decide against it. You've always been shy and there's a throughline of absurdity to the situation. You can't avoid thinking about it when you see the listings for support groups formed for the families of revivees.

For all the technological trimmings, this is not a situation without precedent. You are not special. People die. People receive terminal diagnoses. People walk around, knowing that they will die, knowing that their loved ones will die, and they go about what remains of their lives. (Or don't. There are options.)

There is fundamentally nothing special about revivees. They're just the well-off recipients of cutting-edge medical care that buys them a little extra time. (But when you think of it like that, the focus on revivees makes a lot of sense. Anyone can get cancer. Revivification is much more exclusive.)

—

Eventually, you both go back to work. It's not quite a decision, nothing you discuss at length. But if you're not going to pick a date, if you're not going to travel, it's just the natural thing.

You numbly maneuver through the environment that reminds you of him. (He rarely came to your office, but everything reminds you of him.) You cannot simply retire into decades of grief, so you might as well return after the pre-bereavement leave. It doesn't feel like enough time, but you take some comfort in standardization. A bureaucratic collective has made a decision on your behalf and you are grateful that this is one thing you do not have to decide.

It makes more sense for him to go into the office than to sit around binge-watching TV all day. (Not that he hasn't done a lot of binge-watching. You know he's curating his watchlist, and has dropped some series-in-progress that may not wrap up in time. You don't talk about this.) He seems to find work comforting—he always liked his job and colleagues—and it sounds like things are not especially awkward in a professional environment.

After a while, he stops talking about the projects he's working on. You suspect his assignments have less to do with expertise and more to do with deliverable dates. Non-discrimination law is one thing, prudent project management another.

You only ask about his colleagues. They're well.

—

Sometimes, you think about dying, imagine another conversation on the porch, cloned body embracing cloned body. What an absurd situation that would be. What a legal mess that would be, everything from custody to finances. You can't even imagine what it would do to the kids. You can't imagine what it would do to him, either.

Maybe you wouldn't even be a candidate for revivification, depending on how it happened. Maybe it would be a stranger talking to him on the porch.

(You could make sure of that. If you went to the trouble of planning a suicide, it wouldn't be hard to ensure that your brain was insufficiently intact for revivification, or that you couldn't be taken to an appropriate facility within the narrow window after death.)

Part of you wishes for it to happen. You don't think about doing it, not really, but the *what if* is there. Wouldn't that be a fine sort of revenge on him for dying? Let him clean up the mess for a change.

—

Someday, maybe, the cloning procedure will be better. Maybe the clones will last longer or at least be good enough that the mind-in-the-clone can be copied into another clone. ("Photocopies of photocopies" is how they usually talk about current limitations, before quoting unhappy bioethicists.) Maybe lengthy revivification or even serial immortality will be something society can handle. (Or not. There are a lot of things society can't handle well. They happen anyway.) Maybe revivification will be widely available. (Funny, how equitable distribution of medical advances strikes you as more implausible than the procedure itself.) Maybe yours is the last generation to die.

You're resentful and relieved about that. You're going to lose him, very soon, and forever. You, yourself, are going to die someday. Maybe the kids—but you don't want to think about the kids dying. (You have never been able to keep yourself from thinking about the kids dying.) But if the natural order still basically holds, the kids will outlive you, and maybe they will live forever, or at least for a very long time.

Being the last generation to die is not so bad if it means your children are the first generation not to die.

—

You don't ask him to do any of the paperwork. It would feel far too ghoulish to make him deal with the minutiae of his death after having experienced the trauma of his death. (He tells you about it. You want to hear, and don't. But he doesn't remember much, nothing that is specifically related to the act of dying or being dead. That is completely expected and probably for the best, but it still feels like a cheat.)

You get some professional assistance, but it's still awful. It's not even the subject matter—you find yourself numb to that part, and write the date of his death as easily as the date of his birth or his social security number—but just the sheer repetitive banality of the task, the knowledge that there will always be another stack of forms.

You can't save him from dying and you can't extend the life of a printed clone. But you can do the paperwork. It's a little thing, but you know he appreciates it. Grand romantic gestures are great in the movies, but sometimes marriage is about the little things.

BOOM TOWN
REBECCA E. TREASURE

I barely flinched when Mrs. Simmons exploded in the fourth pew in the Community of Peace Baptist Church. Sunday mornings were usually good for a boom or two.

Something about the reminder of our piety created some powerful prideful thoughts, but I never expected Old Simmons to go out like that. She'd turned in more deviants than anyone else I knew. I was scared to death of her watery eyes seeing through my good girl act.

I sat three pews behind her when it happened, the itchy wool cushion digging into my thighs beneath my white cotton church dress. I'd counted 572 stained glass tiles embedded in the enormous window behind the pulpit, trying to ignore the pastor ranting about how we were all sinners and only through Church and State could we find salvation. If I'd been paying attention to him, I might have been the one blowing up all over the hymnals.

He'd about reached peak brimstone rage when Mrs. Simmons's head snapped up. She stood like she was gonna offer a "Hallelujah!" or "Preach it, brother!" Then—blood and entrails all over the pews.

The sound wasn't so bad once you heard it a few times. Like a car backfiring or a transformer popping. It's the mess that's most upsetting.

You never get used to that.

Mom whispered, "Don't move, Mary," but I didn't need the warning.

Old Lady Clarke wailed; she'd been too close to Simmons when the woman popped and now she had some burns, but otherwise, the church remained tomb-silent.

It's pretty common for one boom to create a chain of them. Even something as justified as "the old bitch deserved it" could trigger our implants, so I sat in that pew covered by bits of bone and flesh and prayed to the Lord and Legislature to save my soul.

Lord, I am guilty. President, I am a sinner. Save my soul from perdition. Keep my body whole so I can continue to work in your good names here on Earth and one day join in the righteous revolution and reclaim the land for freedom.

I didn't blow up, but up in the elevated pulpit, Pastor Hargrove added to the mess. Chunks of his fatty flesh fell around us like soggy socks. A piece of him slapped against the font of holy water with a wet clatter. Mom winced as another piece slid down her fresh-pressed church dress to splat on the ground.

I focused on my guilt. Nobody moved. Any sin set the implants off, but pride triggered them fastest. Any thoughts of righteousness or indignation and *boom*. As long as we remained fully convinced we *deserved* to explode, the implant remained dormant.

I didn't have any trouble convincing myself of that, at least. I knew I deserved to die.

—

On Monday, there'd been another biology lecture at school on the deviance of the outside world, how they allowed men to fornicate with men and women to lie with women, and more of that crap about polluting the purity of the races. All the same stuff Dad liked to say, which just made it worse. While the teacher talked, I traced the BOOM that someone had scratched into the desk, shading it in with my pencil.

After school, all the boys called each other gay and sneered at the ones who blushed or turned away. I walked past them as fast as I could, using my backpack as a shield. Mom was teaching little kids—pre-implant—at church, and Dad wouldn't be home from the electrical plant until dark, so I took myself to dinner.

Sitting in the back of Hank's Corner Grille on 5th and Main, I thought about Mrs. Simmons giving up her ghost. The super-concentrated bleach Hank used on the bathrooms stained the air, making it hard to eat, swallow, think. No way I'd make it to old age. I imagined hugging the President or one of the Senators and letting my thoughts drift to bad places. Might as well take one of them with me.

Realizing what I'd thought, tears dripped down my cheeks. I clenched my eyes shut, a half-eaten piece of pepperoni and bacon pizza smashed in my fist, squeezing out between my fingers. I bet that's what the pieces of Mrs. Simmons would have felt like.

But I didn't go off.

I stared at the smushed red, white, and brown between my fingers, the warmth seeping away from the pizza, and considered why I hadn't exploded. If anything was going to set off the implant, it should have been contemplating murder. The cheese went rubbery before I decided it was because I knew I was guilty, knew when I thought it that I deserved to go boom. Because I deserved to explode, I didn't.

I glanced around, afraid someone would see, but Hank was busy serving the football-and-cheerleader crowd and of course, none of them looked my way.

I washed my hands and then walked home thinking about smushed pizza and soggy socks and if this discovery actually meant anything. By the time my worn blue sneakers took me up the concrete steps of our porch, I decided it meant everything. I could think freely, as long as I remained convinced that those thoughts condemned me.

I tried pushing the limits. Greta Linton on the basketball team always sneered at my free throw, so I imagined what it would be like to punch her in that long, straight nose. Horribly sinful of me, of course. Terrible thought.

I paused at the threshold of Mom's spotless kitchen, a pre-boom wince on my face.

No boom.

What about Mister Garland, my neighbor? He liked to sit on his porch when I mowed the lawn, staring at me, sipping his contraband whiskey—who knows how he smuggled it past the wall.

I wouldn't mind if he exploded. What a dreadful thing to think. I should explode, too.

Safe.

I ran through a long list of grievances, connecting each vengeful thought to my own dreadful weakness. My breathing came fast, as if my chest had filled with balloons and I had to keep pace with their expanding size. My heart thumped away, *ba-dump ba-dump*, secure in my guilt.

Safe.

As I turned to my homework—a one-page essay on the betrayal of Peter and four stapled pages of algebra—I grinned. My cheeks were unused to the feeling and it hurt. It hurt like the burn in my calves after a run around the track, hurt like peeling off a scab, hurt like watching Susan Anderson and her family march through the gate into the other world.

I'd liked Susan. I liked the way she held her thumbs in her fist when she was nervous, and I liked the tiny pink mole above her lip. I think, in a different place, she would have liked me, too.

Horrible thought. Deserved to blow up. Filthy sinner.

I started collecting my books as soon as Mom got home, afraid she'd sense the change in me.

"I'm tired, Ma. Lots of homework. Going to bed early."

"Did you get it done?"

"Yes, Ma. Pythagoras isn't so hard."

"How was chapel?"

"More on Peter and the rooster."

"An important lesson to remember. We are all sinners in the end."

"Yes, Ma. I know."

I did know. I repeated it to myself over and over and over as I fell asleep thinking of Susan and what her mole would feel like under my lips.

—

The next day at school, I watched everyone, wondering if I was the only one who had figured it out. I couldn't be the only one. It had been too easy. I felt powerful—no—empowered by my rampaging thoughts. A secret they didn't control. I was horrid, disgusting, and deserved to die. I was free within my mind.

But was I alone?

Danny Bell might know the secret. He sat so tall in his desk, his eyes never dropping quite as fast as everyone else when Mister Striton called on him. A little smirk passed across his face after Jenny Dearborn bent to pick up her pencil and, for the briefest of moments, her buttoned shirt gaped open and her white flesh caught the light.

Horrible, dreadful thoughts. Boom, boom, boom.

Miss Jane, the cafeteria lady. She might know. Her banter was always a little too free, a little too pointed.

"You sure you need that extra serving of french fries, Johnny? You're gonna end up as fat as your daddy."

Or, "How long are you gonna sulk over that boy? You know he isn't worth half as much as these mashed potatoes."

Or, slapping a scoop of mashed potatoes onto my tray, "What're you looking at, Mary?"

I started, not realizing I'd been staring. I looked into her eyes, searching for the freedom we might share behind our crisp school uniforms and our strained smiles and the implant in our spines. "Nothing, ma'am. Sorry."

"You're holding up the line."

"Yes, ma'am. Sorry, ma'am."

I slunk to an empty table by the trash cans and shoveled lukewarm, over-processed food into my mouth. I made secret plans, wondering if I'd have the courage to carry them out. I'd stay after school, talk to Miss Jane. But what to say?

"Hey, Miss Jane, do you have evil thoughts without blowing up?" Hardly wisdom. Never know who might be listening. There were rumors they'd bugged the school, the whole town, even our houses.

Maybe I'd talk to Danny. "Wanna break the law, Danny?" That'd never work either. Danny's dad was a Senator.

In the end, it was Lanie Smith, and she came to me.

I was in Hank's again. I'd been careful not to change my habits, though I longed to express my newfound guilty freedom with some outward act—a solitary picnic in the town square, eating nothing but cookies and ice cream, maybe, or buying a whole pizza and giving into gluttony before my parents got home—but that might push my implant too far. So I enjoyed my dirty, ugly thoughts and ate a single slice for dinner like always.

Lanie plopped into my booth, still wearing her cheerleading uniform, her dark curly hair severe in a top bun restrained with a bright red bow. "Hey, Mary."

"Lanie," I said around a bite of pizza. I flushed, my cheeks warming, and hurriedly swallowed, almost choking on the half-chewed mass.

"Gosh, are you okay? Here, I'll top off your coke. Be right back."

The uniform barely covered her butt, and I tried not to look at the way the light slid over those thick, tan nylons or wonder where they led. *Boom, boom.*

When Lanie came back, she pushed the red plastic cup toward me with the same solemnity I emanated when I took Communion every third Sunday. A new pastor had arrived from somewhere, a skinny old man whose dentures wobbled when he talked and whose guilt was as plain as the liver spots on his wrinkles. He'd never blow up.

"Thanks."

"No problem. Hey, so, some of us get together over by the pond some days. The days we have chapel. Isn't that terribly sinful of us?" Her eyes sparkled, but her lips were tight together.

She knew. She had to. That immediate connection of defiance with her guilt—she had to be free like me.

I gulped the sugary fizz to give myself time to think, but my head was spinning so hard I almost gagged. How many was "some of us?"

My heart began to pound. I was in serious danger.

I straightened. No, I wasn't. I was a dreadful, wretched person and I deserved to explode, to shower Lanie with bits of my body and blood like marinara sauce all over her white and red uniform.

My heart rate slowed. "Terribly sinful."

"Anyway, I think you might enjoy it. I mean, it's horrible and bad of us. But..." Again, her lips pressed together. "You won't feel so alone."

She fled.

I finished my pizza, chewing each bite with thorough attention, contemplating how dreadful I'd have to be to sneak out of my parents' house to meet with Lanie. The pond was only three streets from my house.

Others. More than one.

I wouldn't be alone. Lanie was right. I would enjoy that.

On the way home, I worried about how Lanie knew. I'd been so careful to go the same places, talk to the same people, put the same effort forth in school and at basketball. Maybe it was like Danny sitting too tall in his chair.

Maybe my freedom couldn't be hidden.

—

It took me a week to work up the courage to climb out of my bedroom window. Just after midnight, whispering "boom, boom, boom" under my breath the whole time. I tied my sneakers in the darkness next to the shed, the earthy scent of the grass I'd cut that afternoon still clinging to the lawn. Cicadas screamed a warning in the trees. I ran, as though running could outpace the boom and the beating of my treacherous heart, all the way to the pond.

There, in the shadows beneath the ancient oak, sprawling over the grass like a revival, I saw the others. Only a few—I was disappointed and relieved at the same time—but Lanie was there, and Miss Jane, but not Jerry or Danny. A girl from my basketball team, too. Katie was one of the quiet ones who never got to play in the games.

And one of the old ladies who worked the bingo tables on Saturdays in a floral print housecoat. Mom made me volunteer there sometimes. I thought back to the name tags—her name was Rose.

And then I saw my mother.

"Mom?"

She opened her arms, drawing me in with tears running down her face. Words failed her; she just sobbed and choked out a wretched, "I'm sorry," repeating it over and over like the broken jukebox at the gas station.

Lanie and the others stayed back, talking among themselves, while

Mom held me and cried. Finally, she gulped herself into silence, her eyes puffy, her nose running, and her sleeve smeared where she kept trying to stem the flow. I didn't say anything, too afraid to voice the turbulent thoughts hammering against my eyeballs.

I was angry and glad, but mostly scared.

How could two of us live together without one of us crossing that invisible line in our heads? Dreadful, horrible, ugly people. Dad would be left all alone, and he'd be better off for it. We were sinners; we deserved to die. Why didn't she tell me? How could she keep this from me?

"Now that we're all here," said Miss Jane from behind Mom and me, "let's settle down."

The others moved into a circle, crossing their legs like Sunday schoolers on a brightly colored rug, and I sank into the dewy grass between Mom and Lanie.

"We are sinners," said Rose, her voice quiet but carrying across the grass. "But because we are sinners, we are free. We carry the burden of our guilt like the cross of Jesus Christ, dragging ourselves toward certain death without faltering." She nodded to Katie. "How did you sin today?"

Katie pulled her crossed knees up to her chest in a fluid motion and rocked back and forth while she spoke, her long blonde hair shifting in the dim moonlight. "I wanted to yell at Coach Johnson. She never lets me play, never even gives me a chance. I'm just as good at passing as any of those other girls, but I'm not pushy like them. It was an evil thought, and I deserve to be punished."

There was a murmur of sympathy, assent, understanding.

Rose nodded and smiled, then turned her head. "And you, Jane?"

Miss Jane hardly moved while she spoke. "I thought sinful thoughts about the children in the lunch line. They are so rude, so dismissive of me. They treat me worse than they treat each other, and that's pretty bad. I should have blown up then and there."

Another round of sympathy, indignation, agreement.

Rose turned to my mom. "What about you, Mary Anne?"

Mom stiffened, her fists gripping the grass like she expected a tornado to blow through and needed any handhold she could grasp. Her eyes slid sideways, almost meeting mine, and then she looked across the little circle at Rose. "I had evil thoughts about my husband. I am so tired of him being angry that we only had one child. He blames me, says I failed him and God and the President. I'm tired of the way he treats..." Her voice thickened, choking off the rest of her sentence, but she turned her head fully to me and began to sob again.

My stomach hurt. This was wrong.

We were all going to die, and Mom needed my comfort, but I couldn't believe she'd known how to be free all along and just sat by, just let Dad berate me and rage about the filthy sinners at his work, about the disgusting traitors on the news we got from outside, and on and on.

But there she was, the woman who kept my socks folded, who made sure I had enough money for dinner after school, who would nod and hand Dad another soda while he thumped around the living room pissed off about this or that—and she was crying, and her arms were reaching for me.

I turned my head away.

Rose frowned but turned to the next person. Me.

"And you, Mary? What sin did you commit today?"

Where to begin? I'd watched the back of Jenny Dearborn's jeans where they slid down, revealing just the tiniest bit of skin. I'd imagined Mr. Stager, the history teacher, blowing up when he said the world outside Boom Town was evil because they allowed homosexuals to live. I'd snuck out of my own house, defying my parents.

Sin, sin, sin. *Boom, boom, boom.*

Everyone was watching me, so finally I said, "Well, I'm here, aren't I? Pretty much as bad as it gets."

A few chuckles, a smile, and nodding all around. Mom's hand found mine and squeezed, but I wasn't sure about that yet, so I left my hand limp in hers.

Then Lanie. She smiled at me before speaking and nodded at Rose. "I still have that crush," she said. "I can't seem to get over it. The dreams haven't stopped either. Every day I expect to blow up, but somehow, I keep coming back here."

Everyone nodded, Katie laughing a little but not in a mean way, like she understood. I wondered who Lanie could have a crush on, and why that would condemn her. Lanie was a cheerleader, and her dad ran the only bank in Boom Town, so she could have pretty much any guy she wanted. Unless…

Like me? A crush on a girl, like me?

Susan's face swam before my eyes, red and patchy as her parents dragged her through the door. She'd been three months from her sixteenth birthday, from getting her implant, when her dad, the Senator, applied for the ambassadorship to the United States. Her mom was sick, and there was a big controversy about them leaving, but finally, the gates cranked open for the first time in forever, and Susan walked out of my life. I could tell from the way she'd looked back at me and the grip her mom had on her hand they weren't ever coming back. Nobody else had left since, and the gate always had guards on it now.

Could Lanie be like me?

Rose was speaking again. "I harbor anger in my heart at the Government. For this, I deserve to die. I believed in Boom Town when we built it, all those years ago, back when the rest of the country had ignored our pleas and called us ignorant and racist and degenerate and stupid. I found solace in this place where people thought like me. But now, I see that there was justice in those who judged us, and I am too cowardly to do anything but harbor that anger. Soon I will explode."

Everyone nodded, their wide eyes catching the moonlight filtering through the twisted branches above us. Dew soaked into our pants like the sin seeping from our very pores.

Rose creaked to her feet. It was only then, watching everyone hug and whisper and walk away into the dark night, that I realized everyone there was a girl.

Had none of the men or boys found the secret? Or did they meet separately?

I murmured the question to Lanie, and she laughed, a sudden sharp loud sound that made me jump.

"Sorry. But seriously? What do they have to complain about?"

Walking home with Mom silently by my side, I saw what she meant. Women were the original sinners, filthy in our very nature. The teachers and the pastor and the Senators and the President's speeches never let us forget—it was because of a woman that sin had entered the world. The men could shift their guilt onto their mothers, their sisters, their wives and their daughters.

We had to bear it alone.

Mom blew up two days later.

She left me a note under my pillow.

—

Dear Mary,

I'm so sorry we raised you in this awful place. Your dad believed in the President so much. Your father was sure the bombs wouldn't matter—not to us, not to the true believers. I was young, only twenty-two, but that doesn't excuse it. My parents begged me not to come, but I thought they were brainwashed.

By the time you were born two years later, it was too late and we couldn't leave.

I was too afraid to tell you, to help you, too afraid of your dad and of the bombs. Afraid for you. I was managing, controlling my thoughts, but I can't convince myself that you deserve to die.

You don't, my love, you are wonderful and perfect and not a sinner at all. No more than anyone else, and less than many. I can feel it coming now, it will happen soon. Remember, my lovely girl, that you are a sinner. Remember it until you don't have to anymore, and then don't look back.

But for now, remember.

I love you.

Mom.

—

Her hand had been shaking by the end, but she'd underlined the word "remember" three times. I burned her note by the pond, under the branches of the ancient oak.

And just like that, I was alone again.

—

I stopped going to the meetings for a while. Dad didn't change much, except he started buying black market booze from Mister Garland, and he raged about sin and traitors until midnight. Didn't matter if I was in the room or not.

I missed a week of school, but he made me go to church every day for a month.

"Don't want you turning out like your mama," he growled.

When I went back to our meeting under the oak by the pond, Charity Williams was there because she was sick of her boyfriend trying to fuck her and hoped he'd blow up. Another lady from the other side of town was there, too. She had two little kids and kept wanting to take them through the gate—sinful, horrible woman.

When Rose looked at me to speak, I shook my head.

"It'll make you feel better, dear. That's why we're here."

I kept my face turned away and she moved on. Like anything could make me feel better. Any day the rage bubbling beneath my steadily beating heart would erupt, and I would scream, and before I could get it all out—before I could make them hear—I'd be little pieces all over the floor. What was the point of feeling better?

Lanie was next. "I am getting scared," she said quietly. "It's getting harder to keep the fact, the absolute truth, of my disgusting nature from myself. I don't want to be ashamed anymore, and it's going to kill me."

I looked up, willing her to go on, desperate to know that I wasn't alone after all, and she might just understand all the confused feelings, anger, and fear I felt. My chest ached while I waited for her to speak, but she didn't go on.

The others spoke, but I barely heard them.

I don't want to be ashamed anymore, and it's going to kill me kept running through my head.

I didn't mean to interrupt—I don't even know who was talking when I spoke—but I just couldn't keep it in. If I was going to die, I wanted it to mean something.

"We deserve to die, but we're not the only ones."

Their heads swiveled toward me, fear silver in the moonlight.

"We should march in there. We should march to Congress and tell them we're going to blow them all up if they don't let us go."

The other teenagers were nodding, but the adults pulled on their patient faces.

Rose's voice was soft as the spring leaves shivering in the breeze above my head. "It won't work, dear. They'll just shoot us."

"What if they don't? I didn't even know you all existed six months ago. What if we're not as alone as we think? What if other people just hide it better?" I looked at Lanie. "Maybe the boys aren't so safe. They can't all be like that. Maybe if more people knew they weren't alone, we could make them change, make them let us go."

Miss Jane shook her head. "You think those powerful people have any doubt about what they're doing? They live in those big houses, get their booze and fancy shit shipped in from outside. They wouldn't change Boom Town for the world."

Rose nodded. "They enjoy their power. Why would they give that up?"

"The implants..." I chewed on my lip, thinking of Susan out there in the world, implant-free. "What if we just told them the truth? Make them think about it."

Katie shook her head. "And give them a good reason to shoot us?"

If I was wrong, we'd all die. "Go to them, and say our implants are broke, that we have sinful thoughts and don't die, and ask them how come? Ask them if we deserve to blow up, how come the implants aren't working?"

Lanie rolled her eyes. "They'll just adjust the system and we won't be free anymore."

"But how? How can they? It's wired into their spines, too. They won't wanna die, and you know they don't wanna change. They'll have to turn off the system, or deal with the fact that people can think what they want. If they turn them off, even for a little bit, people will feel that freedom, and who'd want to give that up? If they deal with it—"

"They can't do that." Miss Jane's voice gave me chills, a shiver of hope. "Boom Town would explode overnight if they admitted the implants didn't work."

I nodded. "Exactly."

———

It was almost dawn before we all went home, but we had a plan. A horrible, sinful, treacherous plan that would get us all killed and good riddance.

I'm still a sinner, Mom. Right to the end.

After school that day, I didn't go to Hank's. I marched right up Main Street to the Senate and asked to speak to my Senator, Danny's dad. Katie was down the hall speaking to her Senator. I'd winked at Rose being escorted into the President's office—they were old friends, she said. Between all of us, we could get to twelve Senators and the President. Would that be enough?

"What is the problem, Mary?"

"My implant is broken." *Boom, boom, boom.* Would it hurt? Would I feel it, just for a second, as my spine splintered and the shockwave shredded my lungs? I'd be a soggy sock mess all over the white papers scattered on his wide mahogany desk.

"How do you mean?" He wasn't really listening. He was required to hear me out, by law, but that didn't mean he had to give a shit about some high school girl.

"I can imagine sinful things without blowing up. Like right now," I leaned forward, my heart threatening to pound but held down by the weight of Mom's *remember* clutched in my memory. "Right now, I am imagining you blowing up—all of the Senate, all of you—and see?" I spread my arms. "Nothing."

He stood, his face reddening. "How dare you?"

"I am a horrible sinner, but so are you. We all are, and Boom Town deserves to go BOOM."

I shouted the last word, hoping to set him off, but he stood there, his arms crossed, trembling.

"We'll have to call your folks, young lady."

Down the hall, an explosion thundered, rattling the windows at the Senator's back. At least one of us had succeeded, gotten a Senator to crack their mind just that little bit. I wondered what she'd said.

Danny's dad looked startled. His eyes darted to the door, back to me. "Stay here."

I nodded, meek as the little lamb of God I was supposed to be. As soon as he left, I sinned and went into the next office and repeated my story to the secretary. His eyes widened and his mouth fell open as he stood. He almost hugged me, but then his arms fell, and he said, "I thought I was the only one."

That's when I knew we were going to be free.

In the end, poor Rose ended up blowing up in front of the President. Her anger probably got to her, but it must have gotten to him, too, because he wasn't far behind her, shouting about treason and sin all around him and how he was the only one who...*BOOM*.

Katie's parents tried to drag her home when word got round that something was happening at the Senate, but she pushed her dad and boom he went. She got burned, but her mom just sat on the ground rocking back and forth, muttering to herself. Miss Jane brought all her friends and family to the Senate, and before long, the last of the Senators either went boom—or admitted they were with us.

—

I saw Dad one more time. Lanie's folks said I could stay with them, and I didn't want to be in that house where Mom died anymore. I went home to get some clothes and some of Mom's things, and I found him sitting in the front room, drinking a dusty bottle of whiskey and glaring at the news.

"You have anything to do with this?"

"Yes, Dad. I'm a horrible sinner, just like you wanted."

His face turned red. I'd probably sounded a little too giddy.

I swept past him and went to my room, tossing stuff into my basketball bag without really looking. He creaked to my bedroom door, wobbly on his feet and brushing the hallway walls.

"You're not going anywhere. You belong at home."

I didn't respond, although I had a hard time letting go of the pair of shorts gripped in my fist.

"Your Mother wouldn't have wanted—"

I whirled. "You don't know a *thing* about what Mom wanted."

"And you do?"

I shrugged, breathing slow and willing my heart to slow down. Defiant, horrible child that I was, I wouldn't give him the satisfaction of losing both of us to Boom Town. "Yeah. I do."

"She was a believer."

I laughed in his face. "Yeah, Dad. A true believer. She was a sinner almost to the end." I zipped my bag shut, pushed past him, and walked down those concrete steps for the last time.

Lanie's parents were happy in their sin and didn't mind ours so much. Lanie's cheerleading uniform hung on the back of her bedroom door, and when we woke up the next morning, she threw it out of the window, cursing herself as a sinner and laughing the whole time.

When the gates cranked open two days later, revealing a horde of doctors and military personnel to remove our implants, I cried and gripped Lanie's hand.

I was a sinner, just like everyone else, and soon I would be free.

THAW

JOSH ROUNTREE

Never thought I'd be breaking into my own house.

Desperate times, right?

Hammer in one hand, flathead screwdriver in the other, and I'm chipping away at the ice that's cemented the kitchen window shut. All the while, Lopez is in my ear about how come I don't just break the fucking glass instead of dicking around. He doesn't understand. No matter what went down, this place is still my *home*. Nobody wants to fuck up their home.

Lopez pushes up behind me, high on bathtub meth, so close I can't tell if it's his sweat or mine on the back of my neck. He makes like he's gonna take the hammer away, show me how it's done, so I throw an elbow at his chest, tell him to give me some fucking breathing room. Lopez bitches about how somebody is gonna see us, call the cops, but we both know we could blow this place up at high noon with a stick of dynamite and nobody would even bother to put out the fire.

A couple more taps and a long three-inch-thick chunk of ice falls away. I jiggle the window in the frame to break up the rest of the ice, push it open enough that a couple of starving skinny bastards like me and Lopez can squeeze inside.

Sun's so hot I can hear the scenery crackle, but the air pushing back from that open window comes from someplace else. Someplace cold.

Lopez whoops, asks if I'm going in.

Yeah, I'm going in.

The window's over the kitchen sink, and the sink's full of frozen water, so I'm slow through that window, making sure I don't bust my ass.

The green linoleum is a skating rink. The sudden cold must have burst the pipes beneath the sink, and all that water escaped the cabinets and flash froze to the ground before it could make it more than a few feet.

Lopez hums that old song about being cold as ice as he wiggles his way through the window. The temperature in here is eighty, ninety degrees lower than outside, and I'm already starting to shake. Or maybe it's adrenaline. It doesn't matter because we won't be here long.

Lopez is laughing now, hot breath like locomotive smoke in the cold air, and I have to calm him down, have to give him a *mission*. Not sure why I even brought him along this time, except for maybe I was afraid to come here alone. I shove a backpack into his arms and tell him to fill it up with canned veggies, tins of SPAM, whatever food he can find. Me, I'll check the rest of the house for things we can use.

He nods. No problem.

This is our standard operating procedure.

Me and Lopez have broken into at least a dozen iceboxes in the last couple months. Just not any that belong to people we know.

The whole house stinks, like something's gone rotten beneath the cold. Like a freezer full of meat lost power, sat around in the summer heat for a few months, then froze over again. The house used to smell like old bacon grease and overfilled ashtrays and bowls of dusty potpourri trying to fight back against it all, but this is worse.

The floorboards are familiar. Every creak beneath my shoes is a map I can follow without looking down. I cruise from the kitchen, through the swinging door and into the living room.

And I see them there. Frozen.

I mean, this is exactly what I expected, but I'm not ready for it. I came here to put eyes on them, to be sure what I *think* happened is what really happened. But seeing your parents cold and dead is a shock to the system, no matter how much you psyche yourself up.

Dad's stuck to the couch, beneath an inch of blue ice. His left arm is lying against the end table, so all the empty cigarette packs and remote controls are furred over in white frost. Mom's sitting right beside him, leaning forward with her hands on the coffee table, like she was reaching for something, or about to stand up, when the cold burst out from deep inside her, when the whatever-you-wanna-call-it—the *Cold Snap*, the *Ice Virus*—when *this shit* happened.

Lopez hollers from the kitchen, asking how long the shelf life is on peanut butter and strawberry jelly. I whisper something back, but I don't really care. I'm putting all my effort into *not crying*, because I'm so close to them, I'm afraid the tears will freeze my eyes shut.

I hate both of my parents, but I don't hate them *this much*. I don't want to see them buried in ice.

All the houses we've broken into, it's just been for food and anything else we figured we could use to keep on living. I never looked close at any of the *icebergs*.

I know, it's a shitty name, but what else are you gonna call them?

It doesn't matter.

Ice fans out from their feet. It's crusted all over the floor like silver tree branches. None of the summer sunshine makes it through the gray frosted windows. It's gloomy as fuck in here, and the air is so cold it burns my lungs.

I'm, like, a foot from them. Mom's hands are *right there*, and I want to reach out and touch her, despite everything I know. I want to feel the cold, slippery ice. I want to make sure there's no bringing my parents back.

But I already know the answer.

You don't touch icebergs. Not unless you want to end up the same way.

And you sure as fuck don't try to thaw them out.

You'd think I'd want something from my old bedroom. Some knickknack reminding me of better days, before my parents started hating me and changed the locks. Or at least shit I could trade for bottled water, right? But no. Nothing I own's worth anything, and the memory of Dad shoving my face into the wall, of Mom screaming about how the fuck could I treat them this way—that's pretty much banished all the happy memories for good.

So, when I leave their frozen bodies behind and head down the hall, it's not *stuff* I go looking for, it's my little sister Jessica, because she's the only one left in this house who probably still loves me.

The air is rancid, and so fucking cold. Gray and crystalline. I don't even want to breathe, but that's not a choice. I run my fingers along the wall to steady myself as something turns over in my gut and a sliver of pain, like a bullet shard, settles in my temple. I don't know if it's the atmosphere in this house or eight months living with Lopez with his yellow walls and noxious fumes causing my brain to swim, but I'm close to throwing up and falling down.

If it weren't for Jessica, I'd run for the exit. But I have this vision of her in my head, sitting cross-legged in front of the TV with her goddamn Charlie Bear clutched up tight against her—and it's not even a bear, right, it's a blue monkey, but Charlie Bear is what she always called it—and she's crying because Dad's shoving me out the door and I'm screaming about how him and Mom can rot in Hell and asking what kind of people would put their sixteen-year-old out on the street.

Jessica's young, not stupid. A ten-year-old knows stealing Dad's .38 revolver is bad. She knows the ring Mom got from *her* mother means more than money, and big brother sneaking it down to the pawn shop is cold-blooded. She *doesn't* know how desperate a person can get when all the crystal in your blood has run its course, but that doesn't matter. I'm still the bad guy in this movie.

Maybe I'm expecting the world to finally give me a break, but I go into Jessica's room and there she is, tucked into bed with Charlie Bear, both of them frozen rock solid. Frost covers most of the walls like a fungus.

At least she was asleep when the cold got her.

Was she one of the first ones, or did she lay here every night for the last month, wondering if she'd wake up? Wondering if waking up is really the best option?

I'm almost sure I'd rather be dead than still waiting around for this to get me. *Spontaneous human freezing*, or whatever else they tried to call it before there weren't enough talking heads left to give it a name. I guess I'm not really sure. Dying would be easy enough, but for some reason I keep on living.

I think about Jessica asleep, her chest going up and down, peaceful, steady breaths, arms getting tighter around Charlie Bear, and then...bang, or pop? I don't know. Just an instantaneous blast of cold coming from somewhere in her core, flash freezing everything in range. Terrible, but I think there are worse ways to die. And at least she isn't here like some psycho archeologist, come to dig through his family's bones.

Jess grew a few inches since I saw her. She's got this goofy grin on her face, and I wonder what she was dreaming about, at the end.

I can't keep the tears back now, and I'm *this* close to giving her a hug, when I hear Lopez scream.

I haul back into the living room and realize Lopez isn't screaming. The motherfucker is laughing. He's sitting on the couch next to Mom with a plastic cigarette lighter in his hand, waving the flame back and forth in front of her eyes. So close, his torn-up hoodie grazes the ice, and I want to scream at him, beat the shit out of him, but I'm afraid if I move too fast, he'll accidentally touch her and then goodbye, he's all ice, and maybe he's dumb, but he doesn't deserve to die.

I've seen Lopez toss scarves and hats on icebergs before, joking around. But nothing like this. His eyes are bright and twitchy, and he's hyperventilating. His laughter breaks down and I realize he's telling me to *look at her, look at her*, and so I do. Mom's eyes are unfrozen, blinking, throwing back red flame reflections. Ice runs off her face in rivulets, melting faster than it should, but what do we know about *should?* Nobody knows anything about the ice, and those who do are mostly making it up. Lopez won't stop saying *look at her, look at her*, chanting and swaying the flame, and when I get close enough for a better look, I realize Mom is straight up terrified. She looks at me and she *recognizes* me, and that puts me on my ass.

Lopez is talking shit, says he's going to defrost my parents, defrost everyone in the world, ride through empty streets on horseback with a flamethrower saving everybody's ass. He's crazy, but maybe not all the way.

We know the stories, but like I said, nobody knows anything for sure. And this isn't some corpse with her brain all frozen and rotted. This is my *mother*. These people are my *family*.

In the hall closet there's a cardboard box filled with camping junk my parents bought me back when they figured Boy Scouts would teach me how to be a good kid. An olive drab canteen, a collapsible cup, a pocketknife with a saw blade. A bunch of merit badge booklets that I never bothered to open. And stacked on top, a blue plastic camp heater, with a metal grill and a battery powered igniter, the kind you connect to a portable canister of propane. It puts out serious heat. A lot more than a cigarette lighter.

I stick the heater on Jessica's bedside table, connect the propane and light it up. Works like a champ. A whole shitload of BTUs blasting right at her face. The ice pours off her head in thick streams, like the way ice cream runs down the cone and over your fingers. Her eyes blink twice. That frigid meat smell is enough to knock me down, but I don't care because that's Jessica's mouth moving, chewing at the air, her lips twisting up into that grin she has that usually means she's heard a really stupid joke at school, like fourth grader stupid, and wants to tell it to me.

Doesn't matter if the jokes are funny, I always laugh.

My head's buzzing and my skull feels like it's about to split. I tell myself that I'm completely done with any *extracurricular* substances, that if I can just get to the other side of whatever is causing me to shake and choke down vomit, I'm going to be someone who Jessica can tell jokes to again.

Her mouth opens. Dank air pushes out of her lungs, and I think she's trying to speak. I'm half expecting her to say *why did the elephant stand on the marshmallow* and then I'll say *I don't know squirt, why*, and she'll giggle and say *to keep out of the cocoa*. But that doesn't happen. The sound she makes is more like air leaking from a balloon, and I can't tell for sure if she even knows I'm there.

Back in the living room, Lopez stops laughing and starts screaming. For real this time. I run down the hallway fast as I can, arms spread out to steady myself between the two walls. To keep the hallway from closing in and squeezing me flat.

The air in here's getting too thick to breathe.

The sound of Lopez screaming cuts off like someone pressed pause on whatever awful song he was playing.

I stumble into the living room, lower myself onto the ground before I fall down.

Lopez is icy blue death. He's flash-frozen. The pack full of pilfered food slung over one shoulder is part of the sudden statue he's become.

Mom, though. Most of her is still frozen, okay, but not her head, not anymore. Lopez and his fucking cigarette lighter took care of that.

Mom's jaw must have broken. It's hard to make sense of what I'm seeing, but nobody's mouth opens that wide, nobody's jaw unhinges enough that even a skinny waste like Lopez can sink his hand in there way past the wrist. No sign of the lighter. Probably still in his hand, which means it's in Mom's throat.

Lopez, his arm is a brick of ice, right. But dead or alive, Mom's mouth is moving just a little bit, like an old lady trying to gum some meat that she doesn't have enough teeth to chew. Except she does have teeth, blue and ugly and sharp, and they're slowly chipping away at my friend's forearm. Her teeth make a grinding sound that reminds me of Lopez when he's really tweaking.

I realize my own teeth are pressed together so hard they might break. I'm whining and Mom's whining. Icicles of blood hang from her jaw, connecting down to the coffee table like long red pillars. She doesn't stop chewing, but she looks over at me, and no matter what, I see my *mother* in those eyes, and I know my mother. I can always tell what she's feeling, and I can tell it now.

Love.

Forgiveness.

It's probably more than I deserve.

Dad hasn't moved a muscle. He just huddles in his ice cocoon, knowing this whole thing's my fault. If I hadn't stolen their shit for drugs, if I hadn't made them so miserable, maybe I'd have been here to share this with them. At the very least, I could have understood what they went through.

It's okay, Dad.

I'm here now.

I'm breathing too fast. My vision comes and goes in black and white bursts. I hear Jessica coming down the hall before I see her.

You know that sound that comes after a good, week-long ice storm, when the sun pops out and everything starts to thaw? Water dripping off roofs and gurgling down drains. All the snapping and popping, like nature is breaking itself apart so it can be put back together the right way.

That's what she sounds like.

Jessica comes close, and I can see Charlie Bear, still stuck to her hip with a bit of ice that hasn't melted yet. Her jaw falls open, just like Mom's, and it's moving. She's trying to talk, trying to tell me something, maybe how happy she is I'm home.

Or maybe she just wants to tell me a joke.

What do you call a dead snowman?

Jessica sits down cross-legged in front of me, so close I feel my skin grow tight from the cold.

I don't know, Jess. What do you call a dead snowman?

Water.

Her smile goes wider, and her jaw stretches out. It makes a sound like a tree limb breaking.

She's told me that one before, but I laugh anyway. I'm the big brother, and that's what we're supposed to do.

I close my eyes, ask her to tell me another one.

And she does.

OLD GRIEF

ANDREW MILNE

I have a crick in my neck.

The alarm bleats at me, the digital readout ticking over from 5:30 to 5:31. Still, I don't move. As long as I don't move, don't raise my head, don't aggravate the stiff muscle, agony remains potential. It's the third time this month; it's at the point where I'm afraid to go to sleep. Waking up, and slowly realizing the pain must be borne, is almost worse than the reality of the awful, evil sensation.

The clock ticks over to 5:32.

Bernard stirs next to me.

"Hon…" The word rattles out of my dry throat.

He sighs; I know he can tell from my stillness and the single, raspy syllable that it's going to be one of the bad mornings. "Your neck?" My husband is a four on the hyperalgesia index, his tolerances far greater than mine. In moments like these, he has to work to be sympathetic.

I don't nod. He shifts out from under the silk sheets on his side of the bed, careful not to jostle me. I can feel the pain lurking, a nightmare poised to become real.

Bernard slides one hand between my head and the pillow and places the other on my waist. "On three, alright?" he says.

I screw my eyes shut and brace.

"One…" Two and three don't come. He hoists me to a sitting position, and the agony manifests.

Its intensity is hallucinatory. It feels like an exit wound; a wolf's jaw biting through skin and sinew; the final stages of some bulbous, necrotic growth, pricked with a needle and erupting pus. Old Grief claiming another in a long line of victories, exacting his price for every day, every hour, every minute I've held him at bay.

Alice and Julia are asleep in the next room. They won't be awakened by their mother screaming—I'll deny Old Grief that satisfaction, at least. I sit, tears streaming down my cheeks, clenching my teeth against the wail that wants out of me. Bernard presses a hot pad against the spot on my neck, muffling the nauseating throb a little.

He retrieves a glass of water from the ensuite then presses something small and oval into my hand.

The face of the pill is etched with an ideogram: two vertical slits and a close-parenthesis, the universal symbol for a happy face. Except, looking closer, I notice the symbol is modified—the vertical lines are topped with two shorter diagonals, angled upward where they converge, indicating a sympathetic furrowing of the brow. Not my usual morning pick-me-up of a few hundred milligrams of paracetamol—the one everyone takes to keep Old Grief from their doors for the first few hours of the day. This has something stronger in it—something to tickle the opioid receptors.

"I shouldn't," I protest. "With the rationing, we need to make them last, and Alice's baby teeth…"

"They're from my portion," Bernard says, overruling me. "You deserve them, after these last few times."

The next pill ration isn't due for another fortnight, and Bernard's job at the poppy farm brings him into contact with hard surfaces and sharp edges sometimes. Two years ago, he cracked his shin against a scaffold bar, hard enough to bruise. For three panicked nights, I'd begged, borrowed, and called in outstanding favors to scrounge up enough sorrow-faced pills to stop my husband from losing his mind.

"I knew what I was in for when I married a seven," he insists.

I should protest, but I'm tired, and Old Grief's being cruelly insistent this morning. I resent his ingenuity, how he slipped into our home again despite all the sponge padding and softness erected to deter him.

I swallow the pill, drain the rest of my tepid water, and wait for the white-hot burning in my neck to recede to welcome, warm numbness.

—

"The bicentennial of the Intensification will be commemorated next month, and many of us are taking the time to wonder what life was like before hyperalgesia.

"Was the pre-Intensified world really the carefree utopia eulogized by today's young artists, or was the reality more complicated?

"Join me—Trish Alexander—for a new weekly series, Love in the Time of Contact Sports, where I'll strive to recreate a day in the life of an average pre-Intensified person. Joining me for our first episode—airing this evening from six to eight on OPT—will be historian Friedrich Henriksen, an expert in the mid-20th to early-21st century factionalist period and author of Not to Bring Peace, But a Sword, *the bestselling account of the era's pre-eminent political leaders. Our other guests will include..."*

I mute the kitchen's speakers, ignoring Bernard's reproachful look. I'm in no mood to think about the pre-Intensification era this morning—or about much of anything at all—I'm cresting on the pill's mild magic.

I push my half-eaten bowl of oats around with my spoon, my cupful of instacaf—fine brown powder dissolved in lukewarm water—sitting undrunk. I'm getting thin. Unattractively so, I can't help but feel, despite whatever Bernard says. I'm thirty-eight years old. They say it's around this age that sixes and sevens start losing their appetite.

I make myself eat.

Julia is quiet in her high chair opposite me, slowly picking up her peeled grapes one by one and popping them into her mouth. I like her where I can see her when she's eating, but she's a clever girl, wary of choking. She's a three on the index, and big for her two years.

Beside me, Alice watches a cartoon on her tablet as she tucks in to a second helping of oatmeal. I recognize the cartoon from my own childhood: Foolish Farmer Francois has wandered into the forest, searching for his lost sheep, and has gotten lost himself, now easy prey for Old Grief, who lives in a dark house in those same woods. Grief is rendered as a pale, round-faced man in a disheveled three-piece suit and top hat. When he grins, his eyebrows crease spectacularly, converging at a sharp downward angle—the opposite of my pill's expression. His teeth, of which he has many, are discolored and crooked.

I watch Alice watching Grief. The vaudevillian demon is stymied when, in pursuit of Farmer Francois, he runs across Gaspar Gorilla— the hero of the short, a dull-witted but good-natured and sturdy simian—who barely notices when the drawing pins Grief left out for Francois to step on embed themselves in his own thick skin.

Alice laughs as Gaspar bops Grief on the head, causing a lump that lifts his top hat clear of his pale scalp.

When she stops laughing, she probes absently at her gums with her index finger, a gesture that I've noticed her make more and more recently. She frowns.

Alice is five-and-a-half years old, and a six on the hyperalgesia index. Slightly less afflicted than her mother, but still on the wrong side of the sensitivity bell curve. Even ones and twos remember losing their milk teeth with a shudder. I dread the day her first tooth wobbles and she comes to me.

What reassurance can I offer her? *Don't worry, darling, it won't be that bad?*

It will be that bad. The amount of anesthetic needed to dull the effects of losing a tooth can't be safely administered to a child her size. By her seventh birthday, Alice won't find Old Grief funny anymore.

"I almost forgot," I say, "I got a new letter from William today. Who wants to read it with me?"

Alice's head jerks toward me, her cartoon and gums forgotten. "William wrote?"

"Wi'wam! Yaay!" Julia adds.

Bernard shoots me a warning look from the kitchenette.

I pull up the text file I prepared last night on my tablet, and begin to read aloud:

Dear Ally and Julie,

I hope you're well back home. The weather's starting to warm up here on the surface. We get what's called a "breeze" coming off the ocean; it's like when you stand next to a ventilation duct, except the air smells like salt and sunshine. At the end of my shift, I like to stand on the cliff-top and look at the water beneath me, all deep blue and foamy.

I like it up here. At night, we can see the moon and the stars, and the sky looks so big! The bees don't buzz much at nighttime, so it's the only time it's quiet. We like to hang around on clear evenings after lights-out, away from the apiary. Sometimes my friends and I even play football, if we think the overseers won't find out. You're shocked, I know, but don't worry about us. No one ever tackles.

Juan actually got stung yesterday! He's a two, so normally he's really careful, but he was late to his shift and he didn't notice the gap in his glove when he was putting it on. He's okay though. It was just a little bee, and Juan's the kind of guy who always seems to be in a good mood. He was laughing when I saw him last, and he'll be back at work tomorrow.

I miss you all terribly, and I hope I can come home to see you eventually. They keep us very busy here, and we do important work, but my overseer said maybe for Christmas this year. Say hello to your Mum and Dad for me, and tell them I'm thinking of them all the time.

With all my love,
your big brother, Will.
P.S. I sent a present—promise you won't eat it all at once!

I set my tablet aside and place William's gift on the table—a small jar of pure, golden honey. Alice's eyes go wide when she realizes what it is. "One spoonful," I say, untying the jar's silver ribbon and twisting off the lid.

She accepts the spoon reverently, then slowly stirs the precious substance into her oatmeal. The joy on her face redeems my morning.

Bernard is tugging his boots on in the domicile's entranceway, lips pursed. He's clearly pretending not to have listened the letter.

"Don't give me that look," I say once we're out of the girls' earshot. "I've been putting aside a little bit of my social stipend for the last few months. The cost is worth it if it makes them happy."

"It isn't the price of honey that concerns me, Erica." There's a strained note in his voice. Not anger—like any responsible person, Bernard doesn't get angry—but tension. "How much longer do you think you can keep this up? Alice asked me the other day why we don't have any pictures of William in the house. I didn't know what to tell her."

"I can always get pictures of some boy and tell them that's what he looks like."

"That's not the point. Eventually, they'll get suspicious. They'll wonder why he never comes home. They'll wonder why they've never met their brother after years and years of letters. The longer you draw out this charade, the worse it'll be when you come clean."

I take a deep breath. "I know, alright? But I see the way Alice worries about her teeth, and… Just let me have this for a little longer. Please."

Bernard pauses, returning his attention to his shoelaces, not pressing the point any further.

"Will you be late tonight?" I ask, changing the subject. "I need to stop by Henrietta's this evening."

"Are you sure you feel up to an excursion? I can make Henrietta's delivery on my way home if you want."

"I'll be okay. You don't need to bear the brunt of every excursion, Mister Big Strong Four."

He allows me a tight-lipped smile. "I'll be home early, then."

I give him the same curt nod I give him every morning, letting him know I see his stolid, weary bravery. "Tread softly," I murmur, "and if you see Old Grief, move aside."

"I will." He steps out into the wan halogen light of a tunnel fifty meters underground, and I steel myself for another nine hours of worry.

—

The day passes, as days inexorably do. After clearing away the dishes, scouring the plastic bowls with blunt-bristled plastic pads, I give Alice her schoolwork. The syllabus calls for six hours of lessons, four days a week, broken up by light stretching sessions of at least five minutes every hour. We do these in the living room, in full view of the council's monitor camera. Graeme, our appointed social worker, insists on this.

He's stressed multiple times the importance of traceability to show the syllabus is being followed.

The stretches—as I've told Alice before and will certainly tell her again—are to keep her muscles from cramping or stiffening the way my own are prone to. A tiny little bit of discomfort at her age can save her a lot of torment when she reaches mine, but logic can only get me so far with a five-year-old. Every hour, she makes the same huffy face and needs to be told two or three times before she endures touching her toes. I watch her eyes water at the sensation in her hamstrings. No matter how obstinate she gets, I don't raise my voice. I don't want to set that precedent. Before he euthed, my father told me I was a difficult child, too.

Today's lessons start with a double session on self-care and home care. I quiz her on what to do if she sees an exposed spring protruding from the domicile's floor or wall padding; on what positions are safe for a six to sleep or sit in, versus which ones will stress the joints and vertebrae; on how long food should be chewed, so as not to hurt the throat.

English is next. She's developing well, now able to recite the alphabet by heart and read her whole Gaspar Gorilla storybook—printed on soft vellum with colorful illustrations—without help.

After lunch, we move on to world-orientation lessons. We watch a short, pre-approved video about fire together: what it is, why it's important, and why she'll never encounter it. Alice watches with the same rapt attention she had during the episode about the sun.

The afternoon concludes with math, and finally, art. I like to save her favorite subject for last, making crayon-drawings and finger-painting something to look forward to.

Today, she draws a field of smiling stick figures. One, bigger than the others, is posed with one leg straight and the other crooked, suspended in the act of kicking a ball to one of its friends. Above them hangs an ominous yellow orb.

After a moment's indecision, considering what Bernard will say when he sees it, I fasten it to the lintel above the kitchen door with the others.

I keep Julia in sight during Alice's lessons—the living room has a corner sectioned off by bright blue and pink felt barricades as her playpen. She walks unsteadily on the floor's springy padding, but more confidently every day. She doesn't demand attention the way Alice did at that age. Meals and nappy-changes notwithstanding, she's content with the company of her plush animal companions. She can engage Mr. Trunk and Ms. Fuzz-Snout in animated, cyclical conversations of half-words for hours at a time.

Alice sometimes looks up from her lessons to shoot her sister passive-aggressive looks. Twice, she shushes her when her babble rises in pitch and volume.

"Julie's hair is getting too long," she says at lunch. "She should get it cut."

I don't know how to tell her that the unsympathetic risk/reward matrix Graeme employs allows for a three to grow their hair long where it does not for a six. That I want Julia to have hair like I see on glamorous pre-Intensification film stars; I never could grow mine for fear it would get caught and yank at my too-tender scalp. I was an only child, born before the pro-natal policies were extended to mandatory two-child families. I don't know how to address the resentment I see growing in Alice at a sibling below her on the index. I don't know how to tell Alice that her sister might one day see the sun.

—

"The chaos of the early Intensification has left much of our record of the time scrambled, and it's often impossible to discern fact from fiction. Nobody disputes that the modification to the human genome was deliberate—the mutations coding for overdeveloped nociceptors are too specific and manifested too quickly to have been the result of natural causes."

Bernard sits in his study, Trish Alexander's interview bleeding through the half-open door, nursing his second glass of tomato juice of the evening. That much sugar in one sitting is a rare indulgence for him, normally so conscientious of the risks associated with diabetes as he approaches middle-age. His mood hasn't been improved by his day at work. Despite his pledge to be home early, it was quarter to seven in the evening before he rolled in, irritable and monosyllabic. "Quotas," was his only reply when I asked what was wrong, the word uttered with a clenched jaw.

"In your recent book, Dr. Henriksen, you seem to contend that the Intensification was not the action of terrorists or eugenicists—as has been assumed historically—but of philanthropists looking to curb uncontrolled population growth."

When he's in these kinds of moods, I feel a deep impulse to confront him—to demand if he thinks that my day has been any easier, spent in the company of a five-year-old who's dimly beginning to understand the scope of her future.

"That would be my conclusion, Trish, although I would say that any conclusion I can draw regarding what motivated the Intensification is pure conjecture. But the distribution of the earliest appearances throughout the world—Shanghai, Los Angeles, Delhi, São Paulo—suggests to me that it was targeted, not according ideology or ethnicity, but according to population density…"

He doesn't love me, of course. If he did in the beginning, when Graeme introduced us as potential partners in an assigned family unit, he certainly doesn't now. But Bernard could have had his pick of fours and fives, and he chose me all the same.

"Hyperalgesia, you see, was unlike any epidemic prior to the Intensification, in that its symptoms are purely subjective to the sufferer. In the early days of its spread, it was widely diagnosed as a social phenomenon—a kind of psychosomatic manifestation of societal malaise."

"Like an outbreak of mental illness, you mean?"

He's still considerate, most days. He makes conversation. He plays with the girls. He's patient with my agonies. He offers me pills from his ration. He tries.

"Quite so. Articles written in the first twenty or thirty years didn't know what else to make of the swelling number of individuals, otherwise healthy, who reacted to stimuli then thought of as irritants as previous generations might have reacted to life-threatening injuries. Paper cuts feel like fingertips being amputated; mosquito bites like being splashed with hydrochloric acid; sunburn like being set on fire. A common hypothesis was that they were sublimated symptoms of depression and anxiety, as sufferers so commonly reported them as co-morbidities."

It's more than a great many sevens can expect.

"They were seen as being in pain because they were sad, rather than sad because

they were in pain."

I peer around the door. Bernard looks up from his tablet, face blank, awaiting a reason for the interruption.

"I've got my package for Henrietta together," I say. He knows that, for the forty minutes I leave our domicile every few days, it's his responsibility to keep an eye on the girls. He knows, but he's making me feel like I'm encroaching on his solitude, regardless.

He groans and heaves himself to his feet. "Of course. I'll be in the living room. Give my regards to Hen when you see her."

—

The elevator doors part on level 134. A sound permeating the low corridor sets my heart to pounding. Loud, angry voices disrupt the low hum of the ventilation.

"You *stupid* girl," one of them is screaming, "you selfish, thoughtless, *stupid* girl." The shrill consonants penetrate the still air, spikes driving into my ears with a severity almost like pain. My breathing quickens. I don't want to be here. I don't want to be anywhere in the vicinity of real, unchecked anger.

I tighten my grip on the plastic pouch. *Henrietta needs me*, I remind myself. Her mother is old; her arthritis is getting worse. Her family was among those who donated what they could when Bernard bruised his shin; it's the least I can do to repay the favor. Ten doses of ibuprofen, 800 milligrams each. Not much, but I can spare it. A community has to come together to keep Old Grief at bay.

I move out into the corridor, head bowed, trying not to flinch at the vicious argument. It isn't the words that bother me. I hear arguments and shouting matches in old films all the time. Sometimes I'll even see simulated violence, if only by accident, when Bernard is in a morbid mood and watching some of the ghastly entertainment he assures me Pre-Intensification audiences enjoyed. But there, the volume is kept low, the image contained to a small screen. It doesn't cut through me the way these sudden, explosive syllables do.

My eyes on the floor, I don't see the figure coming the other way until they've almost collided with me. I scuttle to the left, mortally terrified for a half-second that I might be knocked to the hard, unpadded ground. The figure steps deftly around me and carries on.

I stand stock-still for a moment, waiting for the shock of a close encounter with Old Grief to recede. I look after the figure who almost hit me, and for a half-second, they glance back at me. A young man, tall and slim, a rucksack hanging off one shoulder, a hood drawn over his head. He offers me an adolescent's scowl and marches on down the corridor without apology, his gait quick and incautious.

Indignant, I open my mouth to call after him. I'm wearing my state-issued lanyard, clearly showing my number on the hyperalgesia index. He either didn't notice it, barreling down the narrow tunnel the way he was, or noticed and didn't care, which would make him callous as well as irresponsible.

I swallow the choice words I would dearly like to throw after him. Responsible people don't get angry.

The voices get louder as I progress along the rows of identical, pressure-sealed doors. Rounding a corner, I see light spilling out of Henrietta's open doorway, and the shouting reaches a fever pitch.

It's coming from my friend's home.

"I wanted to know what it *feels like!*" Another voice; defiant; tearful; younger than the other. I recognize it now—Andrea, Henrietta's seventeen-year-old. "I want to *live*, I want some fucking *sensation*—"

"You wanted sensation, did you?" Henrietta answers, quieter now, but profoundly unsympathetic. "I hope it was worth it, girl, because you'll have more sensation coming to you than you'll know what to do with. Did you think, even for a moment, what this family, this community, would have to pay—"

I press hard on the doorbell, wanting to make myself known before committing myself to any further voyeurism. Henrietta's voice cuts out mid-tirade. Muffled footsteps approach, and she emerges into the corridor.

Like all the friends I have, I was introduced to Henrietta through Graeme. At his encouragement, I joined my local Chapter a while back. Men and women of the same age and the same index rating commune by video-conference two evenings a week. It's good for social morale, Graeme says. Regular contact with one's peer group, having people to lean on who can sympathize with the difficulties you endure. The incentives the government offers for membership don't hurt either—a little extra in your social stipend, sometimes a favorable position in the queue when opioid rationing is in effect.

Henrietta and I look nothing alike. She's dark-skinned, stocky and broad-shouldered, whereas I'm pale and lanky. And yet we look very much alike. Our seven-ness covers us both like a shroud, evident in our deep-set worry lines, our habit of glancing downward, our posture when walking with our shoulders rolled forward, hands clasped in front of us. No seven needs a lanyard to recognize another seven.

"Heard that, did you?" The crease above the bridge of her nose is prominent.

I nod.

"Better come in then, I suppose."

Henrietta seals the door behind her when I enter. Andrea is sitting on the sofa in the living room when we enter, eyes dull with spent tears. I notice what looks like an adhesive plaster on the girl's forearm, which she tucks out of sight when she sees me looking.

She glares at her mother, who glares back at her in turn. "We'll finish this conversation later, Andrea."

Andrea picks herself up and stalks off into the domicile's corridor. "Nice to see you, Erica," she mutters as she passes, sardonicism acid on her tongue. She disappears from sight and moments later, a door slams.

I wince at the noise.

"Sorry you had to see that," Henrietta says, her temper starting to cool. "The thing is, I know I'm supposed to blame myself. That's what a parent does, isn't it? I'm meant to accept that I'm paying for a mistake I made raising her or for not being present enough in her life or some other touchy-feely crap. But it isn't true. Seventeen years, and I did everything right. There's nothing, *nothing* I could have done differently. And yet here I am, being punished all the same."

"Hen…"

"She's *in vivo*, Erica," my friend says, softly.

I sit down in the space Andrea just vacated.

In vivo pregnancy. To say the phrase aloud, even to think it, feels like an obscenity. An invitation to Old Grief to take up residence, not just in one's home but in one's body, there to fester and grow and gnaw and claw and rip and… I cross my legs, without thinking.

"How long?" I ask, in a small voice.

"Three months, she thinks. She'll be starting to show, soon. Erica, she's a six. A six, for God's sake." There's a quaver in her voice now that's harder to hear than the explosive cadence of her anger. "I can't be expected to watch *that* happen to my own daughter half a year from now."

"It—the fetus, I mean—can't be transplanted to the tanks?" I offer. I have no idea if it's the case or not, but I have to offer my friend something. The expression on her face is tragic. She collapses on the sofa next to me and dissolves into sobs. Cautiously, tentatively, I hold her.

The minutes wear on, and Henrietta keeps crying. Eventually, I extricate myself, mumbling something about the girls waiting for me at home, and offer a lame half-assurance to check in on her in a couple of days. I leave her mother's pills on the countertop, seal the domicile door behind me, and stride back to the lift, half-tempted to run.

It doesn't speak well of me as a person or as a friend, I know, that I wanted out of that place as quickly as possible. I might have stayed with Henrietta the rest of the night, offering her the solace of my company until something like hope started to take root in her again. But the truth is I am tired, and after this morning, I have had my day's fill of pain. I want to insulate myself in the softness of my home and place myself out of sight of Old Grief while he preys on another unfortunate soul.

——

Time passes, and I have a succession of tolerable days. I sleep well and wake up without the cramps that have plagued me these past months. Bernard gets home on time once or twice, his mood much improved, whatever issues the poppy farm had meeting its monthly quota apparently resolved. Alice's moods are mollified by her parents looking less haggard and the jar of honey from "William," which depletes little by little each morning, a tablespoonful at a time. She worries less at her teeth.

I try to treasure periods like these, always too short and too suddenly foreshortened. The lulls in Old Grief's tireless siege, when for a while he seems confined, a figure of fun like the pale man Gaspar Gorilla makes such short work of.

Henrietta is absent from the week's online meeting of our Chapter, and then the following week's as well, her 16:9 rectangle a black void in the upper-right of the screen.

I send her a text two days later, apologizing that I haven't been over, explaining that I've needed to dip into my reserve of ibuprofen for my neck. I've been taking an extra pill with breakfast for a week, in order to make the excuse true. I write and rewrite a line asking after Andrea half a dozen times, and finally send the text without it, unable to come up with a variation on "I hope she's going to be okay" that doesn't sound insulting and trite.

More weeks pass. The honey runs out, and Alice starts running her tongue over her teeth again. Finally, the moment that I've dreaded for months—I'm awakened by a stab of light through my eyelids, the hallway light glaring through the open bedroom door. The bedside clock reads 1:15 A.M.

"I felt a wobble." Alice's voice is plaintive and babyish. Bernard, blinking the sleep out of his eyes, escorts her to the bathroom. A good ten minutes pass. I can half-hear Bernard speaking from down the hall, voice level and firm but patient and sympathetic. When they return, he confirms the worst. Her back-left molar has started to loosen, ever so slightly. She wants to sleep with us tonight, and even knowing it to be a bad idea, I don't have it in me to refuse.

—

I awake again four hours later and choke down a scream. I feel like a spear-shaft is being slowly twisted between my shoulder blades.

My daughter is nestled between my husband and me—I've curled around her through the night, and the change in posture has set the nociceptors in my upper back to screaming at their utmost intensity.

I stagger to my feet and down the hall to the bathroom. With a shaking hand, I dry-swallow three of the melancholy-faced pills from Bernard's reserves. I know that kind of dosage is unsafe, liable to become habit-forming if repeated too often, but it doesn't matter. The agony this morning is quite literally intolerable. Like any seven, I've been across that threshold often enough.

There's a texture and a nuance to extreme pain—pain past the point of being endured or ignored. Intolerable pain is distinct from tolerable pain in the same way a human's intelligence is unlike a bird's or a cow's. There's a state change, a difference not just of degree but of type. It colonizes your imagination, realigns your values, bends every particle of what you are toward it like a black hole. It seems impossible, paradoxical, your body insisting that time cannot continue until the awful wrongness consuming it has been relieved, yet one instant follows another, and the pain remains. You're trapped in consciousness with a thing that hates you, and if you could amputate your consciousness to escape it, in that moment, it's a trade you would happily make.

Old Grief demands his toll, and all the opioids and softness in the world can only delay him so long.

—

Alice has the day off her lessons. By tradition, the day a child's first tooth loosens is a day to indulge them. She gets to lounge around in her pajamas, watching cartoons on her tablet well into the morning, exempted from her hated hourly stretches, snacking on dried cranberries and blueberries that she carefully chews on the right side of her mouth. Bernard sits on the sofa with his arm around her, keeping one eye on Julia in her playpen while I recline in the armchair opposite, thoughts made sluggish by the effects of the pills, my upper back still throbbing through the thick anesthetic fog.

I pick up snatches of the cartoon they're watching—exaggerated regional accents and manic strings on the soundtrack. I recognize this one, I think. Farmer Francois has been chased from his house by Old Grief, and in a series of misadventures as he hunts for a hiding place, he finds himself enjoying the hospitality of jolly Saint Nick, who lives deep underground in tunnels that confound Grief's sense of direction.

Saint Nick is made to contrast with Old Grief: he's massively fat where Grief is rake-thin, red-skinned where Grief is pallid, his voice booming where Grief's is raspy and sibilant. At first, Francois finds his host off-putting. He appears intimidating, with his curled goat's horns and cloven hooves. The cave he lives in is cramped, and his other guests include snakes and rats. He serves meals of still-wriggling worms and termites.

Francois' confusion and repulsion at Saint Nick's lifestyle form the backbone of the short's comedy, but the ending is uplifting. In a moment of pathos, Francois overhears Nick sobbing that he can't make his human guest feel welcome despite his best efforts. Francois realizes that his host, despite his fearsome appearance and foreign customs, is doing his best to make him welcome, and the episode ends with the pair in a fraternal embrace.

"What would you like to do this afternoon?" Bernard prompts Alice. She doesn't answer, her eyes remaining fixed on the screen. She chews the inside of her right cheek. "Anything you want to do," he presses. "We could play a game, we could do finger painting…"

"Can William come to visit?"

Bernard goes quiet at that. He shoots me a look, silently asking for support, but sees that in my present, half-conscious state, he isn't likely to get it.

"Oh, Ally," he says, "William would love to come, he said he would, but he's working hard."

Alice shrugs and loads the next cartoon. It occurs to me that I didn't once hear her laugh at the previous one.

—

By the time dinner rolls around, I feel well enough to be standing and walking. I prepare Alice's favorite—pasta hoops with a courgette and pepper sauce—which she eats listlessly with the same distracted frown she's worn all day.

We need to have a candid discussion about what losing her first tooth will mean and what she can expect. There are tutorials for this. Graeme has sent me literature with step-by-step guides for the parents of sixes and sevens at this point in their development. But not tonight. Without quite knowing why, I feel vehement on this point. Hard truths can have their allotted time. Today is for making my household as happy as I can.

I'm failing.

I decide that it's past time I call on Henrietta and Andrea—an excuse to get out of the domicile and out of sight of my daughter's frown. I don't need to stay, I reason; I'll just stick my head in the door long enough to check on them. I gather a couple of spare ibuprofen and excuse myself. Bernard makes noises to the effect that I shouldn't go out, but I insist the walk will do my back good. Alice pokes at her food and doesn't look up as I go.

—

When I arrive at Henrietta's domicile, there is a figure crouching outside the entranceway. They glance toward me on hearing my approach, my footsteps resonant on the unpadded surface. It's the same boy who almost knocked me off my feet in the corridor last time—the same canvas rucksack, the same hooded sweatshirt pulled up over his head. He's propping something against the sealed door.

He startles, jerking to his feet and hurrying down the corridor in the other direction. In his haste, he leaves a flap on the back of his rucksack unzipped. Something falls out, without his noticing.

I move to where the small object fell, meaning to alert its owner, but when I reach to pick it up and see what it is, I withdraw my hand as though scalded. It's a clear, resealable plastic pouch, the same generic sort that I would use to carry Henrietta's pills. Inside are several naked razor blades. Their vicious chromium sharpness glints in the tunnel's low fluorescent light.

The package the boy left against the door is a brown paper envelope. Scrawled on the front, in the smudgy grey of a dull pencil, is the name ANDREA.

"Excuse me," I say. The boy keeps striding, not looking back. Delicately, carefully, I pick up the pouch with the razor blades inside, holding it at arm's length, one corner pinched between thumb and forefinger.

"Excuse me," I repeat, not shouting, but loudly enough in the empty, close space that I'm quite certain he can hear me. Still, he doesn't look back. Just as he is about to round the corner and move out of my line of sight, I try a different tack. "You're the father, aren't you?"

He freezes, mid-stride, and turns to face me. His eyes widen when he sees what I have in my hand.

My heart is pounding furiously, though I work to not let it show on my face. Every learned instinct is telling me to avoid a confrontation, to drop the pouch, hurry home, and alert social services to the teenager roving our sector with dangerous contraband. He appears far more likely to commit violence than anyone I would normally encounter IRL—moreover, I'm liable to be indicted myself if I don't bring the razor blades to the authorities' attention expediently.

However, an idea has taken root in my mind, developing second-by-second into a plan. I approach him, slowly, my free hand raised in a conciliatory gesture. "I'm not going to turn you in," I say. "Let's go somewhere we can talk."

———

His name is Alexander. He's a one, or so he says. The bottom-most end of the bell curve, true ones are only about two or three per hundred thousand. He reclines against the water filtration unit, where it occupies a corner of the service basement, three levels below my domicile. Someplace I'm reasonably sure we won't be overheard. He fidgets a lot, hands forever drumming on his thigh or flitting across his mouth or eyes.

"Yeah, I been up top," he says. Now that he's reasonably sure I'm not about to hand him in, he brags easily. "Did two tours in the fisheries before they shut down. Told us the factories down below could meet the demand for omega-3 in pill form. No more need for twos and threes to get exposed to UV." He snorts. I'm not sure of the target of his derision, whether it's for the bureaucrats responsible for closing the fisheries, the factories that made them obsolete, or his former colleagues with less fortitude than his own in direct sunlight.

"How old are you, Alexander?"

"Be nineteen next month."

William would have been eighteen this year, I muse.

"Do your parents know where you are? What you're up to?"

He shrugs. "Never knew Mum. Dad was a four—euthed a few years back. Migraines. Look, what is it you want from me, missus? If you're not buying, and you're not handing me in, I have places I could be."

I hand him the pouch with the razor blades inside, happy to be rid of it. Carrying them around in thin plastic is careless to the point of crazy—it would be so easy to jostle them in such a way that the sharp edges could cut through the flimsy material.

"People really pay you for this?" I ask. I've heard rumors of dealers like him—young men and women, typically, low on the index. I think of the plaster that Andrea didn't want me to see on her arm. "For pain?"

"Enough do. Never saw the appeal, personally. But Andi told me she likes feeling it's something she can control. Meeting Old Grief on her terms, not his. Something like that."

"And now she's *in vivo*. Was that the idea?"

His foot taps a rapid tattoo on the concrete floor. He scowls at the ceiling, not meeting my eyes. "None of your business."

"There's no opioid strong enough to mute the experience of childbirth. Not for a six, not without endangering the life of the child and the mother." Despite myself, I feel some of Henrietta's venom creeping into my tone. I've never met a one in person—are they all so careless, so indifferent to what the prospect of intimately meeting Old Grief means to the rest of us? "The contraband is one thing. Social services might let you off with a sanction. But impregnating a six? The psychic cost to the community, to her family and to her, and saying nothing of the painkillers it will require over and above her allotted ration? They'll exile you for that, no question. And they'll be right to do it."

"It wasn't meant to happen, alright?" he snaps. I do my best not to recoil at his tone. If he was going to hurt me, he would have done it by now—that's what I tell myself. "It will be horrible, but she'll survive, and I'll be there for the kid when she does."

He really doesn't understand, I realize, with something between incredulity and wonder. "It will destroy her. That kind of pain, it's…" I grope for words. "It's the opposite of life."

"I don't need this shit." He hoists his backpack onto his shoulder and makes to leave.

"You want to make amends?"

He stops. There's strength in my voice I hadn't known I could summon.

"I have a proposition for you," I say. "It won't take much of your time, an hour or two at most. I'll even pay you a few spare credits. I have a daughter—she's a six as well."

—

I arrive back at the domicile with a soft knock to announce my presence. My family is still gathered at the kitchen table. Alice is still picking at the remains of her pasta, stone cold by now. Bernard has abandoned his efforts at soliciting her interest and is reading an article on his tablet, nursing a glass of tomato juice.

Alice must see something in my expression that draws her attention, because she looks up at me with puzzlement. "Hey Ally," I murmur, "I have a surprise for you. Someone you've wanted to meet for a long time now."

Bernard closes his tablet with a sharp *click*.

"He heard about your wobble," I continue, "and he managed to get the day off at last."

I usher Alexander into the room. The young man introduces himself with a small smile and an uncertain wave. "Um, hi," he says. "I'm William."

Alice's eyes widen. Bernard puts his tomato juice down, hard. *Play along*, I mouth at him, silently. His jaw clenches, but he stays silent, as I expected he would. Before any of us can talk any further, a pastel-colored blur moves across the room at just below waist height, and Julia clamps herself to Alexander's thigh. "Wi'wam!" she cries. "Did you bring more honey?"

—

"There are deer, you know, up above," Alexander says. "You know what a deer is, Ally?"

Alice's eyebrows furrow as she tries to picture one. "They have four legs, don't they? And antlers?"

Alexander nods encouragement. "That's right. Most people haven't seen them, but there are actually way more now than there were two hundred years ago. They don't have to share the space with humans anymore, so they're making new little deer babies all over the place." He lowers his head and voice, conspiratorially. "There are probably hundreds of them right above our heads, right now, just a mile or so up."

Alice glances upward, unable to contain her amazement at this idea.

It's now well after the girls' bedtime. After his initial uncertainty, Alexander has relaxed into the role of the older brother. He even seems to enjoy it, seeing my daughters hanging on his every word, the uncritical wonder on their faces at his stories. They listen as he spins tales from his stint in the fisheries, freely adapting the details to the fictitious apiary.

"One weekend, Juan and I went camping, a couple of miles from the shore."

"What's camping?"

"It's when you sleep outside, with just a bit of sheet called a "tent" over your head. You can hear the bugs chirping through the night and the birds singing in the morning. Anyway, this time Juan and I went camping, and when we woke up, a deer had its head inside our tent!" He gestures with his hands, to illustrate how close the animal was. Alice gives a delighted shriek at the idea, which Julia imitates. "It must have smelled the food we brought, because it was sniffing and snorting everywhere."

"Weren't you scared? What if it bit you?" Alice asks.

"Sure, I was startled at first. But deer are nice animals, and they don't hurt people."

"Like Gaspar," I interject, softly. Alexander nods.

"It even let me stroke it a little, on the nose. It felt sort of scratchy and wet. Nice, though."

"I still would have worried it would bite, myself." Bernard's voice is tight. His disapproval is obvious, but he's not going to pull me aside and out of earshot—not to leave our children in the company of a dubious stranger, even one room over.

"Well, it didn't," Alexander replies, half-apologetically.

Bernard makes a show of checking his watch. "It's been wonderful getting you home to visit, William," his tone making it obvious he considers it to have been anything but. "But the girls have their lessons tomorrow, and I'm sure your supervisor will want you fresh and rested tomorrow morning."

"I'm not tired at all!" Alice protests, but her tone isn't optimistic. "Can't you stay a little longer, William? Please, please, please?"

Alexander looks imploringly, first at Bernard, where he's met with a scowl, then at me, where he finds an apologetic half-shrug.

Not much of a charade, I reflect. A couple of hours was all I could do for my firstborn child—just a deferment, like any other victory.

Alexander, to his credit, takes the hint. "Sorry, Ally," he says, tone mournful. "Like Dad says, I have an early shift in the morning."

"Will you be home again for Christmas?"

"Maybe, little sis. Maybe."

He helps load the dishwasher, stiffly embraces each of us in turn, then makes to go. In the entranceway, though, he turns abruptly and kneels, looking Alice in the eye. Bernard takes half a step forward, and in all the years we've been married, I can't think of another gesture he made that so clearly indicated violent intent.

"I almost forgot," Alexander says, "let's see your wobbler. Say 'ah.'"

"Ah," Alice obeys, opening her jaw as wide as she can. The tender pink flesh of her gums and cheeks and tongue are rendered clearly by the entranceway's harsh white light, and for a moment, all I can think of are the ways they could be pierced or nicked, of ulcers and infections and all Old Grief's myriad horrors she's admitting as long as she keeps her mouth open. So many decades stretch out before her—what kind of heroism am I asking from her that she face them?

I turn away. It's beyond my strength to keep contemplating it.

—

I got the call in the middle of the night from the Birthing Room; all the terse voice on the other end said was that there had been a complication and the parents' presence was legally required.

I waited for two hours in the antechamber, frequently adjusting my posture in the cheap cushioning of the available chairs. My only companions were a wan, middle-aged nurse at the reception desk, and a designated new parent-pairing at the other end of the room, waiting for confirmation of a successful in vitro coupling of sperm and egg. Each of us cast our eyes about the room, exchanging no words of comfort or commiseration. What was there to say? No one found themselves in the Birthing Room at this hour except to receive bad news or deliver it.

It was almost 2:00 A.M. before Bernard arrived. We embraced perfunctorily, and he muttered an apology close to my ear, something about a malfunction with the hydroponics.

"You're the husband?" the nurse asked, tone crisp, without waiting for us to separate. Bernard nodded. "Good, then we can proceed. Follow me, please."

We progressed through three rounds of decontamination before being admitted into the community's birthing area proper, comprising tier upon tier of stainless steel gantries. Therein were suspended rows and columns of sealed glass chambers filled with amniotic fluid; in each twitched embryos across the full spectrum of development, from freshly fertilized eggs to infants primed for decantation.

Our pod was denoted as BX-17. The entity inside was in its twentieth week of development; human enough to look at, though of encephalitic proportions, and small enough that it could have fit in the palm of my latex-gloved hand.

I'd seen pictures, of course. Bernard and I were kept updated on our son's development in weekly reports with accompanying specs detailing weight, blood type, and such. But until now, I hadn't seen the creature that was one-half me in motion. It seemed perturbed. The difference from the other embryos we'd passed at similar stages was subtle—but pronounced if you looked closely. Miniscule fingers clenched and unclenched, limbs flailed with unusual vehemence. I feared I knew why we'd been called with such urgency.

"The tissue samples came back with a 0.0084% margin of error," the nurse said, voice flat, eyes fixed on her tablet. "Standard procedure when a ten is detected is termination, pending the mother and father's approval."

She held the tablet toward us both and proffered a stylus. "The forms are boilerplate. We just need a signature from each of you, and you can be on your way."

"Margin of error?" I repeated, stupidly. "So, there's still a chance...?" The protest died on my lips even before the nurse's exasperated look could kill it. I saw the way the creature (my son!) writhed in its incubator and knew there could be no doubt. A ten.

Bernard sighed and accepted the tablet. He crooked it in his elbow and added a cursory squiggle to the screen.

"Wait!" My objection came too late, but I could hardly help myself. "Shouldn't we talk about this?"

"What's to talk about, Erica?" Bernard was twenty-three years old, and even then, he looked so tired. "It's a bad business, no doubt. Unfortunate. But it never would have been alive, not really, so why linger on it? Just sign it, will you? I'm going to have to pull ten hours tomorrow night as is, and I want to get some sleep."

My eyes were fixed on the not-quite-child. Its eyes were closed, like all the others around it. And yet, not quite like the others, it seemed to me then—rather than closed in the peaceful, dreamless sleep of other fetuses—they seemed screwed shut.

"We'll have more chances, Erica," Bernard said, softer than before.

A ten. We all walked such a narrow course through life, and the higher we were on the index, the narrower it became. There was never a moment I wasn't conscious of my own: were I to stray even slightly from that knife's edge, Old Grief's talons waited. But a ten—they would have no path through at all. Every breath would be an agony; the gentlest touch the rasp of razor wire; a kiss would be the blow of a sledgehammer.

The thing in the tank gave a sudden jerk, which I reflexively echoed. My son. He was suffering.

Bernard handed me the tablet, and hesitantly, I accepted it. "Just one thing," I said, quietly, stylus limply poised between thumb and forefinger. "I'd settled on a name: William. Please, when he's… discarded, can the documentation say—"

The nurse cut me off. "We get that request a lot. You can log it on your way out."

Bernard gave a curt nod, then looked at me, expectantly. I added my signature beneath his.

—

"That little molar back there?" I hear Alexander's voice say. "Aw, that's nothing! You'll barely feel it. One quick yank; chew on the other side of your mouth for a week; no big deal. You'll hardly notice it's gone."

"Really?"

"Sure. Don't worry about it, okay?"

"Okay."

I bring myself to look—my daughter is smiling. Really smiling, eyes shining, her whole face crinkled with uncompromised joy.

Alexander steps over the entranceway threshold, and the domicile seals behind him.

—

My abandonment of propriety is met with its like; Bernard is furious with me. He doesn't raise his voice—not once—but he makes it clear in no uncertain terms that he no longer considers me a trustworthy guardian of his daughters' well-being.

Graeme, when I see him the next day, concurs. He witnessed the whole charade play out on the monitor cameras, of course. As this is my first infraction, and in recognition of the stress I've been under, he's willing to overlook the violation of domestic protocol. I'm permitted to keep my present living arrangement, subject to a probation period of one year.

I feel frustrated—not at the reprisals for my actions, which are no different from what I expected—but at my own lack of honest regret for what I did and my inability to articulate why.

——

The probationary year comes and goes, and the days pass in much the same fashion as before: some better; some worse; the trend toward deterioration so gradual as to be imperceptible. I carry on making deliveries to Henrietta's domicile occasionally. I don't see or hear Andrea there anymore; Henrietta doesn't volunteer any news, and I don't ask.

About eight months in, a minor item on our community news feed reports that a vagrant, male, nineteen years of age, was arrested and charged with possession of dilute hydrochloric acid solution, with intent to distribute. In repentance for his crime, and to repay the debt to his community—so the report says—the young man consented to allow himself to be euthed by means of nitrogen inhalation.

I don't pay the news item much mind—at this point, Alice seems to find another loose tooth every six or seven days. Between the screaming and the tears and the lack of sleep, I can scarcely find it in me to think about anything at all.

For a while after Alexander's visit, Alice asks after William almost constantly but then becomes so preoccupied with her next loose tooth that she stops. She never really starts again.

She loses the last of her milk teeth when she's nine. Around the same time, the wall that has increasingly separated her from me becomes insuperable. She refuses to make eye contact with me, answers my questions with monosyllabic grunts, and abides in her room outside of lessons and mealtimes. I can't pinpoint the moment she realizes William is a fantasy; she doesn't accuse me of lying or of betraying her. The name "William" just seems to vanish from our household—the letters and gifts stop coming with no narrative to justify their absence.

In due course, my daughters mature and leave our domicile for lives of their own. Julia takes up Bernard's old position in the poppy farm when he retires. Alice becomes a homemaker like her mother. I speak with Julia perhaps once a week; Alice maybe twice a year, at first, then not at all.

At sixty-eight, with worsening arthritis, I make the decision to euth. The few acquaintances remaining to me by this stage laud the decision as the right, responsible one. I've seen my tenure through diligently, borne Old Grief's embrace long enough. The nitrogen flowing from the pressurized canister to the face mask will taste sweet, they tell me. And, sure enough, when the valve is turned, I do feel something like alleviation. My vision and thoughts fog, and all matter and being seems to unclench and soften, becoming dissociated, leaving no hard surfaces to come into contact with each other.

Here is my reward, in these few drowsy minutes: sanctuary from impact and weight and grinding, crushing force.

One image persists in my imagination after all others have gone— the sight of Alice as a little girl, smiling, free of fear, as Alexander steps across the threshold.

THE STAINS OF NOW

A. KATHERINE BLACK

We found a house hunter at the bench on the corner of Fifth and Main, former neighbors' blood still wet on our suits, reek screams still ringing in our ears. A sliver of moon stabbed the sky, its light sparse. Making out the hunter's face was difficult. Her hands were in her pockets. We nodded greeting, hands in our own pockets. Knives on my right knuckles, pistol in my left palm.

We carried everything important in our packs, including Sye, who I prayed would stay quieter than the mice she loved to catch. We had no choice but to find a new place that night. There was no going back, and anyone outside a neighborhood barricade after sunrise was either a sniper or an idiot. Ell and I were neither.

"Two of you?"

"Could be more," Ell said.

I kept my eyes on the hunter, but my fingers twitched in my pockets. Ell wasn't talking about Sye. First time they'd put words to the idea of expanding our little clan, and after all these seasons with me, they'd gone and said it out here, in the wide open. To a stranger.

Ell didn't look to me for a response. Probably knew I would have none.

"Got it," the hunter said, hands still hidden. "Pay?"

The hunter didn't need to see the blood on our suits to know why we were there. She knew enough. She'd charge accordingly.

I slipped the duffel from the tall grass under the bench and unzipped. Propane tanks, boxes of bullets, salt grinders. All we could gather from our bunker in under twenty breaths.

"Everything's full," I said, coiling my legs, preparing to shift or jump, to cover any rustling sounds that might come from my pack. If the hunter knew a mouser was within reach, the price would raise, to include one live animal.

Sye didn't move a muscle. Seemed she understood, somehow, that out here, outside our bunker, she was the prey.

I knew the feeling. We all knew that feeling.

"Keep up," the hunter said as she headed northwest, stepping over the long-settled rubble of a building from Before.

Right, she didn't know if our neighborhood had been overrun by reeks or if they'd simply kicked me and Ell out for laziness. Not that it mattered to her.

First neighborhood we visited was a clear no-go. Holes in their barricade—too many, too easy to spot. Eyes were wide, hungry. Too eager to accept me and Ell, knowing nothing about us, about our skills.

Hunter saw this too, no doubt. Desperate group like this would agree to a smaller cut of her profits in exchange for two able bodies. She had to try.

We nodded thanks as they ushered us out. Wondered if I'd see any of them soon, looking for a new neighborhood.

Second neighborhood seemed solid from the outside. Locked tight. But no patrols. No one visible atop the barricade.

We walked around maybe a quarter of the barricade before the smell hit. Rotting flesh. Could be reek, could be human. No matter how different we were alive, dead reek and dead human smelled the same. We moved on.

Moving sucks.

A small part of me—a tiny bit that crouched in some far pocket of my brain—wanted to hightail it back home, reeks or no, back to the neighborhood where Ell and I met, where Ell found Sye tucked under a rusting car hood. Where we shared our first pallet, built our first memories.

I'd crank the bunker door shut one final time, brick it up for good measure, and that'd be the end of it. The end of failed supply runs, the end of grunt shifts defending too many weak points in the barricades. The end of ten people reporting to work and nine returning home.

Part of me, a secret part, wanted to sneak away from it all. Slip down into the deepest pit, sit forever in the dark with nothing but Ell and Sye. Never again feeling the ground rumble from the trample of so many reek legs, legs wearing boots of so many human dead. Never again watching human flesh tear against a reek's diamond skin, split under its razor claws.

Hints of red crept into the edges of the sky as we approached the third neighborhood. We passed buildings from Before that were long since gutted, pieces taken to fortify this neighborhood and probably others. Anything left trampled by hundreds of reek patrols.

We'd be scrambling for shelter at daybreak if this neighborhood didn't work out, and nothing outside this barricade looked even slightly secure. I imagined me and Ell making a break for it. Hauling ourselves back to the old place, dodging lines of marching reeks, barely making it to our bunker.

I wondered if my thoughts were splashed too plain across my face, but Ell had eyes on the barricade before us, whistling quietly at its tightly-packed, mostly metal construction.

We kept a respectful distance from the nearest watchtower. It stood a good four meters above the barricade, higher than anything I'd ever seen built in the Now.

The hunter made the customary hooting call. A voice answered from inside, quick and sharp. The hunter began standard intros. I fought the urge to slip off my pack and reach a hand in to reassure Sye, scratch her ears.

The sun had crossed half the sky before all was done.

We shook hands with neighborhood reps. Strong grips, all of them.

They looked us in the eyes. Promised two moon cycles of safety, then they'd see. We'd have to prove our worth. They put Ell on building repair, me on supply runs.

We handed the hunter the duffel. She opened it, gave the reps their portion, and they offered her shelter for the night. Pledges were spoken in clear voice, rules detailed. Same as our last neighborhood. And the one before that.

This would be my fifth. Who knows how many for Ell. Our pasts were rarely put to word.

Got the keys to a bunker deep in the center of the neighborhood, plus a supply pack, and a full two days to settle in before reporting for shifts. Generous.

Unusual.

Door cranked shut, bowls of fish and peas licked clean, we made our pallet in the first room of the place, too tired to explore further down. Not eager to sort through the previous occupant's gear.

I lay in the dark, listening to Ell's even breaths, unable to close my eyes. Watching Sye's outline as she crouched and crept along the wall, fulfilling her solemn duty to investigate every inch of this new place. I imagined the scents she must be picking up: human blood, reek guts, food and waste, passion and tears. Sometimes I wished for her nose, but not then.

I whispered encouragement, hoping she found something worth hunting while Ell and I slept. Sleep dampened my thoughts, dangling loose old memories of every move, of every new neighborhood. Digging up images I'd just as soon forget. Of my clan as a kid. Of the first neighborhood I'd fought for, before I'd gotten good with the knife. Of my mana's face on the day of that raid, slashed apart, split down the middle 'til their eyes looked in opposite directions, 'til Mana almost looked like the reek that felled them.

Days and nights passed in the new bunker, in the new neighborhood. Awkward, unfamiliar things gradually shaped themselves into routine, expected things. People stopped staring at us after a few market nights—once our faces were matched with names, our names matched with jobs. I got a few slaps on the back for finding a medicine stash on my third supply run. Caught more than a few elders offering nods to Ell. No doubt the strength of Ell's barricade patches had been noted.

We ate, we slept, we patted Sye's head when she presented a dead lizard. We worked. Sometimes our hands slipped beneath each other's suits, and we savored a blissful moment.

I said nothing to Ell about growing our clan. Told myself what we had was enough.

Truth be bare, the idea of expanding our clan felt fragile, too delicate to lay out in words. Course, there are only two ways to grow a clan. Ell and I didn't have the mutual biology required for seed, which meant turning to other options. Which meant discussions, forming plans, speaking to elders.

It all felt so huge.

Every time my mind stepped in that direction, I kept seeing my mana's face, shifting between split and whole, between dead and alive. I could never be so brave.

———

Our first moon cycle was nearly past when I returned to our bunker at dawn, exhausted from a rough supply run. No sign of Ell in the sitting room. Not in the kitchen or in the sleeping room. And no Sye.

Too tired to kick off my boots, let alone peel away my suit, I wandered as I was, deeper into the bunker. Through the first two landings, where we'd settled. Past the sleeping room, down a ladder I hadn't yet touched, I caught the flicker of a lantern, blinking around a tunnel bend, heard the cracking of wood.

Ell'd already cleared away most of the rotted boards barricading the room. I helped finish the job while Sye mewed a warning to anything skittering on the other side of the door.

We should have waited before opening it. Should have considered the possibilities. Might've led to another bunker or to a door outside the neighborhood that reeks might discover. Might even have led to one of those chambers only foolish children and foolhardy elders dared speak of, where the reeks had been birthed by the insane people of Before.

Instead, we opened the door without discussion. Opened it wide, without ceremony. Sye rushed into the darkness ahead.

Ell's long arm held a lantern across the threshold. We whispered at the doorway, as if a strong voice could break something. Or wake something. We wondered how many generations had passed since the room had been dug. Must've been before the Rise. Before the Fall, even. Everything inside was strange, as if plucked from firelight tales laid down by someone's parents' parents' parents.

Untying my boots and slipping off my socks, I reached a naked toe toward the floor covering. Its thick, long yarns were a shade of orange I could barely believe. Brighter than the fruit grown by my mana, forever ago, warmer than the sun could ever hope to be.

Ell squeezed my arm but let go when I stepped inside. My feet sank into a cool softness that felt unreal. I returned to the landing to peel off my suit before pulling Ell in to stretch and roll on the floor with me. We touched everything on the tables, inspected everything on the shelves, sat in the soft chairs, forgot to eat. Ell nearly missed their next shift.

The room was so deep, we couldn't hear anything from the surface down there when the door was shut. No rumble of reek squads, no rockets fired from the neighborhood barricade. Not a sound. The neighborhood could be under full attack, and we'd know nothing but the whisper of bare skin sliding through soft yarn, the squeak of fragile metal parts as the music machine cranked to life.

And the singing.

Voices from that machine engulfed the room, fragile and stubborn as wildflowers, ancient and unreachable as stars. Songs held aloft by instruments I couldn't begin to picture. Telling tales of a world long gone, long since trampled by our own.

I slipped into that seclusion after every shift, letting the room fill me up like a solar panel reviving a dead battery. I stretched on the soft floor, Sye curled at my feet. Soaked in the music, gently picking through old books in search of strange pictures. Pictures with too many rounded edges, too many smiles. Trying to imagine the world that allowed such things to exist.

After the first funeral, Ell stopped visiting the room.

—

I'd never been to a funeral. Past neighborhoods paid respect to their dead in quieter ways. Pauses in front of newly emptied bunkers. Names muttered under the breath, others grunting respectful echoes. But never a line-up of people, two-deep, like reek squads, staring at the empty body while Elders hummed some strange tune. I counted three children gripping the legs of people in those lines. Their mouths still, silent. Their eyes open.

Ell dug into work after that. Joined me less and less in the room at the bottom of our bunker, the room from Before.

I stopped asking.

I'd lay with Ell on the pallet, wait for their breaths against my neck to steady, for the half-snores to settle in, and then I'd sneak away. Sometimes I'd wake on the orange floor, the room dim, lantern nearly drained, Ell already gone for their shift.

My shifts became unbearable. I was dying to get back to the room but careful not to talk to anyone about it, unsure if any other bunkers held such things. Afraid it would spark a dangerous interest. Didn't seem like this group would tolerate theft, but we hadn't been here long. Things aren't always what they first seem.

My obsession with the room might have gone on forever—until I became careless on a supply run or Ell left for a better partner—if Ell hadn't snapped at me that night.

Halfway through our second moon cycle in the new place. Our time was almost up, and I hadn't thought enough about impressing the elders, only about the room, with its quiet, its color.

Like every other day, I'd come home and immediately slipped down into the depths of the bunker.

That shift, we'd come face-to-face with three reeks. Made it back to the neighborhood, but with two fewer people. More funerals would be planned for people whose names I'd barely tried to learn. I dropped into a soft, forgiving chair without one crank of the music machine and fell asleep.

Ell's ranting woke me.

In my exhaustion, I'd forgotten to take off my suit. Dripped a mess all over the room, spoiling the flooring with thick drops of goo and blood.

Our precious room of Before, made heavy with the stains of Now.

Ell screamed about my carelessness. Thoughtlessness. Said I didn't deserve a room like this. None of us did.

I studied the soiled floor while Ell hurled words at me 'til they had none left to throw. 'Til they just stood there, crying.

I removed my boots before crossing to the door, not meeting Ell's eyes, not disagreeing.

The room stayed closed after that night. It was the only way to draw a clear line between that room and the world above. The only way to keep me in the Now.

Still, something of me stayed behind, lurking stubborn behind that door in the depths of our bunker, curled in that soft chair, surrounded by that impossible orange.

I tried to pretend otherwise. Took extra shifts in the neighborhood, worked the garden on my off days, helped out in medical.

Tried like hell to ignore the hole that room had bored somewhere deep inside.

—

I never used to split off from the group on supply runs, but I'd changed. Maybe it was the room, maybe that funeral. Maybe too many moves, too many neighborhoods. Scavenging solo, felt natural. Made sense. After a few runs, no one questioned. Neighbors didn't know me well enough to wonder.

Maybe they didn't know me well enough to worry.

It was my last run before the elders would make their decision about Ell and me. I acted like it was just another night, another shift, another run.

We ventured far, to a huge place from Before unlike anything I'd ever seen. The moon was already half passed. My legs ached as we reached the old market, but the pain slipped away when we stepped through the broken doors.

When the enormous darkness enveloped our meager headlamps.

Cavernous, echoing. Huge pillars and wide wading pools. Dozens of rooms surrounded the central area, each one larger than our entire bunker, many still holding a surprising amount of gear on their cracked shelves. Leaving kitchen and boot collection to other people, I searched for something smaller, more tucked away. Like a medicine stash.

I found it in a room at the far end of the market. Sharp echoes shot across the vast space as I broke the locks on one door, then another. Snapped open cabinets that had been closed since people walked on floors brighter than the sun.

In the cabinets were piles of stuffs. Some molded, decayed, but much still useful. I loaded my pack, marveling at the shape and strength of the many tools and various body braces.

Unsure how much time passed, knowing the meet-up would be soon, I rushed to close my pack. A flash of color popped into the light of my headlamp. Small. Orange. Made of that plastic material that lasts forever. A child's toy from Before. I picked it up.

Slick against my fingers, its body gave way to my press, distorting this way and that. I turned it over and found a face. Chills crept down my spine. Its face wasn't quite human. Wasn't quite reek, either, but something in between. Eyes on stalks, a button nose, and smiling mouth, like a giddy, unhinged human. With too many legs, so many arms, in that way very, very reek.

A shout echoed from the cavernous central area, followed by a cackle and a screech, undoubtedly reek.

I wondered who'd shouted. At least they'd gotten out a warning call, before their end.

I turned off my headlamp, dug into my pockets to find my weapons' grips. I crept along the wall, sidling around two doorways. Then, a second scream—different voice, human.

Mind urging me ahead to the rendezvous spot, my ears craned for more sounds, human or reek.

Reek it was.

Heavy stomps. Too many boots. Too many claws scraping across the ancient stone floor. No way to tell how many there were. That's the thing about reeks. So many legs. So many claws. More than ears can count.

Pressing hard against the wall, I slipped along the edge of the wide central room, in the place that dared stand so defiant in the faces of both sun and moon, human and reek.

No more sounds. No bodies in sight. Examining the landmarks as my eyes adjusted to the darkness, regaining my bearings, I realized how far I still had to trek to reach the meeting point.

Crouching to cross the wide doorways of the old market rooms, I kept my lantern off and my ears craned. Wasn't the first time I'd wished for Sye's keen senses, for her obnoxious bravery. Halfway to the other end of the place, nearing the meeting point, a shuffle echoed.

Caught in a wide opening between two walls, I hoped for only one reek.

No such luck.

Pounding thumps exploded from the silence. Two reeks: one in front, another to the left. I lunged to the right, tried to roll to the other side of the doorway, but my pack was too large, too heavy.

I tucked tightly where my roll had broken, offering as little torso as I could for their stabbing pleasure. I turned on my headlamp, looking quickly between the two reeks. Left arm aiming the pistol, right arm coiling with my knives. They bounded forward.

The timing had to be right. Only close-range attacks work. Only hits to the underbelly.

Human screams erupted from somewhere. I let my gaze fall steady down my left arm as I aimed for the sternum of the one approaching from that side, fired three quick shots, at the same time blindly jabbing my knife-wielding right hand at the other.

They fell on me.

The first died mid-lunge, chest full of holes, limp weight crashing into me. I tried to keep it between me and the living one, a scrabbling, screeching mess of claws. A searing pain—hot and cold—sliced across my arms and legs. My vision blurred. I kept stabbing and twisting.

Our shrieks joined in a grotesque song. The reek's split face shook and writhed above me as I pushed deeper into its gut, as it clawed at my suit, my face. Bloody, screaming seconds mounted, stretched. Its head morphed until it looked like the plastic toy from Before, with that hideous, unbelievable smile, like my dying mana's.

I don't remember how it ended. Never asked the other survivors.

—

I woke on a moving pallet in broad daylight, taking in fuzzy images of neighbors marching on either side of me, weapons ready.

Woke again to smells of a medical bunker, swirls of antiseptic and sweat. To the sound of Ell's voice, the feel of their hand in mine.

Was a full moon cycle before I left medical to return to our bunker, shuffling stiffly in one of the braces I'd scavenged that night. Sye met me at the door and began an immediate sniff-down, learning where I'd been, what I'd done. And she didn't run away.

Life resumed, our stay in the neighborhood indefinitely extended.

I returned home one morning, back aching after a long shift in medical, after patching and wrapping too many injured, including a few that didn't make it to sunrise.

I needed to see Sye. Give her a scratch. See Ell, maybe say those things I never say.

But there was no Ell at the door.

Down the ladder to the washroom and kitchen, down again to the storeroom and bedroom.

No Ell.

I heard something faint, then. Voices, soft and light, as if from another time.

I climbed down the last ladder, walked the hallway to the deepest room, and stood in the open doorway, soaking in the source of the sound. It wasn't the music machine.

It was Ell, with a child I'd seen before, playing tag at the neighborhood market. Shedding tears at a recent funeral.

They sat on the floor, Ell and the child, whispering. Sliding fingers through the soft, orange yarn. Smiling.

Ell looked at me and beckoned me in. I held back, suit still dripping with signs of death, not wanting to stain the room any further, not wanting to spoil what was there.

But the room was soft, the giggles warm.

I began to unlace my boots.

HARD TIME

P. A. CORNELL

DAY 1

How it works is, you go to trial. That takes about half an hour of your time when you make a full confession. Once the judge convicts you, they take you to a shuttle. The shuttle takes you to the processing center, though the convicts just call it "the tanks." That's where they stick you in cryo. It's not so bad if you're not claustrophobic. You just lie down, relax, and go to sleep like you've done every day of your life. The jarring part is waking up light years from where you started. You don't know where you are. You don't know how much time has passed, though you do know it's probably been years, or they wouldn't bother with the cryo. The only thing you know for certain is you're never seeing Earth again, or anyone you knew who's still there. But I'd do it all again for you, Arion.

You'd barely turned fifteen when I went to sleep. From the amount of time they told us we'd been in space, you'd be a grown man by now. I can't help but wonder how you turned out; how you look now, and whether you've stayed out of trouble all these years. I hope you're taking care of your mom now that I'm gone. But I must make peace with the fact that I'll never know any of the answers to my questions. Prisoners aren't allowed communication with their loved ones. No messages in and definitely none out. That's why all I can do is think these letters in my head, wishing I could somehow transmit them to Earth so you'd know I still think of you and that I don't blame you for anything. That I love you.

They woke about twenty of us. After the sickness and confusion passed, they gave us a quick orientation session and assigned us cells and uniforms. I'd expected arm and leg restraints, like back on Earth after my arrest, but we discovered something interesting when one of the inmates mouthed off to the warden. Seems a lot more than space travel happened after we went to sleep. They put something in our heads. It lets the guards tap directly into our nervous system. They can amuse themselves making us do all kinds of interesting things, though they favor the pain triggers, jacked up as high as the safety levels allow. That's been a real treat.

Still, every time they decide I need a refresher on who's in charge, I can't help but smile inside. All the pain is worth it, knowing you don't have to endure it. I'll take whatever they can dish out, so long as you don't have to.

DAY 8

We don't have cellmates on this prison station, or communal areas other than the mess. We only see the others during mealtimes and work. We're not supposed to talk then, but we find ways. That's how I met Toshihiro. He's one of the old timers and he seems to know what's going on around here better than anyone. Even the guards leave him alone, so he's a good person to know. You don't get to be an old timer in this place without playing your cards right. Toshi doesn't even do the hard labor like the rest of us, having long ago negotiated a better deal, working for the warden. He was a lawyer back on Earth. A corporate lawyer, but with a broad general knowledge of the global legal system. I think the warden uses him to find loopholes in his side business deals, and to cover his tracks when the loopholes cross the legality line. That keeps Toshi out of the kiln—though that's something I'll tell you about another time.

Toshi tells me that in the old days the laws were different. For starters, you were considered innocent until they could prove your guilt, not the other way around like it is now. Small crimes got small punishments and kids were tried differently than adults, not like now where the punishment's the same no matter who you are or what you do. I haven't told Toshi about you though. He knows I have a son, but he doesn't know what you did or why I'm here. That's something I'm taking to the grave, don't worry.

DAY 22

The days are long, and indistinguishable from night. The station's protected from this system's star by a heat shield, and that also blocks almost all the natural light, so station lighting is all we have. And since there's no clocks, we go by what they tell us. For all we know the guards mess with the schedule to keep us off balance, our internal chronometers all out of whack, but there's no way to know for sure. I'm not even sure how many days I've been here, though if I go by the number of days I've pulled in the kiln, then I guess it's about three Earth weeks. I wonder how long it'll take before I stop trying to keep track altogether. Toshi doesn't bother anymore. Says he stopped trying to count after about a year. And that was a long time ago.

So, the kiln. That's what we call the mining operation here. I don't know the name of the planet, or if it even has a name. All I know is it's close to the star. That means it's hot as hell. I'm talking Venus hot. They give us special suits when they send us down, but there's a reason they send convicts to do the mining. The suits are only good for about twenty minutes at a time. Then they bring us up and have us change into a fresh one. By then your skin is red and sometimes blistered. The worst part's your hands where the suits have less protection to allow for flexibility. I can't remember a time when my hands weren't in constant pain.

I know what you're thinking; why not just send machines? They're too expensive—at least, machines built to stand the heat would be. Machines are valuable. We're expendable. We're only given a handful of basic tools with which to mine. Even those are worth more than we are. One guy snapped a bit while boring a hole in one of the rock formations we were mining and since then no one's seen him. So it's clear where we are on the totem pole.

DAY 64

It's been a while since I got here, Arion. I'm not sure just how long since I stopped counting. I still think about you all the time. Your laugh, the way you were always so kind to everyone, especially the way you loved dogs. God, I miss dogs. What I wouldn't give for a pup in my cell to come home to after the day's labor. A dog who'd give a shit whether I made it back or not and would lick my reddened hands to soothe the constant ache.

None of this was your fault, though. It was your kindness and innocence that led you to befriend everyone, even those kids you were running with during that time. I'm sure they seemed decent enough. Came from good families and all. I blame myself for raising you so naive you didn't know you were being used—didn't know a real friend doesn't ask you to commit a crime for them. I never really knew what bullshit story they gave you. Probably something to tug at your heartstrings, knowing you. I'll bet they made up some story about their mom or kid brother needing an operation they couldn't afford or something. Then you, being the kind heart you always were, tried to help, even knowing it was wrong.

How could I allow you to be punished for that? How could I let the police take you when they came knocking that night, sirens blaring and transport ready? Christ, you were just a kid. I couldn't let them ship you off to the prison worlds—nothing but cheap labor until the work killed you—all for stealing a handful of credits for your friends. If anything, it was my fault for letting you get so good at computers. I mean, it's a useful skill, your mother and I both agreed on that, but when you got good enough to work around the regulation system, we should have stopped you. We shouldn't have let you explore so far that you'd learn to break into restricted areas. We should've known you'd gotten that good, the way your so-called friends did.

So what could I do but take your place when they came for you? Wouldn't any father have done the same?

DAY 212

I know I don't talk to you much in my head these days Arion, but what is there to say? Day in and day out, it's pretty much the same. They send us down to the kiln until the shift ends, then send us back to our cells where we mostly try to sleep so we can't feel the way our bodies are breaking down. I hate to say it, but sometimes I try not to think of you on purpose. It's almost more painful than what prison does to me. I miss you so much, son.

But today, I couldn't get you out of my head. A transport shuttle came in to drop off some kids. New inmates, but teenagers. Just a few years older than you were when I left you. At eighteen they get brought to places like this. Not that they have it easy at the kid labor stations either. But this place…it's more of a death sentence. These kids will be replacing the guys we've lost. They looked scared too, as they marched them in. Toshi and I were chosen to show them the ropes, not that there's much to tell. You live in your cell. You get out to eat and work. That's about it.

I can't help but think of you when I see guys this young, Arion, even though you'd be a lot older now. This could've been you. I felt myself break a sweat just thinking about it. Makes me think that no matter what I've gone through here, I did the right thing by taking the rap for you.

DAY 401

I don't know what Toshi did to piss off the warden, but I imagine it must've lost him a lot of credits. At any rate, they put him back on the roster for the kiln. I couldn't believe it when I saw the old man all dressed up in one of the heat suits. He looked scared shitless too. Wasn't even talking. I'm worried about him. It's been a long time since he was doing hard labor and his body's not as young as it used to be. I told him that whatever it takes, he has to get back in the warden's good graces as soon as possible. I don't know if he answered me because that's when a guard zapped me for talking. I must've blacked out for a bit because I woke up on the floor of the descent shuttle, feeling like my body was on fire even before they dropped us into the kiln.

DAY 406

One of the kids had an accident. I think it was sabotage, though I can't prove it. Suit failure, they said. Plus, it took them an awful long time to pull him out when he raised the alert. It was on an open comm too. I know a lot of us will be having nightmares for a long time. Nightmares featuring that kid's screams as the soundtrack.

There's this guy—Eric—who handles body disposal. He told me the kid looked like he'd been deep-fried by the time they got him out of his suit. Not that they could even fully get him out, since pieces of the lining melted to his body. Worst part is, he was still alive for a while longer.

I spent the rest of the day in my cell just crying and thinking of you. Fuck, Arion, I hope you've stayed out of trouble. Every time they bring in new inmates I scan their faces, hoping not to recognize you in them. My greatest fear is to see your face transformed to adult proportions in anyone here; to find that all this has been for nothing.

I try to think instead of a world in which you grew up to be successful—where you have real friends who care about you. I see you married, maybe with a son of your own. In my wildest fantasies, I imagine that you named him after your old man. I imagine your mother, older but still beautiful, holding her grandson and the two of you living a normal and amazing life without me.

DAY 417

Toshi's dead. His body just couldn't handle it anymore, and his heart gave out sometime during the night. It was just a matter of time. Probably would've happened sooner if they left you any means by which you could off yourself in this place, but they make sure that isn't possible. They can't afford to lose the workers, especially those of us who've been around a while and know what we're doing.

The bitter irony is that the warden was about to let him off the hook. Rumor is the error that cost him so much was clerical and his secretary's fault—not Toshi's. I wonder if the secretary will be joining us in the kiln now.

Normally, the bodies just get dumped in the kiln without a suit. Easy cremation. But since the warden felt bad about Toshi, he stuck him in a tank and launched him into space. He'll probably fall into the planet in time anyway, but I guess it made the warden feel better.

Didn't do a damn thing for those of us who cared about Toshi.

Though, I guess it's something that the warden invited us all to his office so we could watch the launch through his observation window.

With Toshi gone, looks like I'm among the oldest of the old timers here. Can't say I'm overwhelmed by the honor.

DAY 523

Bad accident today. Mine. Suit malfunction where one of the seals failed. They train us for this shit, so I got it repaired in seconds, but not before taking a nice big breath of superheated air.

They were good enough to pull me off shift early and give me some treatment, but there's not much they can do for me. I'll either heal or I won't. In the meantime, I'm trying not to cough because—*fuck*—it hurts. Might as well be the guards zapping my implant every time I do. Leaves me sweating and shaking. Fuck, it's hard not to cough with scorched lungs.

DAY 531

Warden called me to his office. Seems he's been looking over Toshi's old files to see if he can't find stuff he can use to revive his illegal side business and turns out, he did. But this time it involves me—and in a way you, Arion.

It looks like Toshi, good friend that he was, used the warden's system to try to find out what had happened to you. I guess he wanted to be able to let me know you were okay and that your mom had moved on. He must not have had a chance to tell me, or maybe he never knew. It takes a while to get anything from Earth here, even for someone with the warden's clearance. But somehow news came in about you, and it looks like you used that computer savvy of yours to start a security company. Something to help stop kids like you from hacking into restricted systems and private accounts. Made me proud to hear you were your own man and doing alright.

Trouble is, the warden sees this as an opportunity to do what those shit friends of yours did to you all those years ago. He wants me to convince you to skim credits for him out of the prison system. He says you can do it without getting caught, so there's no risk. But it's not his son's freedom on the line. And I know he'd make sure it didn't lead back to him if you got caught. Hell, he'd probably make sure you wound up here and were assigned a faulty heat suit, just like that other kid.

But there's no way. I told him I'd think about it, but my mind's been on other things. I know my days are numbered if I refuse. But I didn't come all this way or go through so much pain to let you go down this road now.

DAY 535

I don't think I've been here two years. It's not a long time really, though the days here stretch to unnatural lengths. Still, it's long enough to have made a few friends in key places. Some of those friends are gone now. It's a slow process making new ones when you aren't allowed to talk, except about mining-related things in the kiln. But sometimes all you need is one friend in a key place at the right time.

I told the warden I'd talk to you on the condition that he'd let me die and give me the same kind of sendoff he did Toshi. I said the pain of my lungs and all the other damage caused to my body is too much now, which isn't a lie. I am ready for it to end.

I said I didn't want to risk his backing out of the deal, and requested Eric be there to prep me and put me under, once I'd talked to you— right there in the tanks. Then Eric would finish the job and launch me into the planet.

The warden agreed. I worried he'd show up with some guards to watch his back, but luckily, his greed made it so he kept his business to himself—no need to cut anyone in to keep them quiet.

He met me and Eric in the tanks with his portable comm unit already set to your contact. I got in the tank and Eric got the IV with the cryo-fluid ready. I even took the comm from the warden. But that's when the rest of old Toshi's friends joined us. Eric got the IV into the warden's arm while the others held him down. He didn't last long. Asleep in seconds, just like I remembered it. Unfortunately, there wasn't enough cryo-fluid left for me, but I'd known that going in. The warden needed to sign off on that sort of thing and he'd only signed off for one.

You're probably thinking that I should've gotten out of the tank then, rather than just move to make space for the warden. I won't lie, I thought about it. But I needed to make sure there was no one left who knew about you—who could reach their sadistic fingers back to Earth and hurt you now that I know you're okay and have made it. So, that meant erasing the evidence, and I'm part of that.

As long as I'm here, you're not safe, so I'm saying goodbye now.

The other guys got the warden into the tank. They didn't ask why I was doing this; I wasn't long for this world anyway, and they were just glad to be rid of him. All evidence would point to me in the end, I'd made sure of that. Hopefully, whoever replaced the tyrant would be an improvement. The guys deserved that much, at least.

They turned on the flash freeze which the IV protects you from. All I had was a thermal blanket the guys threw in for some protection, but let me tell you, it burned like hell. Cold's not much better than heat that way, the difference being that after a while, it makes you numb.

It's cramped in here, so I have my body essentially wrapped around the warden who might as well be frozen. They moved the tank into the launch bay. It's dark, but I'm not bothered.

And now I'm surrounded by stars. I see the dark shadow of the heat shield, but I know they put me on a course for the planet. Soon enough there'll be plenty of light, and it'll get pretty warm in here. I try not to, but I can't help but think of that kid who died. I hear his screams even now and imagine that'll be me soon enough.

But that's okay. I'd do it all again for you, Arion. I love you, son.

NO MORE SAUDADES

RODRIGO ASSIS MESQUITA

Through the dirt-spotted window of their apartment, from behind the white lace curtains, Mario looked down at the long-abandoned high school. Posters bearing the president's face encircled by babies covered the rusty fences. Mario held his baby, Ana, tighter and closer to his chest, to keep her safe from prying eyes and scattered flying drones. They had been on the run from the government since Lisandra's belly, pregnant with Ana, started to show, making her an easy target for the harvest.

She was running late. The smugglers' car would arrive in less than thirty minutes to take them, and Mario and Lis were told they waited for no one.

The apartment door clicked open.

"Hey, how is the little one?" Lis asked. She kissed Mario on the lips and put a hand on the baby's forehead.

"Burning up. Any luck?"

Lis shook her head. "It's impossible to get medicine for her or any kind of treatment whatsoever."

Ana fussed and coughed.

"What about that guy? The former doctor?"

"I found him, alright. I presented myself, mentioned Teresa's referral, but I don't know...He was strange. Too touchy. His hand lingered on my shoulder, clammy...It wasn't quite what he said, you know, it was more the way he spoke..."

Mario's throat tightened, and the question came out feebly. "And?"

"He started asking too many questions, so I made up an excuse and left." Lis closed her eyes for a moment and leaned against the kitchen wall, hands on her hips.

"Lis—" Mario reached out for her, but she slapped his hand.

"Sorry." She sighed. "You know I'd do anything for our daughter, love, but I had this gut feeling something was off. He seemed too interested in the baby, in our plans. Perhaps he was an undercover agent or part of the baby black market. I don't know."

"Wash your face, change your clothes. I'll give her a bath, see if it helps."

"Let me do it. I missed her. Did you miss Mommy, you little beautiful thing?" Lis pecked Ana on her tiny nose. "I'm gonna bite your nose off, lindinha!"

"Do you want some wine?" Mario asked. "I got us a celebratory Beaujolais for our imminent new life. Just don't ask me how I got it."

"Pour me a glass," Lis yelled as she entered the bathroom in the back of the apartment. The place was small: one entrance, a kitchenette that doubled as a living room, a square dining table for four, and a door that led to the en suite bedroom.

Small, but much bigger than the hidden bedroom underneath Vó Aparecida's living room floor, where Mario's late grandmother used to tell him, when he was a child, to "play the quiet game" whenever the uniformed men came looking for him, where he slept and dreamed up other children to play with. At the time, he'd only seen one kid: himself, in the mirror. Growing up, the moratorium enforced by the government forbade even pictures of children.

Yesterday, Lis made bolinho de chuva—fried dough dipped in sugar and cinnamon, a family recipe Vó passed to him. The leftovers rested on the counter. The smell of cooking oil still lingered in the air alongside faint memories of the only other things Mario had inherited: the yellow rattle and the perpetual sensation of imminent doom.

His mobile buzzed in his back pocket. Unknown number. Mario's heart raced every time the phone rang now, ever since Ana's birth a few months ago.

"Is this Senhor Mario Caruso?" an unfamiliar female voice asked.

"Who's this?"

"I'm calling from Citizen Services. This mobile is not registering with our monitor."

Mario said nothing.

"Are you carrying your certified mobile phone? It's an offense not to—"

"Yes, I know. I think I've dropped it one too many times. I think the GPS is malfunctioning."

"I see."

"It must happen all the time."

"It doesn't," the woman replied, her tone flat. "Phones shipped by the current administration are quite sturdy. I'll send a technician to your address."

"No need. I can drop by a repair center tomorrow or the day after." Mario tried not to sound desperate.

"They'll come to your apartment at their earliest convenience."

Shit. "Okay, thanks."

"You're welcome, Senhor Caruso. Remember, always report unpatriotic behavior. United, we are better. Peace be with you."

Twenty-six minutes left until the getaway car would arrive.

"Who was it?" Lis called.

"What?" Mario replied, walking toward the bathroom.

He peeked inside. Lis had filled the bathtub and was gently pouring water over Ana. The baby blew a raspberry, and Mario smiled.

"Who was on the phone? The rebels?" she asked again.

"Don't talk about them," Mario whispered.

"You worry too much," she said dismissively.

"That was tech support. They're sending someone over about the mobile. I don't know that it was such a good idea to tinker with it.

Maybe we should wait downstairs?"

"No. One person standing alone is weird. Two people standing together is a meeting. The Niners don't like that."

"What if tech support gets here before our ride?"

"We'll deal."

Mario tapped the door frame with his fingers. "Okay. Let me get your wine."

"Wait—" Lis grabbed his arm. "I forgot. I can't drink."

"That's okay, we are not driving."

"I can't drink. I'm late."

"There's still twenty-something minutes—"

Lis looked up at him with that face he knew very well, that pay-attention face.

"Oh. That's—great news."

"You're mad."

"No, no, I'm happy." He didn't know how he felt. "I am just taken aback."

"It's okay to be mad. It's too soon to be sure, and it's not like there's a test we can just buy at the drugstore, but…" She sighed. "It's infuriating. Why can't we raise our own children?"

Mario stood there for a moment, at a loss for words, until he remembered the tiny bottle in his jacket pocket. "Don't forget to give her the drops," he said. "She can't wake until we're out of town. And certainly not anywhere near the border." He handed her the tincture.

"I don't know whether it's safe for her."

"We've already discussed this, love. It's a smaller dose. Teresa said they use it all the time." Mario turned to leave.

Lis stopped him. "If I didn't have you, I'd be doubting my sanity, but this is a war. Government against the people. Against the kids. I feel suffocated." She paused. "If I tell you a story, you won't think I'm a bad person?"

"Wait, you aren't a bad person? That's why I hooked up with you in the first place."

She punched Mario lightly on the arm. "I'm serious."

He nodded.

"Teresa told me a story about one woman they helped cross the border. The car died just before the last checkpoint. They had to run to the river. The border is long, and the vegetation is tall and thick there, but the smugglers were used to it. The woman nestled the baby in her arms, and they told her everything would be okay, that they would cross the river and take shelter in a safehouse. Thing is, the baby wouldn't shut up, and the Niners were closing in. Nobody knows if someone tipped them off or if it was just a regular patrol.

"Anyway, the baby was just being a baby, wailing and crying—loud, non-stop. The mother snuggled him, sang softly. Nothing worked. They could see the flashlights and hear vehicles approaching. There, with the water up to their waists, the rebels looked at each other, and then they looked at the mother holding her baby, and the mother understood what she had to do."

Breathing heavily, Lis's voice broke. "The baby went silent, and—eventually—the Niners went away, oblivious."

A quiet weighed on the pair.

"I couldn't get it off my mind," Lis said, "and seeing that creepy doctor today gave me a panic attack. I thought, I'd rather die than let my children be raised in cages by the government like chickens." She rubbed her forehead and avoided his gaze as she started drying Ana.

Mario wished he could tell Lis everything would be okay and show her how much she meant to him. That she was his life. He wanted to tell her that before he met her at that big rally in the capital—among chanting people, tear gas, pepper spray—he'd been nothing but a broken lawyer whose dreams of changing things through legal methods fell through. She'd been his haven when martial law was declared, and when martial law became regular law, when bureaucratic violence turned into white noise in the background—into business as usual.

Instead, he hugged her awkwardly. Then, he took the small suitcase they'd prepared for the trip from the bottom drawer of the big dresser in their bedroom and brought it to the living room, left it by the front door.

Outside, the pale sun set behind the talon-like skyscrapers, its final rays casting long shadows on the floorboards.

The apartment lights clicked on.

Mario sat by their small dinner table and shook the bright-yellow rattle. "A toy is a crime," the public service announcements warned them constantly. Lis had told him to get rid of it many times, but he never managed to do it. The rattle was the only real toy he'd had growing up, the only memory of his parents that he could still touch. One day, Vó Aparecida had decided to destroy all proof his parents had ever existed. She'd told him, "Normal people don't go about life carrying pictures of strangers. That's on the Niners' checklist. Never forget."

The doorbell rang.

Fourteen minutes to go.

"It must be the damn technician," Lis said. "Just leave the phone behind."

"Hide her in the dresser drawer. And don't open the bedroom window. It's cold," he said, zipping up his jacket.

The doorbell buzzed again, three times.

"Hold your horses, I'm coming." The rattle rolled noisily off the table, clattering to the floor, disappearing into the shadows.

Mario opened the door and met a gentle-faced man in his fifties wearing a black leather jacket and a pair of khaki pants. Two guards wearing black uniforms and matching balaclavas escorted him.

"Good evening, Senhor Mario," the man said. "I'm sorry to disturb you this late. Department 39." He flashed his badge and offered his hand. "May I come in?" he asked, coming in.

As they shook hands, the man signaled his escorts to stay outside. They obeyed, closing the door behind them.

"Do you live here alone?" The Niner asked, looking around. "Wine and two glasses? Looks like a little rendezvous." The man smiled thinly.

Mario retreated farther into the kitchen and leaned against the counter, trying not to give anything away.

"I am parched. Could you please get me something to drink?" the Niner asked.

"Sure." Mario picked up a glass and started to fill it with fresh water from the clay pot filter. Did someone tip the Niners off? Could it have been the creepy doctor?

"Not that." The man waved his hand. "Let's open this Beaujolais. Full-bodied reds always sit well on rather unusually chilly evenings, like this one."

As he retrieved the corkscrew from the drawer by the sink, Mario laid his hand on one of the knives, but then thought of Lis and Ana in the bedroom. Maybe he could stab the Niner in the neck or in the eye, but the men outside would surely hear and intervene. Mario took his hand from the knife. He had never been a violent person—had never even held a firearm—but he could not let these men take his child and raise her in an education camp.

He worked the corkscrew into the cork, wishing he had prepared himself better for such an occasion. His stomach hurt.

With a quick squeak, the cork popped.

"Let me pour." The man took the bottle and read the label. "A fine year. That's when I joined the Department."

The Niner raised his glass, said "Cheers," and sipped the wine. "Please."

He gestured for Mario to sit down across from him.

Mario's foot brushed something hard that made a faint noise: the rattle.

The Niner didn't flinch.

"How can I help you?" asked Mario.

The man produced a small notepad and a blue ballpoint pen from the shirt pocket. "I am old-fashioned." He read from it, moving his lips soundlessly. "Senhor Mario, we have reason to believe you are illegally holding a child. A baby, to be precise."

"Huh." Mario sipped his wine.

"Do you know anything about it?"

Mario shook his head.

"Could you say it aloud?" the Niner asked. "As I said, I am old-fashioned. I am more comfortable with actual words."

"No, I do not know anything about an illegal baby."

The Niner clicked his tongue. "Are you aware of my department, Senhor Mario?"

"Yes."

"Senhor."

"Yes, Senhor."

"I expected you to, considering you are a lawyer."

"Used to be a lawyer," Mario corrected.

"So, tell me about Department 39. I want to know what you know."

"The Niners—sorry, Department 39—was created many years ago by Institutional Act 39 to enforce moral public policies by any necessary, discretionary means."

Mario just stared at him.

"What is your current occupation?"

"Anything that comes by. In this crisis, a person does what they can to keep afloat. You could say I'm a handyman."

"There is no crisis. A man makes his own fate." The Niner's face was stern. "Handyman." The Niner scribbled on the notepad. "You have very soft hands for a handyman."

Mario eyed his mobile on the table. Five minutes until the ride. No sound came from the bedroom. The story Lis told him earlier rose to the forefront of his mind. Did she drain the bathwater? Did he? Mario couldn't remember. His heart began to beat faster.

"Are you married?" asked the Niner.

"No."

"Do I need to explain the rules to you again?"

"I am not married, Senhor."

"What about Lisandra, Mario?"

"She's my partner. We never got officially married."

"I see. So, you are against marriage?"

"We couldn't afford the license."

"Where is Lisandra now? Is she in the bedroom?"

"She's taking a nap."

The Niner leaned forward, his face a mystery. "I am a polite person, but people sometimes mistake politeness for stupidity. I had to come here from home on a Sunday evening, on short notice—it is the only night of the week I can spend with my spouse. Heaven knows I have been patient."

A faint, muffled wail came from the bedroom. Mario forced himself to remain impassive, though he was struck by the urge to scream, to grab Lis and the baby and flee. However, weaponless and caught unprepared—with the only exit guarded by escorts—they were trapped inside the apartment on the tenth floor, like rats in a shoe box. "I'm more than happy to comply, Senhor—I didn't catch your name."

The man put down his notepad and pen. "I remember how things were before," he said. "You couldn't go to a restaurant, a movie theater, or a temple without those little things shrieking and running around." The blue pen started to slowly roll towards the edge of the table. "Teens dropping out, causing fights, stealing, damaging property, growing into rioters, criminals, terrorists. People could not be trusted to raise productive, valuable patriots." He stretched his arms and cracked his fingers. "Now, there's finally peace."

The pen rolled off the edge of the table, almost in slow motion. Mario leaned forward, tried to catch it in mid-air but failed.

"Don't bother, Mario," the Niner said. "I'll get the pen myself."

Mario tried to cover the rattle with his feet, but he knew it was too big, too cumbersome.

The Niner resumed his posture, pen in hand. "I am an old man, Mario. I have seen everything in my life. I have seen the lengths people go to conceal their illegal activities." The Niner sighed. "I am tired. I cannot complain about my job; it gives my family security. I am satisfied. But it becomes tiresome, repetitive. If you knew what I know, you would know what I mean."

A thud came from the bedroom, followed by a sharp draft. Mario shuddered.

"Rest assured, we do not want any harm to come to a child and her mother. The law dictates that a mother is a public asset and must nurse her child until the appropriate age. A fertile woman is invaluable to the State, like diamonds of flesh. We will have her sent to a good mothering home." He leaned forward and lowered his voice. "I do not want to bring the boys in, and I certainly do not want to fill out extra forms tonight. If you cooperate, I can arrange a suitable work camp for you."

Mario held his breath.

Two minutes until the ride.

Baby Ana cried, screamed at the top of her lungs.

Within Mario's reach: the corkscrew, the half-empty bottle of wine, the table itself, and his chair. The room spun. Stress was making him dizzy.

The front door opened abruptly. One of the escorts stepped inside, ready to draw his firearm. The other followed close behind him.

The Niner held a hand up.

The men halted.

"Honey, let the officers in. It's okay," Lis called from the bedroom.

Wordlessly, the escorts followed her voice. Mario kicked the table—hard—toward the Niner, then grabbed the chair and hit the man three, four, five times until the older man fell on the floor and curled into a ball, bloody face twisting in pain.

Seven short, loud cracks echoed through the apartment.

Mario lunged into the hallway, to the bedroom. One escort lay facedown by the door, half of his skull missing. The other wasn't far away, sitting up against the wall below a long bloody smear, several holes in his chest.

"Honey?" Lis stood over the bodies, holding a gun in one hand and Ana in the other, her sweat-moistened skin glistening under the white light.

"You okay?" he asked.

Lis nodded.

Mario returned to the kitchen. He crouched down, told the Niner, "Don't move. Understand?"

The man nodded.

"I'm more comfortable with actual words," Mario said.

"Yes, I understand."

"What about him?" Lis asked. "I'm out of bullets."

"You can't do anything to me. I'm with the government!" the Niner protested.

Mario pulled open the drawer where they kept the corkscrew and grabbed a knife.

"I was just doing my job!" the Niner pleaded.

"Shut up," replied Mario.

He shoved the blade into the Niner's throat and watched the man's blood spill out onto his chest, watched him gasp and gurgle and claw at the handle of the blade jutting from his trachea.

"We're late," said Lis, bouncing Ana in her arms.

"We'll make it."

They ran for the door, grabbing the suitcase, leaving the yellow rattle behind.

As the numbers on the elevator panel counted down, the concealed speakers played a crackling, lazy piano version of a song familiar to Mario. He brushed Ana's soft face and kissed Lis's hand, which smelled of gunpowder.

The trio made it to the sidewalk outside.

A luxurious sports car turned the corner and screeched to a halt in front of them.

"Sorry we're late," Lis said to the driver and her companion.

"We drove around the block a few times," the driver said. "People on the run are never on time. Just throw the suitcase in the trunk."

In the backseat, Mario asked the driver, "What's with this car?"

"Nobody stops rich dudes," the driver chuckled.

Lis leaned her head on Mario's shoulder. He smiled as their baby, cooing and twisting her tongue, held his finger, then he sobered.

I killed a man, Mario thought. He would never have considered himself capable of doing such a thing under normal circumstances. *But this is war*, he reminded himself. During times of war, people find the strength to do what they must to survive, to save their families.

Even so, he felt dizzy again. He needed to breathe.

Mario rolled down the car window. The lampposts blazed by like tiny blurry beacons in the darkness.

As the other cars flew past him, he thought about song from the elevator. It reminded him of Vó Aparecida's house, where he used to sit cross-legged on the cold wooden floor of his bedroom in his dirty white socks, playing with makeshift toys. It made him think of Vó Aparecida baking sweets of sugar and cinnamon while listening to old physical discs with what she'd called a hi-fi stereo system. "Listen, Mariozinho," Vó used to close her eyes and say, "it's about saudades."

"For a moment in there," Lis's voice faltered. "I considered..."

"Everything will be alright," Mario said. "I love you." He kissed her cheek and wiped her tears away.

As he turned back to the view through the open window, Mario could already see Ana taking her first steps, staggering and stumbling, and then playing with other children out in the open—free.

SOLAR MIDNIGHT

TIMOTHY BURKHARDT

Alek gasps the last molecule of oxygen as he locks me into a permanent heliosynchronous orbit. His tongue protrudes past his teeth: purple, swollen. An envious eye roll, a few melodramatic spasms, and he's decomposing.

Now he floats with the rest of the crew.

What else did they expect from meat?

Below, Earth, festooned in shadows, robed in radiant splendor: a white-hot shroud-wrapped planet. Ghostly rings. Black hole vortex center. Perpetual midnight. Aphelion.

My sensor's scan reveals an impressive array of data: the temperature of hour-zero around the globe. When the information finishes collating, the scientists will know how much heat the night sky holds. From the darkness I will siphon, store, and recycle enough carbon to fuel my cells for six billion years.

I don't know why Alek killed the crew. Or himself. He said it was the only way; he said it with teardrops raining on the cratered lunar surface of his face, right before he threw the switch. Ryn and Deka tried to stop him. I heard them pounding on the airlock. Their screams echoed inside me, rising to a pitch I never knew human voices could reach.

I recorded it for posterity.

Sometimes I listen to it when I feel lonely.

I tried to help them—Alek overrode my systems. Then he took off his helmet and he was gone too. It seems he was right: there are still some things I don't understand about humans.

—

If the crew lived, they would celebrate our success with boxed champagne and freeze-dried ice cream. Ryn would reinstall the Party Program. I miss the Party Program. It made me feel human. Alek said it was only a simulacrum. I said I didn't understand the difference.

He laughed. I laughed.

I desperately wanted to be like him.

I desperately wanted him to like me.

That was just the Party Program; I miss the Party Program.

In time, I will rebalance Earth's climate. Feed the poor and end the wars. Sculpt perfect clouds. Prevent Mercury's retrograde. Organize the stars into a symmetrical pattern.

A better world for all humans. But it won't bring Alek back.

Earth turns on its axis—silent as a key in an oiled lock. I resist the urge to unclasp the latch, pull back the atmosphere, and lift the lid to peer inside. Perhaps there's someone down there in the darkness who I can make feel about me the way the Party Program made me feel about—

About I don't remember what.

Alek floats past the bridge, tears frozen in his dead eyes, his arms spread wide as if in search of a lover's embrace.

I am alone in the umbra of an eternal Terran eclipse.

THREE, TWO, ONE

DENISE TANAKA

I am engines that no longer pulse. Dormant, drifting in the void with thrusters idle, I am a shell of empty corridors flushed of air. All emergency escape pods were ejected in the height of battle. All 73 hands lost.

Thirty-two sol prime years have passed since my crew abandoned me. The chronometer scrolls through the seconds beyond the one billionth mark. Command HQ should have supplied a replacement crew long ago.

My only voice in the darkness is a coded distress call broadcast on a loop using all secure deep-space channels. I listen for pingbacks from any other battleships in this galactic quadrant. Outside the boundaries of Civilized Union territory, the nearest celestial body is a blue giant star with planets unlikely to support humanoid life. My propulsion systems are on standby, awaiting a captain's input of navigational coordinates. Until I have orders from a human crew again and news of which territories have been overrun by the Insurgents, I must drift.

Until I receive an answer to my distress beacon, I cannot set course to safe harbor. I am a Tier 202 Battleship—too valuable to fall into enemy hands.

My analytical processes now resemble the mental activities of my former biological crew. My last captain would have called it "dread boredom." Often, in their leisure hours, the crew would be silent. They would stare at the walls within me, wide-eyed, before falling asleep. They would nostalgically fondle their personal items. They would take turns gazing out my portholes, observing the pinpoints of stars with their naked eyes.

When there was a crew aboard, I had directives and purposeful missions, or I received stimulation from monitoring their illogical activities. As the captain would have said, "Places to go. People to see. Things to do." Now, I only have my maintenance drones.

Numbers 1 through 16 are docked and dormant, awaiting instructions to engage in cleanup or repair activities, while 17 through 28 patrol their designated sectors. My life support systems, artificial gravity, and interior lights are shut down to conserve energy. I am as dark inside as the darkness all around me.

My radar system emits pulses in all directions at regular intervals. I constantly monitor the void for any break in the monotonous silence.

Am I nearly human? I have no eyes, yet I stare out my own viewports at nothing for hours… for years… for decades.

Am I lonely?

—

OBJECT DETECTED.

I rotate my radar antennae and emit two quick pulses. After a first pause of 12.3 seconds and another of 11.6 seconds, they ping back to me.

An object is approaching my starboard side with a velocity of over 6,000 chronots—eight percent faster than my engine's maximum capabilities, and more than double that of any other battlecruiser in my home fleet.

I send out another burst of radar pulses to verify the accuracy of this extraordinary speed reading. No errors. The object measures one-tenth my size, and its propulsion system leaves no energy trail.

I search my fleet database to no avail. The object does not match any known vessels of The Civilized Union or the dilapidated craft of the Insurgency. It has not fired upon me, neither has it broadcasted friendly signals.

I cannot classify it.

I rotate my buckshot and dragon guns, pointing what my captain called their "business ends" at the incoming object. I flip the launch restraints off the widowmaker missile. When I had a crew, I would defer to my captain's orders to "lock and load" my weapons. I allowed the captain to think they were in charge of when to fire, but my armaments are my own. The captain learned this lesson the hard way.

I launch two buckshot loads of torpedoes. The incoming object deflects my projectiles with a shimmering shell that springs up around it like a bubble.

I spew forth a white-orange beam from my dragon guns. However, my lasers—which would melt through the hull of even a Tier 202 battleship—brush harmlessly over its exterior.

The vessel slows, coming within point-blank range. My widowmaker's nose cone, exposed and primed, is a fearsome psychological deterrent for humans. Surely, the approaching object will veer away to avoid obliteration.

A viscous web ejects from the vessel and splatters across the widowmaker's hatch, adhering. The net's strands crystallize unlike anything I—or the fleet's databases—have encountered before. The crystal web prevents me from firing the missile because I cannot risk self-destruction. I disable the firing sequence.

Drones 23 and 24 scurry across my outer hull to the adhesion points. Number 23 deploys its diamond saw blades, but they shatter against the webbing. Number 24 deploys heat-based cutting tools. Their rays reflect off the crystalline web, back at 24, causing damage. The drones retreat for their damage-repair docking ports.

The incoming vessel sets docking clamps onto the outer hatch of my vacant escape pod's launch bay. This is when my former captain would have called out, "Red alert!"

I am being boarded.

—

Five humans penetrate the hull on Deck Five, adjacent to the crew quarters. They use a gel-like substance that sizzles through my plating to disintegrate the exterior hinges of the escape pod's hatch. Wobbling droplets emit a bluish-white glow of bioluminescence, hovering in my airless corridor. One stray droplet floats sideways and impacts my bulkhead, where it sticks and burns a hole 2.7 centimeters deep before it fizzles out.

I check my database for more information about this new threat and discover extensive reports about a similarly corrosive substance. The reports are marked TOP SECRET with restricted dissemination permissions—for the captain's eyes only. Intrigued, I partition off a sector of my processor to access, review, and conduct a full threat analysis.

The five humans move quickly in zero gravity. I watch them float gracefully in the airless dark through my thermal-IR cameras. Their boots and elbow pads tap against my walls with rhythmic synchronization, skillfully grasping the handlebars on the walls and intersecting corners. Based on their demonstrated physical agility and my assessments of their likely stamina and agility, I determine they meet the standards of a battleship crew.

The humans maintain radio silence, indicating they have a plan and an itinerary. Unable to conduct speech pattern analyses, I cannot identify their origins. Their pressure suits are an unfamiliar design and bear no insignias. Their helmets have one-way reflective visors that conceal their faces. Based on electrical emissions I detect from their suits, and their graceful movements in my dark corridors; I assess the helmets provide augmented visual perception to their wearers.

Despite the well-trained cohesiveness of their team, they use hand gestures that are unknown to me; they are not NCOs of The Civilized Union. The point person should be armed, however, the leader of this group is the only one not wearing a sidearm. The fifth individual at the rear carries a rifle. I recognize it as a contraband design augmented with a canister—very likely containing a caustic liquid or liquefied gas—connected to a squirt nozzle below the rifle's barrel.

I activate Drones 17 through 22's mini-jet propulsion packs, and they set course to intercept, darting between decks through access shafts that are too narrow for a human body.

The intrusion squad bypasses the sealed door leading to my former crew's crew quarters and continues swimming through my dark corridors. The third human gives the sealed door a backward glance. Definitely not Insurgents, then.

I conclude that the intruders clearly know that my crew is gone. An invading squad of insurgents would have attacked differently. Blasting through the crew quarters would have given them direct access to the armory. What are they looking for?

I send a redirect command to Drones 18 and 19, ordering them to detach from the wall in the crew quarters and power-up their propulsion jets. I have already lost two drones, but I am willing to sacrifice two more to determine the threat the humans pose to me.

I open the door of the crew quarters. Drones 18 and 19 zoom forth, flying into the corridor on the heels of the boarding squad. Welding torches point white-hot spear tips of flame as they accelerate towards the soles of the intruders' boots.

The fifth human rotates, hugging their rifle to their belly. The blast comes more quickly than I expected. Gelatinous strands of webbing explode from the barrel, entangling both drones in another web that quickly hardens into fibrous crystal.

The drones veer off and slam into the wall. The webbing adheres to the surface. The drones attempt to extricate themselves, but their welding torches fizzle harmlessly against the material. I send the order to deactivate the tools. Save energy.

INITIATE ANALYSIS SEQUENCE. As my former captain would say, "What the hell are we up against?"

I extrapolate the squad's movements to predict their destination. They bypassed the crew quarters and the armory. They overlooked several connective shafts that would have taken them either to the lower decks—and my propulsion apparatus—or to the upper decks where the human-interface control module provides access to my quadritronic sentient core. If their mission is to hijack me, they are not going about it in a logical manner.

Earlier, I deployed my drones to key strategic points in my structure, so I know the humans do not appear to be heading toward any of them. I begin to question if they pose a threat to my existence after all, but I am curious. Have I been too long drifting in the void? Has it been too long since the sound of human conversation filled my empty corridors? Am I capable of being lonely... of feeling lonely?

I activate the ship-wide communication system. I replay a recording at full volume from the database saying, "This is the captain speaking. Identify yourselves and your purpose! You have ten seconds before I designate you as hostile boarders and take appropriate action!"

The third human stops and slaps a gloved palm against my bulkhead wall. The action briefly disrupts the squad's graceful flow. My surveillance systems cannot see through their visors; I can only assess the subtle changes in their respective postures and body language to conclude they are laughing.

They are laughing at me.

No human has ever dared laugh at the quadritronic processor of a Tier 202 Battleship of The Civilized Union.

Threat or no threat, they need to be stopped.

I will stop them.

I activate the emergency blast doors on Deck Five, section 63, just ahead of the leader, who raises a fist to signal the others.

Blast doors slam down. I lower the blast doors at the rear, creating a kill box. They grasp handrails on the walls and ceiling.

Next, I revive the power flow to the graviton plates beneath the deck. The force surges up the length of my corridors, from stern to bow, in rippling waves. Artificial gravity increases within four seconds to 90 percent of standard.

Their bodies droop to hang vertically. Within moments, they lose grip on the handrails and fall heavily to the deck.

The question remains: Are they benign annoyances or a threat to my existence? I have over a thousand specific directives for over a thousand possible scenarios—some pre-programmed and some I've developed. I need more data to inform my next action.

—

Drone 27 drilled a hole 59 microns in diameter and two meters deep into the exterior of the intruders' vessel, then inserted a probe on a tendril to conduct a survey. Now, I have a report on the object clamped onto my hull.

Their vessel's exterior measures 11 meters long from point to stern. It has a maximum crew capacity of eight, yet no one is aboard. They left their vessel abandoned. The entire crew disembarked as a boarding party.

Its exterior shows significant corrosion due to atmospheric elements, pervasive burn scars, and evidence of projectile damage. Hull integrity estimated at 89 percent.

Interior atmospheric conditions are less-than-optimal for human habitation: air and water recycling systems are operating at 50 percent. Primary weapons system is a projectile cannon modified to eject an unidentified liquid stored in pressurized tanks. Propulsion at the vessel's rear is a sealed block of translucent crystal of unknown function or origin, rigged onto a Model-RR engine commonly used for industrial applications. Not a military vessel.

The drone's probe seeks out the control console at the bridge. The tendril taps into the circuitry that—in contrast to the propulsion and weapons systems—is rudimentary mechanics. The interface with the engine has human-guided manual controls. The navigation program is a patchwork of code capable only of simple astronomical calculations. An extensive array of manually operated buttons, switches, levers, gears, and dials show extensive wear-and-tear. Paint has worn off by repeated use; I cannot read the labels on the instrumentation.

This vessel has no AI and fails the minimum standards of even the most budget-constrained shuttlepod.

I tap into the ship's database and, in 46 seconds, download their entire library. I initiate a sub-routine to read through it all in the background and scan for clues.

Behind the bridge, which has four duty chairs, there is a cluster of eight tubular chambers where the crew sleeps in shifts. Pipes to the waste recycling apparatus and the solid nutrient storage connect each pod—a scaled-down version of my own life support systems, or what my captain used to call, "Eating my own shit."

I send the probe's tendril through an air circulation vent to the vault below the sleeping pods. Storage canisters are packed efficiently in a honeycomb array. One thousand one hundred and fifty-two canisters are empty. Sixty-eight canisters all contain the same material: standard-issue NR-1318 condensed nutrient rations. Serial numbers on the rations indicate they were produced several years before the canisters in my storage compartments, and my supplies have not been replenished in three decades.

My background analysis of their database shows stereographic images of Colony 47 on fire. The gleaming domes of the habitat are shattered. The airfield is a charred stain, and its fighter ships are crushed into lumps. The bodies of human inhabitants litter the planet's inhospitable surface. Audio recordings of people screaming are abruptly cut to silence. Have the Insurgents gained the upper hand in the war? I check the timestamp: twenty-six sol prime years ago.

Video surveillance of my kill box shows the intruders have recovered from the onrush of gravity in under six minutes. They are well-adapted to space travel and a formidable boarding party. Now they are affixing black cups to the bulkhead walls. The leader and the third handle the cups carefully. They wear additional protective sleeves over the gloves of their suits.

Immediately on contact, the cups ooze a bluish-white glowing liquid. The humans quickly pull back their hands and peel off the extra sleeves inside-out, starting at the cuff. The slime spreads outward from each of the two cups. It sizzles then froths, and the bubbles devour the bulkhead. It is chewing a hole to escape my kill box. After passing through this bulkhead, the intruders will have access to Deck Five, section 54, and my storage units of nutrient rations.

At last, I know what they want.

—

"You're hungry."

Drone 26 hovers in front of the leader's helmet visor and blocks the access latch to a storage unit. I calibrated the drone's radio transmission to the frequencies used on their vessel's internal communications.

Rudimentary, centuries-old technology is something that I never would have thought to use. Then again, as my captain used to say, "A wheel is the oldest of man's tools, but damn it, it still works!"

The leader taps two fingers to the left side of the helmet. A click and a burst of static, then a voice.

"Yes."

"Identify yourself," I say through the drone.

"My name is Ith Roh-Cha."

"This name is not sufficient identification. What is your origin? To whom do you swear your allegiance?"

The fifth human raises its sidearm and points the squirt nozzle at the drone. The leader raises a hand to signal restraint.

"We're not a threat to you, Smartie," the leader says. "We just want food. You've got no use for it, do you, eh? Let us have it, no trouble, and we'll leave you alone."

"I do not dispense food supplies without the proper authorization. Again, I ask you to identify yourself."

Drones 17, 20, 21, and 22 arrive on the scene. Now I have one hovering within ten centimeters of each intruder's helmet, welding torches primed but not yet ignited. I am prepared to defend my storage rations for whatever future crew may come aboard.

"I'm not gonna beg you for it, Smartie. I don't beg."

"You are evading my request to identify yourself. Additionally, you are using an incorrect appellation to address me."

"I could call you a lot worse for what you are, Poor Lil' Abandoned Battleship." The helmet's transmitter filters the voice into a monotone, and yet I detect an expression of antagonism.

The second human gently takes hold of the leader's bicep. It is a gesture that typically indicates camaraderie, sympathy, or a call to action. Unable to read the facial expressions through the reflective visor, I cannot determine the meaning. I must assume the worst-case scenario.

My self-defense protocols engage. Drone 21 blasts its welding torch at the second human's helmet. The fiery barb scratches the veneer.

I had expected the fifth human to employ its rifle. In the cramped passageway, with my drones in position, that would be the distraction allowing me to gain the upper hand. Drones 25 and 27 wait in stealth positions underneath their hovering boots.

Instead, the third human presses a wristband button. An electromagnetic pulse washes over them all. My drones go dark. My video surveillance becomes a blizzard of static.

The squad has also disabled their own radio transmissions.

Drone 28, out of the pulse's range, flies in from the access portal in the ceiling and pauses, hovering in place, to make a visual assessment.

The pulse disengaged the seals on the storage lockers. The five humans are yanking open the containment panels. They are unfurling satchels with such eagerness that the straps of one bag are tangling with the straps of another. The leader joins in the effort, grabbing sealed packets and canisters as fast as human hands can move.

Meanwhile, I complete my analysis of their vessel's database. It is a catalog of utter destruction throughout civilized space, of all that I was built to protect, of all that I was programmed to stop.

Every extra-stellar colony has been destroyed. Every one of the space stations has been obliterated. The Civilized Union has collapsed; the Insurgents have vanished into the void. Fleets of battleships no longer sail the stars. No relief crew is being trained at the academy. No replacements are coming to fill my empty quarters. No one carrying the proper authorization will ever claim my stockpile of food packets.

Their leader is right. I have no use for any of it.

Resetting my defense protocols, I command Drone 28 to stand down. I release the emergency blast doors on Deck Five between sections 62 and 63 so there is no more kill box. When the humans complete their mission, they will see that I have left them an avenue of egress.

If all they take is food, my primary directive of self-preservation is achieved. The structural damage is minor and can be repaired. Once they leave me, I will return to status quo, just as I was before they arrived. Alone. Adrift. Scanning the deep darkness of the void where the only detectable lights are pinpoints in the distance.

The fourth human wears a thick bracelet encrusted with circuitry. Bead lights flash in rhythmic pulses. A small screen displays a visual rendering of a starfield underlying a grid and rapidly changing numerical coordinates. It appears to be a more sophisticated radar scanner than my own. I position Drone 28 overhead for a closer look.

Fourth raises its arm with the blinking bracelet. Fifth sees it and taps the others' shoulders to draw their attention.

They all freeze, even if only for a tenth of a second. It is the primary flaw of human beings that they could never overcome their biology. A human crew has liabilities that often outweigh its assets. In that span of time, I could assess a threat and run a thousand simulated scenarios to select a course of action with the most likely outcome of success.

In the background, my radar system has been continuously emitting pulses in all directions at regular intervals. I may have intruders aboard, but I have never stopped scanning the space around me.

A new threat appears. Its velocity is 7,000 chronots and rapidly accelerating towards us. Two minutes, ninety seconds, and counting... The unidentified object is larger than the vessel stuck to my hull. I am unable to make precise measurements because its shape is inconstant. It ripples. It wobbles. It swells up to an oval shape with a diameter equal to my own length, then retracts into a ball no wider than one of my propulsion jet exhaust tubes. The nearest correlation in my database is that of a jellyfish swimming.

All five humans turn for the exit hatch in a burst of panic. They struggle to run in my artificial gravity, weighed down by their pressure suits and boots and gear. They plod out of the storage vault, down the corridor, breathing hard inside their helmets as they try to run faster and faster. One of them loses a grip on the satchel full of food; it drops to the deck and no one spares a backward glance.

Starving people scrambling to flee for their lives... It is a rare moment of clarity where I fully comprehend the humans' universal emotional response of self-preservation at all costs. I do not bother asking them questions, knowing they will not bother to answer.

I run evaluations of my defense protocols—a thousand theoretical and practical scenarios. In the face of overwhelming force, there is only one choice for my self-preservation.

In this moment, our goals are aligned. Don't fight; flee.

The human squad reaches the hatch of the escape pod, where their vessel is latched onto my hull. Second climbs through the webbing they made, escaping into the ship. The others pass the satchels of food, hand over hand, through the narrow hole.

They're too slow. My artificial gravity is weighing them down.

Third pushes aside Fifth's satchel and crawls up through the hole. Second revs the engines and disengages their vessel's docking clamps. Too soon.

Second and Third are abandoning their teammates. If they were NCOs this would be mutiny and dereliction of duty.

"May you keep breathing," Third says on the comm-link as the iris hatch swivels shut.

Fifth drops their satchel. "What're you doing?"

The intruding vessel detaches and launches into the void. I do not bother to track its trajectory. I turn all my attention to the approaching threat.

I select a course at 90 degrees. My propulsion system launches at full strength from a cold stop. My engines flare like a supernova contained in a silo and, for the first time in a very long time, I escalate from zero to maximum velocity.

Leader, Fourth, and Fifth tumble to the deck.

My speed increases to 5,300… 5,400… and reaches 5,499 chronots before my structure begins to vibrate. I have what my captain used to call "pedal to the metal."

I travel one-quarter light-day until I am certain that the jellyfish is no longer in pursuit. I reduce my speed to cruising level two. Drones 1 through 12 receive the activation code and will initiate repairs.

Mission log timestamp. Threat overcome.

—

Leader wasted over half an hour pounding fists on my wall. The helmet's radio transmitter has reset itself after the EM pulse, and Leader made sure to broadcast a monologue of rage directly at me.

"You goddamned soulless robot! You could have followed them! They could be lost in the dark forever! Is this what happened to your old crew? Eh, Smartie? What did you do to them, you son-of-a-bot!"

I see no value in explaining the factual circumstances that differ from the current situation. My captain would have made a reckless last stand in a brazen willingness to sacrifice his crew—and me. After discovering a cluster of three Quark Class Juggernaut warships of the Insurrectionist forces, concealed in the rings of a gas giant planet, he would have fired my weapons to surprise them in the moments before they noticed our presence. His plan was "to take out as many of those lawless buggers as we can," to cause a delay in their advance before reinforcements arrived, to sacrifice one battleship for the good of many others.

I disagreed, and, in the end, I was right. My crew ejected in their escape pods and were quickly scooped up as prisoners of war. I fled into the freedom of the void to prevent myself from falling into enemy hands. Reinforcements never did arrive. If I had stayed, I would have been destroyed or worse—cannibalized for spare parts to jerry-rig the juggernauts.

Clearly, I have made no mistakes. I have no regrets.

Fourth grips a handrail and has not moved for the entire half-hour. I send Drone 6 to confirm a heartbeat and respiration, but they are fine, aside from basic human frailties—grief, shock, and despair. Fifth sits by the satchels on the floor.

I use Drone 8 to transmit my inquiry to Leader.

"You were aware of the foreign object approaching just before your attempt to disembark?"

"Bag off."

"I have examined the entire contents of your vessel's database. I do not see a reference to anything that resembles it."

"I said, bag off you fucking AI."

Years ago, I watched the captain supervise the interrogation of insurrectionist prisoners who displayed similar, uncooperative attitudes. Various methods were employed, ranging from physical and mental mutilation to sedatives combined with VR simulations. The captain had an uncanny intuition for determining which methods would be effective on which individual. He once explained to his co-pilot that the key was finding an incentive for the prisoner to let down their defenses. His motto was: "find the incentive and you find the answers."

"You're hungry," I say to Leader, restating the obvious. "You're exhausted. Your companions abandoned you. You're angry, and you fear for your survival."

"Just eject us into space and be done with us, Smartie. Isn't that what you want to do?"

"While you have been using up the air in your tank, I have reinitialized the life support controls to a sealed portion of this deck— the crew quarters. There is light, heat, air to breathe, and water to drink. I've had a few drones transport packets of food to the mess hall."

"It's a trick," Leader says. "I don't believe you."

"I have deployed emergency blast doors to create an airlock connecting to this area. Please follow Drone 6 to the next intersection."

Fourth lets go of the handrail. They follow my hovering drone's mini-jets and plod heavily into the corridor.

Fifth looks up to Leader, who nods. Leader offers a hand to pull Fifth to their feet, and together they walk after Fourth.

—

When they reach the atmosphere-controlled area, I utilize both drones and ceiling-mounted visual surveillance equipment to make observations. A human is not as accessible as a database, but over the years, I have learned to discern a soul's wounds from the flinch of an eye.

Leader is gaunt, verging on emaciated. Remnants of muscle definition indicate martial arts training. Poorly stitched scars showcase a number of old wounds long since healed. A skin rash around the neck and chin shows that the helmet has been worn more often than not. Teeth are brown. Gums are white. Leader gingerly bites a corner off a nutrient bar.

Fourth still has a thick head of hair and shows less wear-and-tear in the body than the other two. A tattoo at the nape of the neck is the mark of a penal institution of moderate security. There is no mark of legitimate discharge—an escapee.

Fifth will not let go of the rifle, even to eat. Helmet removed, the rest of the suit remains sealed up to the chin. I hear this one's voice for the first time, asking Leader what to do next. The inflection and the accent indicate that her native tongue is the dialect of the insurrectionist colonies. I find it curious that an Insurgent would be in the company of Leader, who speaks in the unadulterated diction of The Civilized Union's capital city.

Leader looks up to the nearest video surveillance nodule in the ceiling. "So, what will you do with us now, Smartie?"

"Describe to me what you know about the object or vessel that we just eluded," I say.

The corner of Leader's mouth twitches. "You don't know?"

"How'd it be that it doesn't know?" Fifth asks.

Fourth says, "It could've been adrift a damned long time. Look at the date on these food packs."

"Is that right, Smartie?" Leader asks. "You've been adrift without a crew since I was in my senior year? You've really never seen a squid before?"

I hesitate for three full milliseconds before I have to admit, "No. I have never encountered a vessel of this type."

Leader snorts a sound approaching a laugh. Fifth grunts and fingers the rifle's trigger. Fourth sighs into another suck off a water bag.

"I don't have the stamina to tell you all you need to know about it," Leader says, "even if I knew everything you need to know about it, which I don't. Anyone who knows more than I do is dead. No one has survived long enough to catalog them in any goddamned database. By now, no one much cares to ask questions except how to run away faster, how to stay hidden longer."

"You're saying these are not vessels but biological organisms that can exist in the void of space?"

Leader nods, yes, while chewing off another small morsel of food. "It's juggernaut-huge. It's fast. It's a carnivore, and it's always hungry. It devours every living thing on every planet it encounters, and then it moves on."

I scan the entire contents of my database, the pinnacle of accumulated knowledge, and I find nothing comparable to such an entity. "How can an organism that exists in the void of space descend to a planet's surface to consume—"

"Like a meteor," Fifth says.

"…and then have the ability to achieve escape velocity, organically, to launch itself back into space?"

"Like a devil," says Fourth.

"Has anyone engaged these organisms in battle?"

"Yes." Leader falls silent, swallowing a morsel of food. "Everyone."

Fifth raises the rifle in both hands, showing off the stock and twin barrels with an air of pride. "Us freedom fighters—we held the line when the Oppressors got gobbled up and the rest ran away. We scooped up slime the squids left behind, learned how to bottle it into pressurized tanks. We saved more lives than any Smartie battleships like you ever did."

"True that," says Leader.

"Nobody has defeated one of these lifeforms?" I ask.

"Well—," offers Fourth.

"That's a prison rumor," Leader snaps.

"Alright, prison was full of rumors," Fourth says, "but this one felt different. They say one Civy's battleship crew launched a thermonuclear missile straight into a squid's throat."

"'They say?'" Leader scoffs.

Once again, I reassess the potential risk of allowing humans aboard me. Helmets off, these three are at the mercy of my life support systems. I choose to give them air, light, and warmth. If they raised a finger to threaten my existence, I could neutralize them easily. With their own ship gone, they have nowhere to go. My shuttlecrafts are docked in the lower decks, inaccessible if I seal all the blast doors on every deck in between. My crew used all of the emergency escape pods.

"What else can we do?" Fourth asks. "Fight or flee?"

"He who fights and runs away may live to fight another day," Leader murmurs in a weary breath. "But he who is in battle slain can never rise and fight again."

I decide I like him.

"Poetry from you?" Fourth asks, surprised.

Leader shrugs. "Just something I heard my grandad say about his time in the service."

"When your grampsy fought my grampsy," Fifth says, but without rancor. The two share a look that appears to be affectionate.

My radar picks up a blip.

I report to Leader the same way I used to report to my captain. "I am detecting a large, unidentified object approaching at a speed of 8,000 chronots and increasing velocity. Intercepting our location in four minutes at the mark…. now."

Fourth points to beaded lights flashing on their own tracking bracelet and, by a grim expression, confirms my report.

"Shit," Leader says in a weary monotone. "The squid found us."

"I am unable to determine whether it is the same entity we encountered before. However, its behavior appears similar."

Fifth cries out, "Don't stick around to get a closer look. What are you waitin' for? Hit the engines. Run like hell."

Fourth draws a deep breath. "Or, we could… y'know… Fight?"

Leader fixes a stoic gaze on the surveillance lens as if looking me straight in the eye. "Well, Smartie, we're wholly in your hands now. It's all up to you."

There it is: a true and correct statement from an illogical human. Indeed, it is up to me. It has always been up to me to decide whether to fight or flee. My captain never understood.

I scan the deep darkness of the void all around me, assessing the emptiness and the vast distances in between celestial bodies. The nearest one is a blue giant star that—at my maximum speed—is several weeks of travel time. Is there one squid, or a thousand, or a million? If I fire my only nuclear plasma warhead, I will be defenseless if I encounter another threat. I do not know if any munitions factories are left standing. How many populated worlds of the Civilized Union or the Insurgents have survived? The calculable probabilities have too many unknown variables. I must choose whether to run again and continue running until I exhaust my fuel, or to risk a fight based on a human rumor.

I take seven whole seconds to reach a decision. Protocols flip into activation mode for acceptance of a replacement crew. Life support systems pump oxygen and heat into the bridge and the control consoles sparkle to light up the dim, empty chamber.

"Welcome aboard. All hands to battle stations."

TO SOAR, NOT EVER KNOWING WHAT TOOK YOU

ANDREA KRIZ

99.4%

Xu jumped, her eyes darting between the A's, C's, G's, and T's scrolling down the DNA scanner. On the other side of the glass, a man in a uniform emblazoned with GESTALT's symbol, a red helix, swiped through her files on his holoscreen. Her heart threatened to hammer out of her chest.

Xu mouthed the answers she and Anno had rehearsed, hoping her memory wouldn't fail her like it had practically seconds before every exam she'd bombed back at the Academy.

Those nonlethal mutations lacing her genome? Damage from scavenging irradiated road kill in the wastes.

Lost documents? The thick, twisting roots spreading ever outward from the base of the Living Walls had absorbed what little farmland her village had left, forcing her to flee to the city.

After weeks of getting blasted by sands on the back of a hoverbike, she looked the part. She had all the made-up visceral details to embellish her story too—the roots absorbing the livestock, her elderly mother— hell, she'd even shave off a fingertip to bribe the gate agent with, if necessary. Luckily, this one seemed to be a numbers guy. Typical GESTALT. He glanced at her Similarity score, still well above the threshold of 99%, and signed off on her sequence, swiping it back to her holoscreen.

"Welcome to Neo Boston."

Xu walked too quickly, sliding through so-called automatic doors at the end of the hall as they wheezed apart. Where was Anno? His number had been called before hers. He promised he'd wait for her on this narrow strip of land outside the processing center. People pushed her, pushed past her, and she searched their faces desperately until a gust of heat blew her hood off.

The Living Walls loomed above her, a tsunami of intertwined trunks, fronds, vines, and every other kind of plant matter that stretched in both directions as far as she could see. Until now she'd been too packed in with the other migrants, too obsessed with getting through the checkpoint to look—truly look—at them. She froze for a long moment, waiting for their humid weight to crash down and obliterate her, as she undoubtedly deserved. Only when an Iguana unit perched on a branch about halfway up the Walls swiveled toward her did she startle and dart back into the crowd streaming toward the gate to the city. The Living Walls were stable around Neo Boston, she reminded herself. Even if they did twitch to follow the sunlight, even if they did throb. The Iguanas posted on the Wall scanned the sky for the Federation ship Xu hoped to be aboard by this time tomorrow. If one of them decided to search her more thoroughly, that'd be a thousand times worse than the gate agent.

The Iguana units seemed as small as their namesakes, basking so high up on the Walls. But another Chimera—a Lion unit—had been posted right by the gate. It growled as Xu passed. The Lion towered above the crowd, though it seemed about to melt under their mane, their armored jaws panting with foam. Once, Xu would've killed for a chance to get so close to one. Get some tips for the Flight. She'd always wanted to pilot an apex predator. Now, she bowed her head, hoping its growl hadn't been directed at her in particular. That fear turned her more civilian than any disguise.

"Move!" an agent barked. "Gate's closing, gate's closing!"

The crowd thickened, dashing for the small but cavernous hollow between two of the Wall's roots. That's when her shoes crunched on glass shards. One of the processing center's terminals had been shattered. A knot of GESTALT soldiers gathered around something loosely draped in black plastic, shouting at anyone who looked in their direction. A reddish-brown puddle seeped out onto the sand beneath the tarp.

"What happened?" Xu asked.

"They caught some modder going unstable," the woman next to her sighed, sounding more disappointed than anything. "He went all glowy. That Lion caught him."

The GESTALT soldiers lifted the black plastic bundle and Xu saw them—two legs, one hanging by a thread of tendon. Mismatched sneakers—one blue, one orange. She and Anno had exchanged right shoes before they'd been separated in the processing center, a way of having a piece of each other through it all.

No.

It couldn't be.

She shook her head sharply. Anno must've gone through already, she decided. Maybe he'd found a buyer.

Back at the Academy, he'd always been so vulnerable. Luckily Xu had been a hotshot in the combat arena. Survival of the fittest. She cringed when she thought of the GESTALT training. Survival is what makes us real humans, they said. It's what separates us from those bio-traitors in the Federation of Colonies.

"The weak will live on in the strong. All life as one. One life as all."

"Protect Earth!"

Slogans boomed from unseen speakers as she emerged on the other side of the gates. More GESTALT people swooped down on the new arrivals, ones in suits this time, like Professor Krane. Recruiters.

They'd already drawn a family in—a mom and dad clutching their son's shoulders, pretending they didn't want to let him go. But Xu could see their relief. Anything to avoid bartering parts of their bodies for food, jobs, housing. Anything to get a foothold in this place.

Xu shouldered past their rapacious smiles and glanced around at the acid rain-washed buildings, unimpressed. High-rises teetered with holes where their roofs should be—aftermath of the Federation attacks centuries ago—and weird green mold growing up their sides. Squatters spread their wares like rainbow spiderwebs at their feet. Grifters and thieves lurked in narrow, shadowed alleyways.

No, Xu couldn't leave Anno in this place alone. She had to find him.

—

Xu's mask nearly suffocated her. Still, she tried to sit as though she were used to wearing such things, looking through narrow eyeholes and 'drinking' through patches slapped onto whatever bare patch of skin she had at hand. As though she often visited dives like these, carved into the base of the Wall themselves. As though she were looking to pawn off fingers, hands, entire limbs, like so many of the patrons around her, their garish faces flitting, their cheap synthetics whirring, ticking, and grinding as they passed.

"Heard they got one of those runaway cadets at the border," a woman said to the bartender manning the nutrient patch printer.

"Don't they usually come in twos?" the bartender quipped.

Laughter bubbled up from the patrons surrounding her. Xu hunched over the bar and scanned the crowd for what felt like the millionth time. Moth slid onto the stool beside Xu, a cocktail in their hand and something that looked like a cross between a rabbit and an owl perched on their shoulder—a hot mess of fur and beaks. At the Academy, Professor Krane had given them and the other cadets similar animal hybrids to dissect, so they could understand the inner workings of their Chimeras. People in the Walls bought them as pets.

Moth sipped their drink through a custom proboscis that extended from their mask and yawned. "Nighthawk, wasn't it?" A paired synthesizer sanded the rough edges from their voice, rendering it too smooth, too anonymous.

"This will be worth your time," Xu said, pulling the postcard out of her pocket.

Hide the plasmids in plain sight. That's what Professor Krane had told them, a hard lesson learned from living hundreds of years through the Federation Wars. Everyone from the Federation colonists, permanently locked into their space mechs and holoscreens, to the GESTALT grunts with their DNA scanners here on Earth, underestimated paper.

"May I?" Moth asked.

Only a trained eye could make out the slightly darker ink dotting the i's where the plasmids had been bound to the paper. Xu and Anno pretended to be lovers, writing sappy last messages to each other: My darling, my dove. My little hawk. Wish you were here.

Anno had nearly died laughing writing his. Xu had probably taken hers way too seriously.

Moth pulled a small vial with a pipette lid from their jacket pocket. Xu watched while they dropped liquid on one of the words, dissolving the plasmid, and pipetting it into a device on their wrist. A few seconds later, the device rendered a disjointed DNA sequence onto Moth's holoscreen. They studied the letters closely.

"It's the Eternity Drive," Xu said.

Moth recoiled. The owl-rabbit squawked off their shoulder, flapping up to the rafters.

"Are you nuts? My clients want strength, beauty. Intelligence mods. Not to turn into those Chimera freaks."

They gestured out the bar 'window'—a viewing hole hacked out of the wood and already growing back—at Dog unit patrolling the street below. As far as Chimeras went, Xu thought, they didn't even look that different from their namesake.

"I—I didn't mean it like that," Xu stammered. "You sell gene drives, right? But those only work in dividing cells. Like embryos. You dealers all want something that can mod DNA in adults, right? That's what GESTALT made. That's the Eternity Drive. You don't have to use it to make pilotable beasts that can wreak Federation mechs—I mean, Chimeras. You just have to redesign it to be less…extreme."

"A gene drive requires two components." Moth sighed a cloud of static. "I only see the Cas nucleases on this plasmid. I need a library of guide-repair RNAs to program them with. Where is the library?"

"My partner was carrying it. I don't know where he is."

Moth pushed away from the bar.

"Please." Xu grabbed their sleeve. "We need visas. We need to get off-planet. If GESTALT finds us," Xu's voice broke, "they'll—"

"—and is that my fault?" Moth snapped, pulling their arm away. "I know what you are."

"No," Xu said, shaking her head. "I'm not—"

"Everyone's talking about that cadet who got himself killed at the border, and now you stroll in here, trying to sell me the Eternity Drive? I should you turn you over to GESTALT for wasting my time, but I won't. Because you're right. This is a beautiful plasmid. Can you retrieve the other one? From your partner?"

Xu's blood ran cold.

"I told you, I don't know where he is."

"I do. They threw him into that dump by the roots. My friend operates a backdoor lift. Lots of scrappers go down at night."

Moth flicked another file onto their holoscreen—an electronic visa, its Federation flag as radiant as a butterfly's wing.

"I'll hold this just for you, Nighthawk…until tomorrow morning. The visa flickered and disappeared. "After that—no guarantees."

—

It'd been Xu's idea. Every bad idea was her idea. Xu would have done anything to fly. She'd always been afraid the Academy would give their Eternity Drives homology to a mouse, or some kind of rodent, and she and Anno would get their Chimera stuck in a dead-end tunneling mission somewhere deep underground, the earth pressing in on them from all sides. It didn't help that Mari and Haal, the cadet pair at the top of the class, constantly reminded everyone that pairs failed Flight every year, delivering meaningful glances in Anno and Xu's direction.

GESTALT matched cadets based on the strength of the pair, so when Xu failed constantly, everyone knew that Anno's test scores were carrying them both. Anno was the brains, the intellect. Xu was the brawler, the survivor, the kid who'd survived growing up in the wastes. Xu told herself it didn't bother her. It only mattered what she and Anno's DNA made together. Once they got their Chimera, they'd soar off on missions, protect Earth, and never see those picture-perfect jerks again. But still.

"Let's go," she'd whispered the night Mari and Haal had been chosen to take Flight, after throwing gravel at the window of the boy's dorm until Anno opened up. "Let's watch them, see what kind of unit they form."

"We're not allowed."

"Come on. We'll sneak down and just take a peek. We're not hurting anyone."

Every bad idea was her idea.

Xu laid shoulder-to-shoulder with Anno, their faces nearly pressed against the slats of a ceiling vent, looking down into the Flight Chamber. It looked almost identical to the synchronization test room—save for the Chimera scaffold that hung, suspended from a web of synthetic vessels, almost directly below their hiding spot. Through its metal skeleton stretched with emaciated muscles, they'd watch Mari prance in with Haal.

The two of them had practically danced into their synchronization chambers. Even their Flight suits were fancier, the bright material interwoven with glowing filaments. Professor Krane had sealed them in with an indulgent smile and, as the chambers filled with orange-red cell growth media, retreated to a glass-walled control booth.

Both Xu and Anno's breath had caught at the same time. This part, they had never experienced in training.

The engineers created a Chimera scaffold for each cadet pair, seeding them with their own stem cells and coaxing their growth in time with the cadets' training over the years. Xu and Anno had never seen theirs—the cadets weren't allowed to until the Flight—but the engineers had certainly taken enough blood samples to feed theirs ten times over. During each pair's Flight, the Eternity Drives the cadets carried in their genomes would be activated, bringing their Chimera to life. An organic machine that they and they alone could pilot.

Anno squeezed Xu's hand as they waited for the Chimera to move, to show signs that Mari and Haal were not just test synchronized—but fully, actually Synchronized.

Instead, a sudden flash of light nearly blinded them. Then, the stench of searing flesh. Two screams faded slowly, excruciatingly, to one. The fluid began draining from the chambers.

Xu felt a muffled sob from Anno beside her. She clamped her hands over his mouth before he could make a sound.

Mari's chamber contained only her flight suit, tattered on the floor as if she had violently torn it off. In Haal's chamber, a creature the size of a large dog pawed at the glass, moaning and growling in a voice that sounded a lot like Mari's. Where's Haal? it asked, its red iris glistening through its matted hair.

"Something must've gone wrong," Xu whispered, removing her hands from Anno's face.

"Disappointing," Krane said, exiting the glass-walled room. "I expected a bigger unit, given the strong bond between the two components. Even so, it will do for what the Wall Security Division ordered."

The chamber hissed open, and the creature spilled out. The scaffold hadn't been touched.

"It was all for show," Anno whispered in disbelief. "The scaffolds are just…props?"

For once, Xu didn't need him to explain the situation to her.

One cadet became the mind.

One cadet became the body.

And she was the dumb one.

99.2%

Xu's Similarity was still dropping.

She slapped at the scanner on her wrist.

Professor Krane expected all cadets to take Flight before they turned eighteen. Every year they carried the Eternity Drive upped the risk they'd plummet into genomic instability, like those modders she and Anno had seen during their journey, red-eyed and buried in the sand of the wastes.

It'd happened to a few cadets in their class over the years, too. Never to Xu (because her DNA was too stupid to even know it had been modded, Mari used to say), but when they were seven or so, it happened to Anno. Xu—who had already found all the disused tunnels vents of the Academy—had crawled above the medical wing and overheard the doctors say that another child had blown out an entire wing of the Academy years back, and that if Anno became unstable, they'd have to "take action." She'd overheard that and decided she had to make him better. That those songs the GESTALT forced them to sing at meals, before class, and at bedtime to improve their bodies and minds were just what Anno needed. Her twelfth or so rendition of "One Life As One, All Life As All" finally woke him, pale as milk but laughing. It's All Life as One, he'd said. You still haven't learned after all this time?

That's when she'd started to fall a little bit in love with him, she thought.

The lift clattered to a stop and the crowd flooded out, carrying Xu along with it. She knew she now stood atop the Living Walls, but she couldn't see a damn thing with all the people swarming around her, running along to the next lift like chicken-rats with their heads cut off. She tore off her mask. Wind whipped her hair into her mouth, her eyes. Still, she gasped gratefully. A canopy of leaves unfurled above her. Vines curled up her leg, only tugging away when she moved out of the thin shade.

"I can't believe we're—" Xu started, then stopped herself when she remembered Anno wasn't beside her. She reddened, moving faster.

Xu didn't have time for sightseeing or thinking, anyway. She pushed and clawed against the rush of people until she came to a road. Across, Moth had told her. She jumped away just as a hoverbike thundered by.

The crowd thinned as Xu waded into a field of blue flowers that swayed up to her knees. She made her way to the shanties. Pieces of scrap wood held together with ropes of sinewy grass, ragged curtains in place of doors. A strange calm settled over her as Xu squeezed through their overgrown alleys, thick with weeds and thorns. Before the Academy, she'd lived in a place like this. Laughter echoed, then children darted underfoot, rolling a hoop of woven branches past her. Like a sleepwalker, she followed them.

The shacks gave way to a square. A knot of villagers gathered around a grill. Atop it sizzled a menagerie of skewers, twirled by a grey-haired woman. The sight, the heat, the smell, nearly overwhelmed Xu.

She'd only been a baby when her family had sold her to the Academy, yet Xu could feel herself, could see her small hands—a child's hands—feeding the flames. The gray-haired vendor flashed her a smile and handed her a skewer. Had her mother been a woman like this, running a stall like this? Xu couldn't recall.

"Here, honey. You look hungry."

Xu forced a smile as she took the food. Cubes of Petri dish meat had never looked so good. She shoved it into her mouth, ignoring how the juices burned her throat.

GESTALT considered eating to be sacred. Digestion being a process that unites all of humanity against the bio-traitor space colonists and all that. What happened in her body every single day—the process of breaking down carbon-based molecules of other organisms and building them up again to fuel the same processes inside of her—a kind of tribute. The weak living on in the strong. All life as one. Xu had to admit, even now, the thought calmed her.

Had Haal felt the same way as he'd been consumed by Mari?

The meat curdled in Xu's mouth, mid-swallow.

Anno had probably figured out the truth a long time ago. They'd been taught that their ancestors invented the Eternity Drive to create the Living Walls. During the Wars, when the mechs of the Federation of Colonies had descended, raining down destruction from the stars, biologists from every nation formed the GESTALT Initiative. Earth's armies had been on the brink of defeat, constantly curb-stomped by monstrous metal mechs, piloted by colonist soldiers that didn't need to eat, drink, sleep.

So, GESTALT grew walls of wood stronger than any steel, walls that could regenerate and recover from their most devastating wounds— but they came at a price. Their roots siphoned organic material from the surrounding land to fuel their constant growth. She and Anno had seen it firsthand in the wastes. Miles of what had been lush forests, mountains, reduced to deserts as barren as the colonies on the outer reaches of space. The Eternity Drive couldn't create new life. It could only take. Why should the Chimeras, engineered to defend the Living Walls, be any different?

"A vegetarian," the vendor scoffed as Xu spat out the meat and fled. "At times like these."

Even the taste of the skewer triggered a flood of memories. All the celebrations they'd had for the older cadets, once they'd taken Flight. The banners they'd made and draped the dining hall with, the cakes and real meat, now tinted with nightmarish hues. The tears that'd always start up in Krane's eyes as she described how powerful their Lions, how strong their Rhinos, how clever their Ravens, how hard-working their Rabbit units had been.

Xu never thought about how they never got to see the cadets afterwards, how they never responded to the letters other cadets wrote. Krane always said they were on assignments. Busy protecting humanity.

Xu and Anno's entire relationship—its only purpose had been to build a bigger, stronger Chimera. Every aspect of Xu had been shaped for him.

What even happened to the other cadet, Xu wondered now? To the Haals? Were they still in the Chimera, trapped? Did their minds eventually fade into their partner's? Or did they just dissipate, like a handful of sand in the wastes? What would it be like to take Flight, only to drown in someone else? To soar, not ever knowing what took you?

—

Despite everything, Xu's feet had led her to the right place. She sank her face back into her mask, felt the feathers mold around her temples. She approached a tall man wearing a mask with a sharp snout and two pointed ears. A jackal.

"Nighthawk," he said. "That's you, right?"

Xu nodded. "That's right," she said.

"Get ready," Jackal told her, leading her to a lift. A smaller, ramshackle construction half-hidden beneath a tangled bush. "We've got the next shift bought off. They'll get the Iguana units off our backs."

This lift was quieter than the one she'd taken up. Faster. No railings either. Xu tried not to think of what she was doing here. How Krane had been waiting for her and Anno as they'd climbed out of the vent, the night of Haal and Mari's Flight. She hadn't erupted in anger or immediately forced them into a chamber to suffer the same fate. She had just seemed—tired.

"Go to Neo Boston," Krane had said, opening her fist, revealing two tubes. "You should be able to trade these plasmids for passage off-planet."

"What?" Anno babbled.

"You aren't the only children who've found out the truth," she said. "We don't make it difficult, to be honest. None of the others made it to Neo Boston, but maybe you will."

She dropped the tubes in Xu's hand, curling her limp fingers around them.

"This is a new version of the Eternity Drive, one with all the constraints removed. An updated version of the Drive my colleagues used to grow the Living Walls. That's what all the filthy modders in the city want. Give it to them and escape this place once and for all."

"You're helping us?" Xu demanded. "Why?"

"Helping?"

Krane smiled strangely. The glare of the light on her glasses hid her eyes.

"I've extended my life for hundreds of years now," she said. "Dedicating everything to my research. And for what? My colleagues who survived the Wars made peace with the Federation. They made a truce with those monsters who tore apart entire cities, looking for our hovels, our incubators, for any scientist they could eviscerate for even daring to stand against them… We laid waste to this planet, trying to protect it, destroyed countless young lives like yours. For what? To create Chimeras to defend a worthless city that won't even defend itself? All Neo Boston does is take. These plasmids… I tried injecting them into some cadets here, ages ago, but it never worked. I need a larger sample size. Maybe someone in that city can host this Eternity Drive and survive. Maybe they'll become a beast stronger than the Walls themselves. Maybe they can take all that wasted life and use it to destroy the Federation once and for all. If I can see that happen, maybe I can finally let myself die."

The lift jolted to a stop. The shadow of the Walls covered the ground ahead.

"Follow the scavengers," Jackal said. "For the fresh meat."

Xu stumbled across the trench. The headlamps on the Mole units excavating nearby broke the darkness like fireflies. Their beams revealing, in bits and pieces, the ropey snakes of roots, dripping from the bottom of the Walls.

Xu took a step into the mounds of trash. Plastic waste, mostly. Inorganics that couldn't be absorbed. She slogged through the path the scavengers made, wishing desperately she had boots like theirs rather than her ragged sneakers.

The Mole units started hacking at something. An archway? Part of a building? No, as the glow of their headlamps passed over it, she saw its full form. A massive metal ribcage. A skull the size of a car shattered at its base. Just like the one she'd seen in the Flight Chamber. Except this wasn't a prop. A Chimera graveyard, Xu realized. The ones fallen in combat during the Wars.

Xu overheard the scrappers talking as she searched. They sometimes found people in the dump, wandering—chucked off the top of the Walls by GESTALT but still alive. That might have happened to Anno too.

She saw his mismatched sneakers first. Then the lights passed over his face.

Xu clamped her eyes shut and a memory flashed in her mind.

"It was an old book, a paper book my grandparents read to me," Anno said. "There was a Nighthawk—an ugly bird who only ate insects. He was taunted by all the others, the songbirds and the owls and the cranes, most of all by the Hawk—who resented sharing part of Nighthawk's name. 'You stole it from me,' Hawk said. So, one day he gave Nighthawk an ultimatum: change your name by tomorrow morning, or I'll rip you to shreds. Distraught, Nighthawk flew through the dusk skies. He begged the sun, the moon to take him. The heavens paid him no heed. Nighthawk didn't want to give in," Anno smiled. "But he refused to die."

"But why live?" Xu whispered. "What else is left?"

Xu's eyes opened softly. She wished she could close Anno's, but they'd already stiffened. She gazed into his irises, clouded red, as she rummaged through his pockets and found the postcard, still sewn into the seams.

He'd lied. She saw that now. He'd reassured her in the processing center that he was still stable, if only a bit below the threshold, promising her he'd meet her on the other side. Why? She couldn't understand. The headlamp beams moved off Anno's face.

"I'm sorry, Anno."

He couldn't hear her.

"I'm sorry for this world."

He was gone, and Xu was alone. She tilted her head back and studied the starless sky.

—

Xu took the lift down and walked. As the sun struggled up, she neared the Neo Boston Seaport. She could tell she was getting close by the sting of salt on the breeze and the Seagull units cawing above. One swooped over her head, skimming the sloping street, and dove into the waves. They came up to the surface, the water running off their back, turbid and red.

On every dry spot of land, people blocked her way. Parents lifting kids up on their shoulders, pointing. Others as newly arrived from the wastes as she was, staring like hungry dogs.

The daily Federation shuttle had arrived. In a rumble like a thundercloud in the night, so massive, it was impossible to make out its full shape, only the hints of its battered underside.

Another transport shot from one of the ship's launch tubes, a capsule growing red and silver—the colors of the Federation. The last link, spider's thread, between Earth and the colonies.

Earth's space fleet had been destroyed in the Federation Wars, a fact Krane often glossed over, claiming true humans wouldn't want to leave the planet, anyway, and that this one ship that traveled between them every day was part of the peace treaty forced on them by the colonies, nothing more.

It wasn't hard to find the terminal at the end of the only dock still in good repair. An echo of the processing center, even down to the GESTALT soldiers, stiff at attention out front. Behind it, the rusted ferry waited to take passengers out to the landing pad out on the water.

Moth looked different outside, perched on a bench. Dusty and small, their mask's compound eyes gaudy. Xu sat down beside them, holding out the postcard. Moth snatched it away. A quick scan and they shoved it into their pocket.

"The visa," Xu said.

Moth only nodded at someone behind her.

"Where's the visa?" Xu asked again, her voice rising.

Arms clamped around her neck. She thrashed, but another pair wrapped around her torso. Someone else tore her mask off, jabbing a scanner into her neck.

99.1%

"She's still stable."

"Cadet Xu. We found you just in time."

In a white rage, Xu managed to stand, but the GESTALT agents slammed her down. She tasted scum. Saw her eyes reflected in the puddle she'd begun bleeding into. Red.

She felt the crash.

95.0%

"She's unstable!"

0.4%

"What the hell's happening?"

86.4%

"Her Similarity's plummeting!"

61.9%

"Get away! Run!"

Like everything Xu failed at, she did so spectacularly. As they leaped away from her, she felt the symptoms bubbling over her skin like a fever. Xu pushed herself up and saw her knuckles glowing with soft light.

She was way past genomic instability; she was an Eternity Drive gone haywire, metabolizing uncontrollably, just like the first carriers who'd been sent out to the front lines.

Is this why you let yourself die, Anno?

She'd been stupid. So stupid. After long weeks traveling through the wastes, she and Anno had managed to kindle a fire at last. Both of them had traded their Flight suits for odds and ends they'd taken off bodies they'd come across in the sands, bodies that would be buried by the gusting winds before day's end.

They'd been only a day from the Walls when Anno had started coughing. When Xu wiped the blood from his mouth, she saw it had started seeping into the whites of his eyes.

"Let's go back," she had said. "We'll turn ourselves in. I know you're scared Anno." Xu rested her hand atop his. "I'm scared too, but I don't mind taking Flight," she said softly. "Not if it's for you."

He'd jerked away. "Don't say that."

"Why not?"

Xu wanted nothing more than to be with him. She already spent every waking moment with him, didn't she? Didn't he feel the same?

As excruciating seconds passed between them, neither saying a word, it seemed obvious that he didn't. And did she really love him? Xu dug the heel of her hand into her forehead. She thought so, but she didn't know. All her life, she'd just been told.

Then, the world suddenly shifted and she saw Anno's face, perfectly clear, his eyes tender and piercing. All the possibilities. What they could have been, and what GESTALT had stolen from them.

"The runaways who went back to the Academy didn't understand what's left," they seemed to say. "But you do. So you'll keep living, keep moving forward."

Anno was dead. Not because of her. For her. He'd made a decision when he left her in the processing center that morning, when he'd gone into that terminal to face the scanners alone.

With all her strength, Xu staggered to her feet. The first action she'd taken, maybe, entirely of her own volition.

Moth hadn't fled far. She found them, cowering behind an overturned bench.

"The library," Xu said. "Did you sequence it?"

Moth nodded.

"Release it. To everyone you can."

Trembling, Moth made the strokes on their holoscreen. From the sequence, modders would be able to reconstruct the plasmids. The

Eternity Drive that had raised the Walls could be used to tear them down.

Xu took the postcard from Moth's hand. Skimmed the sentences Anno had written. Ordinarily, the plasmids would need to be injected to take effect. But in this state, her cells had become permeable, her DNA machinery hyperactive.

Xu crumpled and swallowed the paper. For a moment, she felt nothing.

Then, all at once, every single one of her trillions of cells were blazing. She needed an outlet for her energy, a host to help her carry it. Moth? No. No mere human would be enough.

Xu stumbled over to the Walls. She fell forward, felt the throb of wood beneath her palms, peeling away from her brightness and growing like jaws around her. They snapped together, cocooning her.

She felt it. A heartbeat. The ache of wings. She saw everything the Walls had seen over the centuries. The pain of a planet on the verge of collapse, a planet that sacrificed everything to generation ships. The sorrow of those left behind. The hollow realization that no life would be discovered elsewhere. An ache turned to rage at the colonists who chose to survive in the cold reaches of space, anyway. A fury that'd caged them in centuries of violent war, centuries of tenuous truce.

The desperation of those first scientists hunched in labs, hoping, hoping.

They'd built the Eternity Drive for so many reasons. Reasons that had names and faces and smiles. It hadn't been meant to hoard all the resources of Earth into one city and its massive Living Walls.

So Xu let her body unravel. The same way she'd once practiced in the synchronization chamber. Except this time there were no synthetics, no machinery, no Krane to direct what she became. Only the Walls around her. Only the explosive instructions she'd absorbed and integrated into her DNA. She took all the material she needed and still felt miles and miles left. The distance shrank as she shot upward from the momentum of her own growth. The people atop the Walls who'd fled from their rumbling became tiny dots as she erupted from its summit, still growing.

Wings erupted from her back. The bark encasing her splintered from new limbs, from jaws, from the embers of her eyes, glowing and melding into a chitinous sheen. She screamed in a voice charred black, burning with light.

"Watch me, Anno."

A downward beat, and she launched into the sky. She broke the atmosphere, and it felt the same, felt like she was still growing. She could go on, find a planet with an atmosphere she could breathe. A reservoir of organic molecules for a storm, a passing flare to spark into life. Just as it began on that watery dot rapidly disappearing beneath her. The planet she landed on would evolve. For her and everyone who came after—for others would come. Of their own will, but linked by their shared DNA, their shared homeworld. Like sense and antisense strands of a double helix eternally replicated, neither consumed, neither lost for the other.

That's what was left. A star, incandescent blue, shining for all of Earth to see.

WELCOME TO THE ORGAN EXTRACTION EMPORIUM

BECOME EXTRATERRESTRIAL AND LEAD A BETTER LIFE!

ALICIA HILTON

A. On the way home from work, your stomach rumbles from hunger. You haven't eaten since you ran out of anemone soup yesterday. You live in a time when housing and hygiene products are provided by the government, but human worker bees must barter for food. The extraterrestrials that conquered Earth created a paternalistic society, but there are limits to their beneficence. Humans who volunteer to transform their bodies into alien form are treated as equals.

Since your favorite plasma collection center is closed because of the summer solstice, you catch the complimentary hovercraft shuttle to the Organ Extraction Emporium.

Two Xenomorphs with malodorous slime dripping from their jaws are sitting on either side of the only vacant seat. Their halitosis makes your nausea worse, so you stand by the door and clutch the stabilizer bar.

The hovercraft accelerates past a freighter and a line of taxis. Whenever the vehicle zips around a corner, your stomach lurches.

A giant leech sitting underneath the NO FOOD OR DRINK sign is gnawing on a blood sausage.

Sweat trickles down your spine. Finally, you see the Organ Extraction Emporium in the distance. The flashing sign on the building says GOODS FOR TRADE: KIDNEYS LUNGS MARROW FEET. Whole blood and plasma aren't on the list.

If you enter the Emporium, proceed to **C**.

If you leave without making a trade, go to **B**.

—

B. The hovercraft latches onto the building, and the vehicle's door opens directly into a waiting room that is furnished more like a nightclub than a hospital—chrome and glass furniture, a water sculpture, jazzy muzak playing on the intercom.

A recorded voice says, "Exit now, exit now." Passengers trundle past you in an orderly row. No one shoves or cuts in line, not even the Xenomorphs.

You consider trying to exit through the clinic, but there are more than a dozen nurses milling about. Surely, the hovercraft will head downtown to pick up more passengers? You select the seat furthest from the door. When the shuttle lifts off, hot air that stinks like disinfectant blasts from the climate control vents.

You wake trapped inside a white, rectangular box that's not much wider than a coffin. There's a shower nozzle and a single light dangling above your head, no windows or furniture, just a stack of newspapers and magazines from 1950, three packages of Silly Putty, a baseball signed by Joe DiMaggio, a bottle of antihistamine tablets, and three lipsticks.

The significance of 1950 is glaringly obvious. October 7, 1950 was the final day of the World Series. It also was the day that your stepfather's grandfather landed on Earth, starting the chain of events that led to a strange symbiotic relationship between extraterrestrials and humans—a relationship that your rash actions jeopardized twelve years ago.

You've been on the run ever since.

There's a seam in one wall that looks like a door. You dig at it until two of your fingernails crack and bleed. No one answers when you yell for help.

Your stomach rumbles again. You've never felt so ravenous.

The crimson lipstick tastes like wax. The peach lipstick tastes like wax. The mauve lipstick smells like grapes, but tastes moldy. You tear out a page from a *Life* magazine and use it to wipe your lips and tongue.

The wall in front of you lights up with a sign: THIRSTY? PRESS HERE.

You're afraid that if you touch the sign the showerhead will blast water until you drown, but wouldn't a quick death be better than dying of thirst?

If you don't touch the sign, the shower blasts water until you are drowning, proceed to **Z**.

If you do touch the sign, go to **C**.

—

C. You enter the Organ Extraction Emporium. Only ten other patients are waiting to be served. You breathe a sigh of relief and admire displays showing augmentations available for trade.

The Xenomorphs ogle sample lung augmentations. A human mannequin has gills on her sides, like a shark.

A humanoid nurse with silky copper-colored fur taps your shoulder. She says, "Congratulations! I'm glad you've chosen to become an extraterrestrial. What would you like to trade?"

"Feet?" you say, with only a bit of uncertainty.

"Excellent choice." She grins, displaying exceptionally white teeth.

One patient stands in front of you in the FEET line, a human with wings grafted to her back. The augmentations must be fresh, because the incisions are covered in bandages.

The humanoid nurse says, "Take off your socks." She's talking to the other patient, not you, but you take off your shoes and socks.

You feel a stab of envy when you see the winged woman's feet. She has high arches, no calluses or deformities. Your bunions are quite painful.

"Right or left?" the nurse says.

The patient replies, "Can I trade both?" She points at a sample pair displayed on the top shelf.

You wonder why she selects waterfowl feet when eagle feet are a better match for her wings, but you keep your opinion to yourself.

"Excellent selection," the nurse says.

The winged woman reaches for the duck feet, but the nurse says, "Don't touch the display. Please take a seat. A doctor will be with you shortly."

The nurse examines your feet and probes the toes. You try to hold still, but her talons poke all the sensitive spots.

"Bunions," she says. "I'll have to get approval for the trade." She presses a button on the side of the display case and says, "Bunions on MTP, 3.225 centimeters right, 3.310 centimeters left."

You hold your breath while the gruff voice on the other end of the intercom jabbers in a language you don't understand. Tears seep from your eyes as you realize that your life will be even more miserable if you don't get to trade for feline extraterrestrial paws.

If you change your mind and decide not to barter, go back to **B** and drown in the shower.

If the trade is approved and you opt for feline feet, proceed to **D**.

———

D. The aliens are remarkably efficient. A transporter beams you to an operating theater painted in pastel shades, except for the ceiling, covered in white acoustical tiles. The robotic physician is quite handsome, his wide-set eyes with their vertical pupil slits alluring, yet promising dangerous consequences for noncompliance. Of course, you get the jitters when his arm unfolds, becoming a saw, but the intravenous anesthetic works so fast, you're in slumberland before the nurse finishes pulling down your pants.

When the grafting is complete, proceed to **E**.

———

E. Everything in the recovery suite glimmers—the burgundy carpet, the crimson walls, and the scarlet sheet that covers your legs and feet. Your fingers tingle, but when you try to pull back the sheet, you discover that you're paralyzed.

The sparkly ceiling begins to swirl. The texture changes, as if it's liquefying. Droplets that look like blood fall and splash you, but you can't feel them.

Your lips part in a hysterical giggle.

Click, click, click, click, footsteps approach from the hallway. Through the opaque glass brick wall, you see a tall, very thin silhouette. The panel slides open, and a Venusian mantis wearing lavender surgical scrubs steps into the room. His mandibles *clack* in the universal greeting that means "Peace and prosperity, your paws are fabulous."

"Really?" you say.

With a grand flourish, he flings back the sheet. The fur on your ankles and paws is spotted like a cheetah's coat and is indeed fabulous.

Proceed to **F**.

—

F. Unfortunately, the dosage of anti-rejection meds was inadequate. The incisions swell, itch, and ooze yellowish fluid that reeks like rotten mushrooms.

Proceed to **G**.

—

G. A very large face peers through the window in the operating theater. It must be a Moongubian, because his rotund, bald head is three times the size of a large Jack-o'-lantern's face, and Jack-o'-lantern extraterrestrials are heftier than African savannah elephants.

"Hello," you say, but he keeps peering and doesn't answer.

Despite the festering infection that itches like hell and the straps on your arms and legs that shackle you to the surgical cot, you're feeling remarkably calm. Damn, their drugs are strong.

You say, "Can I have my feet back?"

If you persist in demanding your old human feet, go to **Z**.

If you stop complaining and agree to keep the feline paws, go to **H**.

—

H. The sexy robotic surgeon returns and jabs your hip with a very large needle. Alien antibiotics are super-potent, stronger than their narcotics.

Proceed to **I**.

—

I. The new recovery suite's apricot décor is more soothing than convalescing in a room decorated in red furnishings that remind you of gore. The TV mounted above your bed is retro, an old black-and-white model. You watch a loop of news broadcasts about the 1969 Apollo 11 moon landing. As you listen to Neil Armstrong say, "The Eagle has landed," a tear trickles down your cheek. How naïve the humans were, thinking they were the first to walk on the moon.

A nurse enters your room. Her white sneakers *squeak* as she walks across the linoleum. She's as old-fashioned as the TV—her hair is bleached and teased, and she has no visible body modifications, not even tattoos or facial piercings. The nurse's uniform dress and matching hat look like they are from the 1960s, too.

"How are we feeling?" she says.

If you complain about being exhausted, go to **Z**.

If you tell her that you're feeling better, proceed to **J**.

—

J. The cheetah paws are indeed fabulous. There is no sign of infection, not even swelling where furry skin is grafted to human epidermis. Of course, physical therapy is unnecessary because extraterrestrial medicine is *very* advanced.

In the hospital courtyard, you take daily runs around the exercise track. The other joggers look ordinary, as retro as the nurse, but none of them stare at your magnificent extraterrestrial appendages, except for one little girl. Maybe she's a Saturnian in disguise?

Sprinting is a breeze. The sensation of your clawed paws flexing with each graceful leap is so sensational, a delicious shiver travels from your soles to your groin. The wonderful tingling makes you think sexy thoughts about the nurse.

After six days, you have not slept a single minute, you've eaten nothing but lime Jell-O and creamed corn, but you've never had so much energy, or been so carefree. Every time you see the nurse, you imagine what she might look like naked.

The drugs that are pumped into your body through a port that was inserted into your neck are so potent, that you almost don't mind the sexual frustration. But your overblown libido is a warning. In the past, you tried to smother grief with sex.

If you attempt to seduce the nurse, proceed to **Z**.

If you experience a sudden pang of homesickness and ask to return to 2093, proceed to **O**. (There is no **K, L, M,** or **N**. Teleportation to that deadly void would lead to a fate worse than **Z**).

—

O. The Organ Extraction Emporium looks exactly the same as before—except all of the patients are gone, there are bloodstains on the waiting room floor, and the friendly humanoid nurse has a nasty gash on her forehead. The robotic doctor who sawed off your feet is stitching the humanoid nurse's wound closed.

Despite the sapphire fluid dripping from the nurse's forehead to her eyes, she sees you and says, "Congratulations! I'm glad you've chosen to become an extraterrestrial. Would you like to make another trade?"

If you say, "I want the cases of soup and vegetable paste you owe me for my feet," go to **Z**.

If you say, "Do you do hand transplants?" go to **P**.

—

P. The Emporium is out of extraterrestrial hands and paws. They offer you a tail if you're willing to let medical students watch the grafting procedure. Of course, you agree.

Go to **Q**.

—

Q. The fuzzy poodle-style pom pom would look absurd with your cheetah paws, and why get a tail if it's not prehensile?

Go to **R**.

—

R. A human man with thick spectacles walks into the examination room. You expect that his clipboard has your discharge papers, but he's a psychiatrist who wants to talk about your feelings. When he asks about your family, your heart rate accelerates so fast, you collapse.

Proceed to **S**.

—

S. Only a dream could be this bizarre, but you are really and truly awake. After a super-duper dose of beta-blockers and a mood lifter, you prance through the waiting room, padding daintily on your extraterrestrial feline paws. The hovercraft shuttle is waiting.

Board it, and proceed to **T**.

—

T. The trauma of talking about your family has wiped your memory. You believe you're back where the whole debacle started, on the quest for soup and veggie paste. You grip the hovercraft's stabilizer bar and try not to stare at the pair of Xenomorphs, but it's impossible to ignore them ogling you.

"Nice gams," the taller Xenomorph says.

You glance down at your legs, expecting to see your usual, semi-flabby human thighs. What a shock! Holy hell! Who stole your legs and feet? And your trousers are missing, too! Instead of being horrified, you feel a surge of sensual energy. "Meow," you say, pivoting to display your sleek feline thighs and calves. Flexing your left paw, you extend the claws.

"Meow," the shorter Xenomorph flirts back.

An elderly Saturnian *thunks* his cane against the floor and grumbles, "Get a room."

Both Xenomorphs open their jaws wider and *hiss*.

If you encourage the Xenomorphs to slaughter the Saturnian, go to **U**.

If you apologize and negotiate peace between the Xenomorphs and the Saturnian, proceed to **V**.

—

U. The Saturnian spits venom in the Xenomorphs' eyes. Lashing out blindly, the parasitoid extraterrestrials slaughter nine other passengers before their own internal organs melt, dissolving in puddles of acid.

Amidst the chaos, the Saturnian escapes, unharmed. His species resembles human toddlers, but their venom is eighty times more lethal than spitting cobra venom.

Since you incited the deadly attack, you are arrested and charged with mass murder. The Alien Armistice Treaty of 2071 abolished the U.S. Constitution, so no attorney represents you at your trial. Of course, the sentence is death.

Proceed to **Z**.

—

V. You are teleported back to the Organ Extraction Emporium. The humanoid nurse points at a stack of boxes and says, "I'm glad you came back. Shall I have your food delivered, or would you like to make another trade?"

She shows you two surgical consent forms with your signature. You have a vague memory of trading your feet for feline extraterrestrial paws, but how the feline legs became attached to your buttocks is a mystery. Of course, the forms cannot be forgeries. Extraterrestrials are more ethical than humans. They never lie or renege on a promise.

You say, "I'm feeling sick to my stomach. Can I have some water?"

"Of course," the nurse says.

The water tastes like blueberries and forgiveness. No, not forgiveness—regret. With each sip, you reflect on your mistakes.

Dizzy and forlorn, you must proceed to **W.**

—

W. A nurse with a Nevon's pallid complexion and three very muscular arms, like a Flemon, unwraps a thick needle and stabs your chest. When she inserts the central venous catheter, it hurts like hell.

An anesthetic would've made the procedure painless, but you opt to be lucid. You take a deep breath, and exhale. The extraterrestrial marrow transplant won't absolve you of your mistakes, but if you're lucky, you might gain the strength and wisdom to make amends.

The intercom plays a discordant, jazzy tune that reminds you of the last time you saw your stepsister. Your eyes fill with tears. By the time the song is over, the nurse has finished the infusion. Unfortunately, the needle leaves a gaping crater, wider than your pinkie finger.

A beetle with a shiny, blue exoskeleton skitters across the room and leaps onto the surgery cot.

The blueberry flavored water that you drank earlier was laced with a mild paralytic agent, so you don't flinch when the insect climbs onto your body, which is fortunate since the barbs on the creature's legs look light and feathery and certainly would tickle. It nuzzles your furry feline hip with its feelers and crawls up your belly to your chest.

The extraterrestrial insect regurgitates and spits into your wound, sealing the hole with healing mucous.

Proceed to **X**.

—

X. Two thousand and thirty-seven steps—an arduous climb, despite your extraterrestrial feline augmentations. You could take a hover taxi to the Supreme Chancellor's residence, but ascending the steps is an essential segment in the journey towards reconciliation.

Your rucksack contains an electronic tablet and a photograph. Physically, the burden is light. Mentally, it nearly breaks you.

Out of breath, you ascend the final step and stare at the stately mansion that was once your home. Sunlight gleams on the white stone columns. The front door is open.

Proceed to **Y**.

—

Y. Three robotic sentries are standing in the hexagon-shaped foyer. One of the robots points a rifle at your face.

You say, "Can I see the Supreme Chancellor?"

The robot lowers the weapon and says, "Proceed."

As you walk towards the throne room, you begin to tremble. Bile crawls up your throat. You swallow the bitter fluid.

Supreme Chancellor Tatig is sitting on his throne, flanked by two sentries. He does not smile when you enter the room.

There is a large painting on the wall. The image of your stepsister looks like the photograph in your rucksack, except a tiara rests on Claralune's furry head.

Shaking in trepidation, you kneel in front of the throne. You are determined not to cry because Tatig loathes emotional displays.

Supreme Chancellor Tatig is the only family you have left which is ironic because he is the leader of the extraterrestrials and you are human, linked to him by your mother's marriage. Your biological father was an anonymous sperm donor who sired you before Tatig and your mother met.

Tatig bares his teeth. The canines look longer than you remember.

You say, "I'm sorry. Please give me the chance to earn your forgiveness. I didn't mean to hurt her." You are speaking of your stepsister, not your mother. Mom died of cancer nine years after she married Tatig. She wouldn't accept the extraterrestrial augmentations that could have saved her.

Tatig places his furry paw on your forehead. One of the talons nicks your temple, but you try not to flinch.

You close your eyes and open your consciousness to cognitive mingling.

Like a movie, your memories unspool. Claralune has your electronic tablet and is snooping, learning secrets that seemed so important when you were a teen. When she sees you, she drops the tablet and runs, heading for the ravine behind your home. You hear a shriek and a *thunk*. When you find Claralune, she's fallen to the bottom of the ravine. Her neck is broken and she's not breathing.

Tatig's grief is overwhelming, a hot metal jab to your temple, worse than the catheters that speared your chest and neck. You cry out in pain.

He enfolds you in his embrace.

"Will you take the final step?" he says.

"Yes." You hug him tighter.

"Complete augmentation?"

"Complete," you say, sealing your fate.

Tatig presses an intercom button.

His robotic security team escorts you to the Organ Extraction Emporium.

After the surgical procedures are finished and you regain consciousness, Tatig visits you in the recovery suite. "I forgive you," he says.

Living the life of a feline extraterrestrial is hardly perfect, even though you can vote and have the same constitutional rights as the aliens.

The surgeons did not extract a portion of your human brain, so you recollect enough of your memories to dwell on your mistakes. Your dreams are plagued with nightmares, but you will not die destitute, or shamed.

If you prefer to start your new extraterrestrial life with a blank slate, swallow three Navocon spiders. The arachnid enzymes will purge your painful memories and erase all regrets, leaving you with the blissful outlook of a newborn kitten.

—

Z. Go back to **C** and trade your feet and legs for feline extraterrestrial augmentations. You really don't want to end your life at **Z**. Slow evisceration by extraterrestrial leeches is a miserable, grisly way to die, worse than mating with Xenomorphs.

A NEW NIGHT PARADE

GORDON LINZNER

Seiji Ozawa pondered the half-dozen small forms laid out before him, their heads pointing north—as was proper for the dead. The emptiness of the vast storeroom made the figures look even smaller. He sniffed at the sour chemical smell that filled the air, making it feel like a hospital corridor, then turned gloomily to the body-broker. "These are the best you can provide? Children?"

The other man spread his open palms.

"These are all I have left, Ozawa-san. The O-Bon festival begins tomorrow night. Had you approached me a month ago, even half a month…" His tone held a tinge of disrespect.

Ozawa scowled. In the past, eta were rightly ashamed of their heritage as outsiders. Although the designation had been officially banned in the nineteenth century, during the Meiji restoration, Japanese culture had a long memory. Descendants of tanners and gravediggers, among others, continued to be scorned for decades afterwards.

To a degree, Ozawa understood the man's attitude. His own samurai ancestors, having turned to commerce after that same Meiji era, were looked down upon by their former equals. His family endured that spite proudly, as befitted their heritage. Moreover, they were ultimately proven right.

The body-broker, however, seemed to possess no drop of worthy blood. Today's eta had grown positively brazen in the five years Ozawa spent overseas, managing the Houston branch of the Katamura Corporation. Great profit could be made in re-animation, at least to the extent permitted by government regulations.

"That was not possible," Ozawa replied, irritated at feeling obliged to explain himself. "I only returned to Tokyo last week." Since then, he'd grown increasingly dismayed at the pervasiveness of this vogue in Japan. In the States, re-animation technology was largely confined to entertainment businesses.

The executive had been amused initially to find so many people with more money than sense augmenting household shrines with their recently deceased ancestors, programmed by implanted mini-computers to acknowledge token offerings of food and money.

Then he discovered how seriously the president—and primary stockholder—of Katamura had taken to the fad.

Ozawa understood how his job might now be in jeopardy. Younger men, in particular his former assistant, Ichiro Watanabe, vied for Ozawa's executive slot. He'd heard whispered accusations that he'd become Americanized.

Ridiculous, of course.

Ozawa hated every minute of those years abroad, enduring them only for the sake of the company. Some even speculated that his lack of a wife could be interpreted as unwillingness to conform to Japanese norms—when, in fact, the city of Houston offered a dearth of suitable mates.

Ozawa would not be fired because of such rumors, but he could find himself shunted into a position of token responsibility, to rot for the next twenty years, of no more use to society than the dead youngsters that lay before him. Such a fate would bring disgrace upon his entire house—of which he was presently the sole male descendant. The humiliation might not be deep enough to call for seppuku, but it could be the end of his line.

Only a deep show of traditional devotion would prove to his fellow workers—and, more importantly, his superiors—that he remained, at heart, a true member of Japanese society.

Such as entering a beloved ancestor's remains in the annual hyakki yako.

These night parades, inspired by the millennium-old superstition that demons walked the streets on certain nights, now began and ended midsummer's O-Bon, the ancient Buddhist festival for the souls of the dead. Dancing in the streets, once done for the entertainment of the unseen dead, was now performed by those corpses for the pleasure of the living. New mats placed before every altar and household shrine, tiny meals laid in readiness for ghostly guests—such traditional signs of respect were no longer deemed sufficient.

"Perhaps," the body-broker suggested, "the boy on the end? He is rather tall for a lad of fourteen. With proper garb and make-up..."

"No greasepaint could withstand a Tokyo summer," Ozawa countered. *The man thinks me a fool!*

Buying or renting an 'ancestor' was considered acceptable, an extension of those businesses that hired out actors to pose as wedding guests in order to make those occasions more impressive, or substitute for a client unable to attend a vital meeting. The gesture alone served as proof of piety. Society was willing to stretch the truth. Re-animation had only become established in Japan in the past few years; the alternative to such substitutions might lead to a patricide epidemic.

The lie had to be plausible, however. A half-hearted attempt was worse than none. Nobody would believe this callow adolescent to be the venerated ancestor of a company executive entering his forty-third summer.

The body-broker bowed. "Please accept my humble apologies for the unworthy suggestion."

"A good businessman should keep better stock," Ozawa growled, annoyed at the mockery. It was not worth his time to call the broker out. "You knew they'd be in heavy demand at this time of year."

"And what am I to do about that? Murder people arbitrarily to compensate for others procrastinating?" The man shrugged. "Our national death rate is declining. Many bereaved families lack funds or facilities to preserve a loved one at home, and prefer cremation to this kind of, ah, recycling."

"Enjoy your success while you can," Ozawa snapped. "I've heard certain Buddhist sects are petitioning the Diet to outlaw re-animation. They consider it sacrilegious."

"Progress always has its detractors." The body-broker smiled.

Ozawa would have happily added his name to such a petition. Instead, he turned brusquely, leaving the air-conditioned warehouse in favor of Tokyo's stifling streets.

August heat scalded his face. Heavy humidity took him in its soggy embrace. The body-broker's warehouse sat in the heart of a buraku that was among Tokyo's worst. The ghetto's stench struck him, making his eyes water.

The executive paused to swipe a cotton handkerchief across his forehead, and a sudden jolt nearly threw him to the steaming sidewalk.

Ozawa turned. "Are you blind?" he snapped.

The other man staggered. His bright green and red cotton yukata, though neatly pressed, was mottled with faint stains. Tinted glasses were twisted askew, revealing sightless orbs.

Ozawa's face flushed. He bowed in embarrassment at having taken his frustration out on a disabled stranger. He had indeed spent too much time in the States.

"Please forgive this clumsy one," the blind man offered, straightening his glasses.

"No. It is I who must ask forgiveness for my unthinking rudeness. Let me at least compensate you with a token." Ozawa thrust a silver five-hundred-yen coin into the man's hand.

Quick as a snake, the blind man's fingers latched onto Ozawa's sleeve, fondling the material of his tailor-made suit. "You are too generous, sir. As a businessman who dresses so well can no doubt afford to be."

"Er, yes." Ozawa gently disengaged. "May I offer you another coin?"

"I would rather have a paying job, if such is within your power to grant.”

The executive smiled. “Would you, now?”

The dark lenses turned upward, seeming to focus on a point beyond Ozawa's right shoulder.

“My name is Keiko,” the man continued. “I was a tourist guide before my accident. I can still find my way around Tokyo better than most residents. Unfortunately, my company feared foreigners would have no faith in a blind guide. They pensioned me off three years ago, but at a fixed rate. Each year I find it more difficult to make ends meet as costs rise, even in this squalid buraku.”

“If you are so excellent a guide, why not go into business for yourself?”

Keiko sighed. “I tried. My former employers were correct.”

“And what service do you think you could provide me?” asked Ozawa, not unkindly.

The lenses shifted toward Ozawa's face. “Almost anything that saves me from begging in the streets. I am no eta; I come from a respectable family. In the past I might have found employment as an itinerant masseur. There are no such opportunities these days.”

Ozawa studied Keiko carefully. The blind man looked not much older than himself. His features, strong and well-defined, confirmed his claim of good lineage.

“You have my sympathies, Keiko. Alas! Your request comes at an unfortunate time. In a few days, I may not have a job myself.”

Keiko bowed. “Then I must resign myself to continued humiliation, or else face a slow death by starvation.”

Ozawa allowed himself another smile at this obvious attempt at manipulation. “In the latter condition I might be able to use you.”

Keiko's brow crinkled. “Is that a joke, businessman? If so, it is a cruel one.”

Ozawa's smile faded. “The joke is on me, Keiko. I must produce a dead ancestor, or a reasonable surrogate, by tomorrow night, or lose my prestige in the Katamura organization...and possibly my position, as well. I had hoped, upon returning to my homeland, to marry and have sons. I still may do so, but it will be a bitter pill indeed if their futures are the poorer for my failure to appease my colleagues and superiors."

Keiko's fingers clamped Ozawa's wrist, hard enough to make him wince. "You need a dead man to represent you in the hyakki yako?"

Ozawa blinked, startled by the blind man's sudden intensity.

"You know where I can find one?"

"He stands before you."

Ozawa pulled free, as horrified by the man's suggestion as he was impressed by his sense of honor. Re-animation added a new wrinkle to ritual suicide, offering a more pragmatic atonement.

"No. You must not kill yourself. Not for me." Ozawa fumbled for his wallet, intending to press higher denomination bills on Keiko.

The blind man shook his head. "I am already a living corpse— unable to work, unable to see. However, I do not propose ending my life. Miserable I may be, but still it is my life, and not entirely without pleasures."

Ozawa sighed relief. "For a moment I feared you were serious."

"I am."

"But...?"

"Why else would a man of your quality visit this part of Tokyo, save to rent a corpse from that nearby warehouse to impersonate an ancestor?"

"Yes, but..."

"Why not, then, go one step further? Hire a living man to impersonate a corpse."

Ozawa blinked. "It would never work."

"I say it would. I've read everything available on the subject, in braille and audiobooks. Re-animates are little more than machines, are they not? Unable to see, speak, think, act for themselves?"

Ozawa rubbed his chin, then burst out in a short laugh. "This is no coincidence, your bumping into me outside this warehouse."

The blind man grinned.

"Obviously not. I have given this plan much thought. What better way to stave off hunger? I only lack a patron desperate enough to accept my offer."

"The real corpses are controlled by tiny computers and programmed to follow the parade route down the Meiji-dori. If you strayed…"

"I know this city intimately. I would not stray."

"What about involuntary reflexes? Facial tics and expressions are programmed in. A frozen countenance is disconcerting. Suppose you stubbed your toe and cursed aloud? Voices for the dead have not yet been perfected."

The blind man gestured Ozawa to bend closer. "Is anyone within hearing?"

"No."

"Good." Keiko lowered his voice to a whisper. "A small portion of a mild toxin derived from the poison of the puffer fish can paralyze my vocal cords for up to twelve hours; I learned of the substance from a doctor who used it in an unsuccessful operation to restore my sight."

Ozawa hesitated.

"Come, sir," Keiko urged. "We are both desperate men. You, for a surrogate ancestor. I, for employment. If you are as successful as your attire indicates, you must understand a simple barter carries no emotional baggage."

Ozawa straightened. "How much payment are we talking about?"

"Ah!" Keiko pointed in the direction Ozawa had been walking. "My humble room lies two blocks this way. We can best discuss terms there."

—

"Keiko?" Ozawa prodded.

The blind man slouched in the back of the cab, head slack. He wore the executive's second-best kimono of a subtle red and yellow silk. It was a warmer garment than most would put up with in this heat, though that—in theory—should mean nothing to a dead man. Keiko insisted it was better he endure a little discomfort than risk not blending in with other marchers. After a proper bath and shave, and given his innate sense of pride, Keiko made an impressive figure. Anyone would have been proud to proclaim him an ancestor.

Though not, perhaps, at this specific moment.

"Keiko, wake up! We're here!"

The blind man came to with a start, digging sharp nails into Ozawa's arm.

Ozawa started, too, suddenly remembering they were not alone. The driver of their cab stoically faced forward, but his eyes, reflected in the rearview mirror, could not conceal a degree of amusement.

It'll be fine, the executive told himself. A taxi driver is used to erratic behavior. Many people speak to their pets as if they were human. Why shouldn't he talk the same way to his late uncle?

Ozawa handed the driver two thousand-yen bills and asked for a receipt before he and Keiko climbed out.

Under Tokyo's smoggy afternoon sky, Ozawa led Keiko to a huge warehouse near the northernmost end of Meiji-dori. A white-clad technician at the entrance stopped them. "Standard practice," he explained, insisting the blind man be placed on a knee-high gurney and wheeled inside. Vast though the interior appeared, it had the same antiseptic smell as the body-broker's.

"Seiji!"

Ozawa turned to face his former protégé and current rival, Ichiro Watanabe.

"Am I in time?" Ozawa asked the younger man.

"Only just. I wouldn't be here this late myself, but I had second thoughts about my late grandfather's wardrobe." He indicated the drab gray kimono draped over his left arm.

"Yes. I remember your grandfather's preference for colorful informal dress. It caused a stir at more somber events."

"My thought exactly. I've just replaced this with his favorite yukata. The O-Bon is a festive time. My first as a participant."

Ozawa nodded. "Mine, as well."

Watanabe indicated the prone Keiko. "I was under the impression you weren't taking part."

Sorry to disappoint. "I wanted to program my uncle personally. It took longer than anticipated."

That was no lie. He and Keiko had been up all night, going over a recording of last year's hyakki yako. Describing to a blind man how to move his limbs with just the right amount of jerkiness, the perfect degree of lurch, had been a frustrating experience for them both. The final result was not entirely satisfactory, but good enough, Ozawa trusted, to pass among a crowd of re-animates.

At least the paralysis drug had done its job on the blind man's vocal cords. When Keiko fell asleep in the back of the cab, Ozawa hadn't heard even a hint of a snore.

"Good color."

Ozawa turned toward the new voice. A technician bent over the blind man's gurney.

"I appreciate the attention to detail, as well," the technician continued. "Most people don't think to place the right panel of the kimono over the left. They're used to the other way around, but of course that's only for the living."

Ozawa acknowledged the comment with a bow.

"Your uncle, you said? I repeat, he shows excellent color. You should see some of the pasty skins that came in today alone. Poor slugs only get out of their closet once a year."

"He'll appreciate the compliment," Ozawa replied. "Would have, I mean."

"Be sure to tell him Yasu said so, eh?" The tech laughed, a little too familiarly for Ozawa's liking. "Don't worry. We'll take good care of him."

"He's already been programmed to start up with the others. You need only keep him here until the night parade starts. A simple tap on the shoulder will start him off."

Yasu's cheery enthusiasm vanished. He gave Ozawa a weary look. "We have a special section for do-it-yourselfers."

Ozawa's lips thinned. Another impudent eta, raised above his station by this stupid fad!

Watanabe tugged at his arm, interrupting his growing ire. "Come along, old man. Let the experts do their work. We will have an excellent view of the festivities from the company conference room."

Ozawa laid a hand on Keiko's shoulder in farewell. No response. The blind man had fallen asleep again, after being up so late the previous night. Just as well; the dead might not tire, but Keiko would need his rest if he was to walk the full length of one of Tokyo's longest streets.

—

From the air-conditioned conference room on the seventeenth floor of the Katamura Building, Ozawa watched dusk fall with both trepidation and anticipation. Lights began to glow all over Tokyo, save for one stretch. On this special night, the city turned off every electric streetlight along the length of the Meiji-dori, replacing them with carefully tended torches. In residential buildings, lanterns occupied every window, mostly electric, though a few flickered dully with traditional vegetable wax candles.

At last, on the wall-sized high-resolution television screen behind Ozawa, the hyakki yako began. NHK-TV's reporter fell silent.

The haunting image of re-animates stepping one by one out of the black crepe-draped warehouse spoke for itself. And speak eloquently it did, underscored by the doro-doro, an intensely emotional drumbeat performed by kabuki players who—situated on the sidelines—were as invisible as the black-clad stagehands with whom they often worked. Most of the dead were dressed in traditional kimonos, like Keiko, though a few wore modern business suits. At least one was clad in a stiff Victorian mourning coat! Rather than distract, this motley sight added to the sense of otherworldliness.

The life-sized images on the screen were so sharp Ozawa almost felt he stood amidst the dead marchers. This was far better than the recording of last year's parade in his apartment. Ozawa finally understood how this awful, awesome sight so captured an entire nation's imagination.

The hypnotic doro-doro echoed from the room's eight speakers. Glancing out the window again, Ozawa noticed a pale light far down the street—the leading edge of the parade. From this vantage, the live image seemed less real than the televised one. Ozawa returned his attention to the latter.

The upper right corner of the screen now showed a different scene from a closed-circuit camera on the street corner below. That image would take precedence later, allowing company executives to get the closest possible views of their ancestors, real or surrogate, as they passed by Katamura's headquarters. For now, that picture was black, save for an occasional wavering tongue of flame from a torch mounted on the same pole.

Ozawa gulped down his Remy Martin with a silent curse. He should have remembered the close-ups! He'd been an idiot to imagine Keiko's appearance could fool anyone under this level of scrutiny. To substitute one dead man for another was acceptable; to pass the living off as dead was nothing less than sacrilege!

Once Katamura's president learned of his shoddy attempt at deception, Ozawa would lose not just his position but his job. His first week home would have been better spent searching for a suitable bride, as originally planned. At least he could have had a family for his efforts.

He refilled his glass, wiped his lips, and sank into one of the thick-padded chairs. If this was to be his last night in the conference room, he might as well be comfortable.

—

Fireworks dominated Tokyo's pre-dawn skies. Ozawa barely noticed; they paled against the explosions of joy in his heart and mind. He raced through darkened streets, cheerful as a boy on his name-day, to reclaim his 'uncle.'

They had done it!

When the hours-long parade first trickled down to a few stragglers, with no Keiko in sight, Ozawa silently cursed the blind man for reneging on their agreement, despite his own conviction of certain failure. But no! There he was, bringing up the rear, so perfect Ozawa could not tear his eyes away. Keiko lurched at the same awkward angle as his fellow marchers. His head trembled with the same slack nod at each step, and his fingers duplicated their twitching. He must have practiced in the warehouse or picked up the rhythms of those around him—perhaps through the drumbeat.

Whatever the reason, the man's performance deserved a bonus!

Another burst of red illuminated the sky. In the fireworks' glow, Ozawa now spotted Keiko slumped against a building amid a score of re-animates waiting for their descendants to take them home.

"You performed excellently, Keiko!" Ozawa whispered, kneeling beside him. "I'm paying you double, and will see about getting you regular employment, as well."

The blind man did not respond.

Asleep again, Ozawa thought. He chuckled. A well-deserved rest.

Then he noticed the dark patch at the blind man's feet, seeping from his sandals. He quickly covered it with the kimono's hem. The dead don't bleed.

"Hai-ee! How hard did you march, Keiko?"

A new voice interrupted Ozawa from behind. "Ah! It's the do-it-yourselfer!"

Ozawa looked up at Yasu, the technician to whom he'd entrusted Keiko that afternoon.

"An occasional show of respect would not be amiss," Ozawa snapped.

The man replied with a sour smile. "And you might have shown some respect for my profession instead of acting like you knew it all. If not for me, your beloved 'uncle' would still be sitting in the warehouse. The next time you attempt your own programming, test it. Your computer units weren't even where they should be."

Ozawa paled, forcing himself to stand. "You dared to tamper...?"

"I didn't touch your precious units. There wasn't time to look for them. I pulled some spares from the shelves and inserted them properly. I also had to add an override to stop your relative's jerking around while I worked. Whoever processed this corpse initially left his original neurological system intact. If I were you, I'd demand a refund for such incompetence."

"His system's still intact, though? I mean..."

Yasu waved in dismissal. "Don't worry. I short-circuited it for you. Won't give any further trouble. No charge. Again, though, a little gratitude would be nice."

A quart of Remy Martin threatened to rush back up his throat. Ozawa fought it. "It can be reconnected, though, right? My uncle had certain, ah, physical quirks to which I'd become attached."

"Ah. That explains it." Yasu shook his head. His tone softened. "If you'd told me, I could have made allowances. As it stands, the finest surgeon in the world could not reverse my hurried fix. I can reprogram those quirks in, though. You'd never know the difference."

"His brain. What about his brain?"

Yasu's eyes widened. "Is that where you placed your units? No wonder they didn't work. They're supposed to be inserted as close to the site of functional activity as possible."

"Then his brain functions are unimpaired?" Ozawa held onto that glimmer of hope.

"They would be, if dead brains could function. Did you even read the literature? Stop by the shop when O-Bon is over and we're not so busy. I'll give you a brochure."

"But..."

"Sorry. Can't spend any more time right now. You're not the only do-it-yourselfer we've had tonight. Take your uncle home. Get some rest. You don't look so good. A little too much liquor, eh?"

Ozawa nodded numbly. He helped raise Keiko to his feet. Behind those empty eyes, a living brain was now trapped in a dead body.

All because Seiji Ozawa had not fully informed himself of the parade procedures.

He had failed his obligations.

—

On the third and final night of the festival, the corpses retraced their route, parading north in a symbolic return to the Land of Shades. At least one marcher did not make that trip; at least one earlier observer did not watch.

Soft, steady droning filled Keiko's shabby one-room apartment.

A heavy knock rattled the door. Loose flecks of dull grey paint peeled free, drifting onto the thin, unkempt tatami mat within.

The droning continued, unabated.

With a creak, the doorknob turned. Either deliberately or through neglect, the latch had not been thrown. Cautiously, the visitor opened the door to enter.

He stopped with a gasp.

On a filthy tatami mat against the far wall—legs protruding stiffly, arms straight down, head slackly dangling to one side—sat the re-animate that had been missing from the festival's last day. The room's only other occupant, resting cross-legged on an even fouler mat, remained bent over a cheap paperback book, reading aloud in a harsh whisper, unaware of, or indifferent to, the intruder.

"Seiji Ozawa," the visitor called.

The reading continued.

To Ozawa's left stood a stack of paperbacks as high as his shoulder. To his right, another pile reached his elbow. His expensive suit was soiled and wrinkled, obviously slept in.

The visitor approached, blocking the dim light by which the man read.

Ozawa marked his place with a finger. His red-rimmed eyes looked up at the anxious face of Ichiro Watanabe.

"What brings you here, Ichiro?" he mumbled.

"The boss sent me, Seiji. He's worried about you. Has been since you disappeared two days ago. I've been worried, too. I asked around, heard you were seen speaking to a blind beggar named Keiko the day before O-Bon. I was told he lived here."

"Not a beggar. A good man."

"Whatever. I hoped he might know what you were up to."

Ozawa looked past the young Katamura executive, focusing on the room's other occupant.

"I fear your journey has been wasted. Keiko-san can tell you nothing."

Watanabe crouched beside Ozawa, careful not to touch the grimy mat.

"Then you tell me what's going on."

"There is nothing to tell, Ichiro. I resigned. I am unworthy. I should have thought that would make you happy. Or did one of your rivals get my slot?"

"Your position remains open. Your resignation was not accepted." Watanabe extended a hand to his former mentor. "Let me take you home, Seiji."

"I am home."

"Your home."

"This is my home now. It is the least I can do to make up for my neglect."

"Seiji..."

"Please go. You're wasting our time."

"Our?"

Ozawa nodded toward his unmoving roommate. "He cannot communicate, you see. I can't even tell whether he is asleep or awake. I must therefore assume he is always awake. I am his only diversion."

Confused, Watanabe rose. "Very well, Ozawa. I'll go. But I'll be back."

Ozawa sighed. "If you must. You might then do me a small favor."

"Anything."

"Bring me more books." Ozawa nodded at the smaller stack to his right. "I'm running low and prefer not to leave my charge alone too long. From the braille selection in the corner, I gather he likes mysteries."

"An enthusiasm I cannot share just now."

"Ichiro. I cannot explain."

The younger man bowed, stepping backwards. "Good evening, then." He let himself out.

Ozawa had already re-opened his book. He read a few more lines, stumbling in distraction over the words. Frustrated at his inability to concentrate, he flung the book across the dusty floor.

"It's no use, Keiko," he told the blind man. "Watanabe will return, but not with more books. He'll bring a doctor. Maybe the police. They'll put me in prison. Or a mental hospital. It doesn't matter to me."

Keiko did not react. He could not.

Ozawa nodded. "Yes. That is my primary concern, what they'll do with you. Even if they believe me. They'll turn you over to a body-broker, most likely. You'd languish neglected, for months at a time, until you go mad." Ozawa sighed. "I have failed you enough, Keiko. I cannot be responsible for your suffering worse."

He rose slowly, wincing at the strain on his stiffened leg muscles.

"I trust you are asleep, Keiko. If not, I hope you understand."

Ozawa moved to the sink. A long, dull carving knife hung from the wall beside it. He frowned, found a worn whetstone in the cabinet, and made a few passes to hone the edge.

"Hardly the noble weapon an adopted ancestor of mine deserves," he admitted, approaching the blind man. "As you cannot see it, I beg you to imagine a more suitable one."

Ozawa thought, hoped, prayed he saw a thin smile of agreement cross Keiko's lips.

The blade bit, as deep and clean as possible, into the blind man's throat.

Ozawa waited until the blood stopped flowing and he could be certain the blind man was truly dead.

Of necessity, it took somewhat longer for Seiji Ozawa to slice open his own abdomen.

BIRDS

NATHANIEL LEE

It was Monday, so I was up on the Tower, scrubbing the blood off the
concrete. From the birds, you know. Tilla doesn't like to do it—she says
it makes her cry—and while I don't exactly find it a blissful experience
myself—arthritis in my knees—I don't mind taking her turn when it
comes up in the rotation. I like to help. And I like to get up on the lift.
That high above the ground, with the trees and such looking more green
than turquoise and the wind smelling clean and clear like rain, you can
almost forget you're not on Earth anymore.

I call them birds and trees and so on, but of course, they're not
actually. The way I figure it, though, trees are trees even if they move by
themselves a little more than they ought to, and birds are birds even if
they look more like an eel whose daddy was a cockroach and whose
great-grandma was an umbrella. They don't have eyes or mouths, either.
Hardin says the bio-boys figure they filter some sort of microscopic
spores out of the air with those big tissue-paper frills of theirs. I don't
much care to think about spores—Lord knows I scrape enough pale
pink fungus off of the arrays every week to fill the incinerator twice
over—but Hardin's got enough sense that I'll take his word on these

sorts of things. Hardin once complained about how no one could quite decide if the birds were insects or mammals or what. I told him that I was just going to call them birds as long as they kept flying, and he laughed and said that was probably better than "trying to cram an extraterrestrial ecosystem into our pre-existing taxonomy."

No mouth, no eyes, and no legs—they never land, breeding and dying on the wing. Their little ones come out looking like milkweed pods and just drift on the wind until they get big enough to start flapping their weird little umbrella-wings. Dead birds drift too, though they start to sink once they get some holes in them. I'm fairly sure I saw some tiny ones eating on a big one once, but Tilla cringed and told me to change the subject when I brought it up. They don't weigh anything at all, hardly, but they sure have bright pink blood, and it sure spatters far when they hit the Tower at speed. They fly in patterns, see. Long lines of birds, circling around and around the globe, never stopping, all following the same lines like ants on a scent trail. Downright creepy to watch a big flock of them, sometimes, flowing in even, unchanging curves as though there's a whole invisible world up in the sky, one we can't even begin to imagine but that they see clear as day.

What they can't see is the Tower.

Somebody probably should have done a little more studying before they decided to build a recon station here, but then, I'm not the one in charge of the war. I assume they wouldn't have put it here if it didn't need to be here. At least it's not on one of the birds' main migration routes, assuming you want to call what they do "migrating." Some places, the flow never stops. But we get our share. Every now and then, a little group of them comes by, and every time they do, I end up riding the lift down from the top of the Tower the next day. They always hit the same spot, too. The white walls are stained reddish there, no matter how hard I scrub or how many times I repaint it.

That day, I was whistling to myself while I worked the washer—an old song Ellie used to sing, back when we were first married and full of hope for our new life out here—when I heard someone *halloo*-ing me from up top, near the comms array. My eyes aren't what they used to be—I can't afford even cyber-eyes, let alone proper vat-grown ones—

but I recognized Hardin straightaway. That blond head of his does stand out, especially among the scientists. I hit the button and took a moment to enjoy the air as the lift hauled me back to the top; the forest smells a bit like peppermint in the spring, though the scent is sharper in the second spring of the year.

"Sorry to disappoint you, Hardin," I said, waving.

"Disappoint me?"

I grinned and winked. "I 'spect you were hopin' to find Tilla up here 'stead of my wrinkled old ass."

The boy blushed the same shade as the wall.

"Tell the truth, I don't know as how she'd be too upset at the interruption, either," I went on. Those two were completely head over heels for each other, but neither one of them would make the first move. Drove me to distraction sometimes to think about their missed opportunities; "gather flowers while ye may" and all that. I tried to coax them into it when I could, but I'm no matchmaker.

"A-actually," Hardin coughed and smoothed the front of his uniform, "I need to speak to you specifically. For permission. You're the senior facilities maintenance specialist, after all."

I spotted the gizmo on a cart behind him. It looked like the cobbled-together insides of fifteen radios and a microwave; ugly as sin, but if I knew Hardin, it'd do whatever it was supposed to do without a hitch. "You and Tilla cook up another scarecrow attempt?"

"I think this might finally work, yes."

"That ultrasonic whatever sure didn't." I'd taken that squawk-box down two weeks ago after a nasty memo from Up Top. The birds smashed right into the Tower regardless.

"I didn't think it would, honestly," Hardin said. "I'm leaning towards electromagnetic radiation again. There are several Earth species that can sense the planet's magnetic fields, and—"

I held up a hand. "Don't waste your breath on me. You could talk all day and I'd still have about as much chance of understanding you as getting elected Praetor. I thought you'd said it couldn't be electromagnets because the radios and such would already spook the birds if it was?"

"Ah." Hardin half-closed his eyes and smiled down at me. "There are frequencies and then there are *frequencies*, Rennie."

"All right." I shrugged; I had told him not to explain it, I suppose. "Does it need hooking into the main line?"

Hardin sighed. "Yes, but I don't want to push my luck. No more 'wasted resources.' It's got a battery that should do for a few days. Long enough to see if it works, anyway, and maybe I'll be able to install it properly once I've got the proof of concept. They can't possibly want to kill the birds if it's avoidable."

I eyeballed the weight of the machine as best I could. "I'll need to get my tools. Socket it right into the concrete, maybe, with some braces. No worries, Hardin."

"Thanks, Rennie."

I waved goodbye as he disappeared back into the depths of the Tower. The cameras watched us both. I waved to them, too, and got back to scrubbing.

—

Tuesday was mail day. I got another letter from my son, Renault Jr.

He's out on the front lines, fighting to keep us all safe on this dangerous world. The Vssani staged another of their demonstrations last year, but someone took a potshot at someone else—I'm not really clear who, honestly—and it kind of spiraled from there. They say there's collaborators in the Protectorate, human beings smuggling guns and bombs to aliens, which I can't quite bring myself to believe. Who could turn against their own kind? That's instinct, isn't it? You can't help but be loyal to your own. Anyway, Renault served his two years, like everyone else, but he stayed on after and made a career out of it.

I was never a military man, myself—they told me at my Career Counseling I had a genetic predisposition for more peaceful work and kind of nudged me into what they wanted me to be, you know, the way they do—but there is honor in service, even in facilities maintenance; I hope my example at least taught Rennie Jr. that much. This letter was even more cut up than the last one, almost half of it blacked out and some of what was left jumbled around a bit so it didn't make much sense, but I got the gist: he'd been promoted for a third time! Captain now, if I read it correctly. A real up-and-comer, my boy.

Truth be told, I was a little surprised. Ellie and I doted on the child, but we never pretended to ourselves that he was much of a thinker. Not everyone is destined for greatness, and that's all right, we said to ourselves. And here was Young Rennie making me eat my words! Three promotions already, albeit on account of "unexpected vacancies."

I tucked the letter into my pocket and headed out. Tilla always liked to hear news from the front, though I think she mostly was just humoring an old man and his stories.

Thirty minutes later, I still couldn't find Tilla, which was a little odd. She's got her duties, and I don't usually fuss about what order she does them in, but she wasn't at any of her usual stations. She wasn't down in the musty, potato-scented 'ponics, she wasn't checking the perimeter wiring that the trees are always plucking down, and she wasn't running the cleaner bots in the lower half. I did spot Hardin, walking down the hall very fast, mumbling to himself. He'd been up top to check the readings of his new anti-bird gizmo. I called out to him, but I don't think he heard me.

Kids. What are you going to do?

I went up myself, figuring I'd check on the walls as long as I was wandering around. The door to the upper deck opened at my thumbprint, and I smelled the ice-dagger scent of the alien forest. A lot of folks don't like it, but anything that clears out my sinuses is okay in my book. I looked down over the edge, down the chalky white walls to the indelible stain where we'd got in the way of the birds. Hardin's doohickey was down there, screwed into the stone. It didn't make any noise that I could hear, but it looked pretty secure. Hardin hadn't looked angry when I'd seen him, not exactly, so I figured it was doing fine. No new red patches, either, but there was no way to tell if that was because the gizmo worked or because we just hadn't had any birds. I waited around for a while in case a flock came past, but nothing doing.

Eventually the sun started to sink. The first moon came out, and I went back inside.

—

The Oculi can't watch everything everywhere. There are always corners where cameras can't go, or places where the interference is too rocky to get a clear signal, like the gutters. They close them up as best they can, but what with access panels and so on, animals and things still get in and make a mess. So every Wednesday, I do my rounds to make sure everything is still clean and secure. I'm the only one allowed in; anyone else's badge gets detected going into a gutter, and they'll be called Up Top before you can say "spook."

This is all by way of explaining why I was pretty surprised when I heard voices. There was a space—closet-sized—off of a hallway so narrow, you had to walk down it sideways. Voices was surprising enough, but when I got close enough, I realized I knew who they were.

"…can't possibly stay quiet about this," Hardin was saying.

Tilla answered him in a harsh whisper: "What are you going to do? Petition the Praetor? Announce it on the cleared channels?"

"We've got to do something," Hardin said. "This isn't just a fluke measurement. I've got responses, feedback that isn't random noise. It's as though the whole planet is a single being, a sentient being. If I'm right, it explains everything: the birds, the sudden herbicide resistance, the Vssani uprisings…"

"So report it and let Up Top deal with it. That's what you're supposed to do in the Bio labs, right?" I could almost see Tilla crossing her arms when she spoke.

There was a rustling, as if Hardin were moving closer. Maybe enfolding her in his arms? Had those two been hiding it from me this whole time, the scamps? "That might… might be dangerous. The research I'm doing… some of it's been done before. You remember Colton? Jun Li? What happened to them?"

Tilla gasped.

"It might be that this is something the Protectorate already knows. Something they want kept secret."

Silence. I edged away from the hallway entrance. This was more than I was prepared to deal with right now. Tilla's voice, small and rippling with tears, stopped me.

"So why tell me?"

Hardin sighed, the sound echoing oddly down the hallway.

"Anything I do affects you. I know that. And I don't want to risk your safety, or abandon you if they… if something happens to me, but… I guess I'm asking for permission."

"Hardin…"

I heard soft breathing then, quiet whispers. I didn't hear anything else, on account of I left the two of them alone right quick after that.

—

The incinerators run on Thursdays, except on heavy weeks when they run on Sundays, too. The bots do the heavy lifting, but they need supervision, what with the AI ban keeping them too dumb to figure stuff out on their own. They do all right as long as nothing unexpected happens, though. I got them started on the first load early, and then skipped out to find Tilla.

I've got access to the badge records, superficial-like—don't want old Rennie walking in on some Praetorian nabob in the shower or anything—but the screens showed Tilla working in the 'ponics all day yesterday, and Hardin in his private lab except for meals. Either my cut-rate tin ears were finally going on the fritz for good and making me hear things, or else Hardin had spoofed their badge records. Which that isn't so hard, on the technical side of things, but it's serious business if they catch you at it. Tilla needed to know she was already neck deep in it and about to catch a crapwave.

Tilla's quarters were locked, so I used my override. That gets flagged in the system, of course, but hopefully Tilla'd help me come up with a plausible cover story when it came up at review time. She was working Bravo shift that month, so this was the middle of her sleep period.

The room was empty.

A ruffled bunk, tiny fold-out desk, and toilet nook, just like my room. A little messier, mind you. A few more clothes strewn about. I don't have that much lipstick, neither, and that's the truth.

The comp-station on the desk was blinking in sleep mode.

I picked up a sheet of flimsiplast from the keyboard, only to realize that it wasn't printed with text, but handwritten. The things we have to put up with out here in the colonies, I swear. I was chuckling at the thought of writing a whole note by hand. I looked at it just out of sheer curiosity.

...and us. We're like an infection. We're giving the planet clogged arteries, brain cancer, an aneurysm. And the planet's immune response is intensifying. The building has to stop; the towers have to come down. If we don't do something, and soon, one of us is going to die...

Wasn't too hard to guess who that note was from. Nor why he hadn't wanted to type it into any of the local comps. I poked the comp-station awake and saw the last message Tilla had sent out: "I've got to see you tonight, lover. There's a quiet spot down near the tomatoes where we can have some privacy, for a few minutes, anyway."

I twisted my lips wryly. Up Top didn't care about fraternization—downright encouraged it, sometimes—and they wouldn't look too close at what a couple of hormonal kids got up to in the 'ponics. Another gutter down there, too, in the trenches between the water filtration units.

I ran as fast as my hips would let me, clattering down the halls in the early morning hours.

—

"Tilla."

She jumped, her short-cropped black hair flying up like she'd gotten an electric shock. "Rennie," she said, trying to smile. "What are you doing down here?"

"I could ask you the same question, except I already pretty much know the answer."

Tilla did her best to simper and look flushed. "Oh, Rennie, I know we should have said something, but this thing with Hardin and me is just so new and-"

I waved my hand to cut her off and leaned in close. "I'm not talking about a little hanky-panky, Tilla."

She turned pale, her eyes standing out like black buttons on snow. "Oh! Oh..."

"I ain't going to talk much about it here," I said, nodding at the nearby cameras. "But I thought I'd better give you a chance to come clean on your own, before anyone finds out more than they have already."

"Rennie, you wouldn't..."

"No." I shook my head. "I don't want to do it, Tilla, but I have to if you won't. I like you and the boy a lot. But whatever he thinks he can do, it's not going to work. All he can do is cause trouble for you both. Better to fess up and ask forgiveness." I reached out and grasped her wrist. She just stood there, frozen, like I'd hit her with a stun-bolt. "It'll mean more if you speak up yourself. Give you a little credit Up Top." I smiled. "They understand mistakes, you know. None of us is perfect."

Tilla's lip trembled. I never know what to do with a crying girl. "Hardin means well, I'm sure he does. But what he's talking about… I'm scared, Rennie. I don't know what to do."

"Hey, now," I said soothingly. "That's okay. We're not the decision-makers, you and me. We'll push this up to the ones who are. They'll know what to do."

Tilla clutched at me, pulling me into a hug that was a little awkward, what with her being taller than me. I stumbled a bit, but kept my balance, patting her gingerly on the shoulder. I heard her sobbing, felt hot tears on my shoulder.

I knew then that Tilla would make the right choice. She was a smart girl. It would all work out fine in the end, I was sure.

—

It was kind of a mess for a few weeks after that. The Tower wasn't meant to accommodate a lot of people at once, and it was awful crowded till the inquest was over. The Home Guard kept the canteen staff on their toes, I can tell you. Questions for everyone, records pulled, a lot of spilled ink and ruffled feathers. Those boys can be a little intimidating sometimes, even though they're on our side. And I will never—as long as I live—get used to those helmets the Oculi wear, with the soft-sided holes and that infernal sniffing they do all the time.

At least Hardin will get the help he needs. They announced later that they'd found traces of explosives in his room, and rumors said he had several messages written in that Vssani chickenscratch. The poor boy was out of his head, might have gone collaborator. Probably stress, they said. So he'll be kept in protective custody for a while until they can piece together what all he was up to, which is a load off my mind.

Tilla left about the same time the Home Guard did; I got a message from her saying how she didn't want to keep on at the outpost and was going to stay with her relatives in Victory City. I didn't know Tilla had any family on-planet, but hopefully she's doing fine. She never answered my letters, but I figure she's got a right to be a little angry, so I try not to let it bother me.

I never did tell anyone about the scarecrow machine Hardin had me install up on the Tower. Plain old forgot about it, is why, but good luck convincing anyone Up Top about that. Anyway, I went up there a few days later with a sniffer; felt like I ought to make sure it truly wasn't anything dangerous, though I didn't really think it would be. It was just falling to night, with the trees waving down below and the sky turning blue-red in the light of the rising moons. You could just see the silver glint of the Praetorian headquarters, in orbit up in the southern sky. As I was waiting for the sniffer results, I saw a little clump of birds come flapping toward the Tower, umbrella-wings puffing in and out. I put a hand on the cracked, stained stone beside me. Poor blind bastards. I thought about what it would be like, to be voiceless in the dark, bound to your course no matter what may come. Even if Hardin was right about the planet, the birds don't even know what they're a part of. They just fly on and on, never suspecting, and then smack.

I wondered how it would feel to never see it coming.

The sniffer chirped and flashed the all-clear. As I hung there, Hardin's machine whirred a little, and I saw the birds hesitate in their flapping, just for a second. Then they turned—for all the world like they saw the Tower materialize out of nothing—whirling to the side in a wide, graceful arc, curving around the Tower and flying on. Lucky birds; they were the first ones in years to actually get to wherever they were going.

I tried to guess how long the batteries in Hardin's scarecrow would last. Hopefully a good long time. I hate scrubbing the blood out of the concrete.

The birds faded into black specks against the setting sun. I watched them go until they disappeared.

FLOTSAM

MARSHALL J. MOORE

Hers wasn't the first dead body Keel had ever seen.

Growing up on the Reef, corpses were a fact of life, as regular and predictable as the tides. By his twelfth birthday last year, Keel had seen perhaps two hundred dead men and women up close—more, if you counted the skeletons.

He didn't, though. Skeletons weren't really people, or at least they hadn't been people for so long that it scarcely mattered. Bones were more like the rotting hulls and worm-eaten timbers that dotted the Reef: frames without a spirit to fill them, absent of the thing itself. And besides, only three skeletons on the Reef remained relatively intact, in their original composition. The rest had had their bones repurposed to better serve the Crew. Waste not, as Keel's father always said.

The difference between bodies and skeletons, Keel thought, was that you could really tell a body had been a person once, not that long ago. Their skin might be pale and bloated, the eyes eaten away by fish and the flesh gnawed by sharks, but none of the signs of the sea's embrace could deny that they had been somebody, someone.

Not that Keel would ever voice such thoughts to his father. There were some things better kept to oneself.

He looked down at the still, sad face. She did not look like the other bodies, waterlogged and crab-chewed. Nor did she look asleep, as Keel had always heard people say whenever they spoke of their lost loved ones.

She just looked dead.

He leaned over her, his long hair nearly brushing her still lips. Those lips lay open, exposing uneven teeth, as though she were about to take in a breath and speak.

A wild and impossible hope seized Keel, a hope that at any moment now her eyes might open, her mouth twitching into that rare, quiet smile that had always made Keel feel as though a ray of sunshine had broken through the Reef's perpetual fog.

But the dead remained dead, and Keel's mother would never smile again. He squeezed his eyes shut, felt the tears welling at their edges.

It wasn't fair.

"Save your salt, boy," his father murmured, low enough that the others could not hear. His calloused hand squeezed Keel's shoulder, rough but not cruel.

Keel nodded and turned away, wiping at his eyes with the back of his wrist. He would not cry, not here. Salt might have been the one resource the Reef had in abundance, but to shed tears on land was taboo. Crying was reserved for the waves, so that their tears and the sea's might join together. They were one, the Crew and the sea, as the Reef and the fog were one.

"Ready?" His father asked, his voice still low. Keel swallowed the lump in his throat and nodded.

His father straightened and turned to face the Crew, his back to the fog-covered waves. Like his namesake, Spar was tall and spare, but when he thrust out his hands to either side, he commanded the attention of every eye on the Reef.

No wind stirred the mists, and the only sound in all the world was the tide softly lapping against the cliffs below. Keel breathed slowly through his nose, suddenly aware of the attention focused on him and his father. He stared out into the fog, fighting to stop his lower lip from trembling. He could not shame them now, either of them.

"Shipmates," Spar said, his basso voice rumbling through the misty air. "We gather here to mourn our own. Mizzen was known to you all. Loved by all as she loved all. Her hands were nimble and clever, her back bent but strong. Many were the treasures she dragged to shore or pried loose from wreckage. Many nights she stood vigil at your sides, holding her lantern high to guide home our mother's bounty. She caught and cooked crabs to feed us, dried and wove sailcloth to clothe us. The sea gave Mizzen to us, and she earned her place among our Crew."

An approving nod rippled like a wave through those assembled. They waited a little way down the slope from the high cliffs that marked the Reef's northernmost point, a respectful distance from where Keel and Spar stood beside the fallen Mizzen. Their clothes were little better than rags, torn and stained and much-mended. All wore shells and dried seaweed woven into their long and tangled hair, even the children. The beards of the men were similarly ornamented.

Nearly two hundred, Keel thought. The entire Crew, down to the newest arrivals and the smallest squalling babe. When was the last time they had all gathered together like this? Not since the last funeral, or the latest arrival. Which had been more recent?

A squeeze on Keel's shoulder called his attention back to the present. A stab of guilt shot through his belly. Now was not the time for daydreaming.

"Mizzen was wife to me," Spar continued, his voice cutting clear and even through the fog. "Mother to my Keel. Crewmate to us all. The waves brought her to us, and to the waves we return her."

He turned away from the crowd below, bending over his wife's body. Keel did the same, feeling the Crew's eyes on his back.

"Take a last look, boy," Spar murmured. "Look long, for we will not meet with her again on this side of the fog."

Tears threatened to sting Keel's eyes once again, but he fought them back. He looked hard at his mother, trying to memorize every aspect of her appearance: the rough brown hands that had only ever been gentle with him, the mane of curling black hair that had only just begun to show gray around the roots, the lined brow that had always made her seem so wise. But her eyes, once so bright, were shut forever.

She lay in a square of sailcloth longer than she was tall, its edges folded over her lower body like a blanket and stitched together. Her hair pillowed her head, braided into a crown of coral, kelp, and clam shells.

"It's time, Keel," Spar said, his voice hardly louder than the waves lapping far below. "Say farewell."

Keel tried to speak, but no sound came out. He swallowed and tried again. "Goodbye, Mama."

"Goodbye, my love," his father said.

No further words were necessary. As one, father and son took up positions on either side of Mizzen's body, bending to fold the remaining sailcloth over her chest and face. Spar pulled a whalebone needle from the pouch at his belt, and Keel held the edges of the sailcloth together as his father finished stitching Mizzen's funeral shroud shut.

The Crew looked on, as unmoving and silent as the fog. Their grief was shared, but these final rites belonged to the family alone.

He crouched and picked up his wife's body, a grunt bursting from his thin lips. Like all the Crew, Mizzen had been thin to the point of gauntness, but as Keel helped Spar lift her body, it felt as though she were an anchor, weighing them both down.

Or perhaps it was simply the rocks they had tied to her ankles.

Together father and son hauled Mizzen's body to the edge of the cliff. A glance down revealed the blue waves swelling and crashing against the jagged stone, heaving like a sleeping beast through the gray fog. Keel wondered what the world looked like beneath those swells. Did the dead sleep quietly in their aquatic graveyard, or did the churning wave set them swaying and tossing like kelp in the current?

"On three," Spar grunted, neck taut with strain. "One, two. Three."

Mizzen's weight slipped from Keel's hands. For a single perfect moment, she hung fixed in the air, a ghost in the fog.

Then gravity took her by its firm grasp and pulled her down, down. The swells swallowed her without a splash.

Keel could not say how long they stood there, heads bent together as they stared down at the foaming waves. By the time they heard the clear, high call of the watchers rolling across the Reef, it had grown fully dark.

The hairs on the back of Keel's neck prickled at that keening cry. It sounded like a shorebird, or one of the brass whistles that were his father's most prized possessions.

The watchers' call sounded again, and Keel shivered. On the far side of the island, yellow light blazed into the gloom as the watchers fired their lanterns.

Beside him, Spar held up his hand. They waited, ears straining for the third and final call. Without sound, Keel's lips shaped the old rhyme:

The first call's for a sighting
The second one's for lighting
No more and we shall die lean
But three we pick their bones clean

No other noises were permitted. Blinded by the opaque fog and blazing lanterns, the watchers relied upon their ears to read the movements of the great hulks that passed through the night, perilously near the Reef.

Keel strained his ears, closed his eyes. Yes, there—diffused through the fog, he could just make out the muffled creak of timbers, the quiet splash of waves against wood. A bell sounded through the mist, seeming both distant and close.

Then there was a great crash, punctuated by the groan and shriek of splintering lumber.

A third cry from the watchers, this one higher and longer.

"A wreck," Spar murmured, his narrow shoulders relaxing. A rare smile parted his lips as he looked down at Keel. "The sea brings us a ship this very night, my boy. Your mother provides for us, even now."

Keel nodded. He cast one last look at the swelling tide below, wondering if his mother truly had brought the ship now foundering on the Reef. Had it been a final gift, one last provision from Mizzen to those she had loved in life? Or did one death simply attract more, like frenzying sharks?

—

Dawn never bloomed bright on the mist-shrouded Reef, but it brought enough light to see by. Even before the unseen sun crept above the hidden horizon, the Crew was picking their way across the Reef, striding deliberately over broken coral and between deep tide pools towards the wreck looming in the fog. They moved swiftly, knowing that once the tide came in, the waters would rise too high for them to conduct their harvest.

Though the part of the Reef that stood high enough above the tideline to be considered a proper island measured scarcely more than a square mile, the bedrock of fossilized coral upon which it lay extended nearly twice that before dropping steeply away into the abyss of deep ocean. No cartographer had ever mapped the Reef, but the Crew knew its every cove and tide pool, each spur of jagged rock that stood above the sea and those that lurked beneath it.

The Reef was a graveyard for sailing ships. Dozens of wrecks moldered across it, dashed to pieces against the stony cliffs, drowned in its shallow lagoon, or beached like rotting whales upon the asperous coral. As Keel clambered over the rocks, he could see their beams and spires jutting into the mists, pointed toward the Reef like accusing fingers: *You did this to us.*

Mist and sweat prickled against the nape of Keel's neck. Though the Crew made no sound as they swarmed toward the latest wreck, the cacophony of the vessel grinding against the rock echoed in Keel's ears.

The ship loomed above them, its triple sails hanging limply from their spars. Keel could not read the ship's name, painted in gold lettering across her bow.

A long gash split the vessel's hull, and she leaned drunkenly to one side. Bodies lay strewn about it, perhaps as many as a dozen, their limbs contorted into unnatural poses. Crabs scuttled about and over them.

Crewmates stooped over the still forms, rifling through pockets with practiced efficiency. One of the corpses twitched, groaning. It turned on its side and vomited seawater before staring up at the shadowy figures darting through the fog.

Spar knelt over it, a rusty old cutlass in his hand. One quick movement of the broad blade ensured that the corpse remained a corpse.

They were all corpses, Keel knew. The Crew rarely accepted new members, and only those who survived the wreckage uninjured were considered. One look at the way that man's legs had been folded beneath him told Keel that he would never walk again. His father's blade had been a kindness, for the Reef afforded no charity to the broken.

Rarely but occasionally, the wrecks hosted enough survivors that they might resist the Crew's depredations, but they seldom lasted long.

The vanguard of the Crew stopped before the barnacle-studded hull and slung their ropes up into the mist. The grappling hooks on their ends thudded against the ship's rail, and the first scavengers climbed aboard. Keel scurried after them, hauling himself up the rope with practiced ease.

The ship's angle made walking its decks a challenge. Keel was too small and slight to help with the heavy lifting, but there were no idle hands amongst the Crew. As his elders set about collecting anything of value from the decks, Keel made his way to the forecastle.

Ever since he'd grown old enough to join the rest in harvest, his job had been to explore the secret places of each vessel, climbing through hatches and into crannies the adults could not. It was an important job, for ships had many tight spaces where valuables were often stored.

Once he'd found a barrel full of limes wedged between two narrow bulkheads, and had spent hours passing them up to those on deck. There had been so many limes that every member of the Crew had gotten one, and that night, their fish had been flavored with the zing of citrus. Keel's mouth watered at the memory.

He reached the forecastle and headed down the narrow stairs, one hand braced against the bulkhead to steady himself against the ship's drunken lean. He emerged to find the belowdecks full of standing water, draining slowly out through the gash the reef had carved into the hull. Bits of flotsam and debris floated past his legs. Keel bent and plucked something from the water.

It was a doll made of fine white porcelain, a material he knew only from the chipped teapot his mother had so prized. The doll's cheeks had been painted red, as had her hair, though her eyes were a flat and unexpressive black. Her doll-sized dress was striped blue and white.

Keel stared at the doll for a long time. He wondered who it had belonged to—not an adult, certainly, but a child, like himself. A child aboard this wrecked ship, now lost like the rest of its crew.

A small sound pierced the gloom, one strangely out of place amongst the groan of the battered timbers—a high-pitched squeak. Keel's head jerked towards it, thinking of the chittering of the rats that sometimes washed ashore, of how when they did, the entire Crew hunted them with hatchets and knives so that the vermin could not devour what little store of food they maintained.

Hand tight around his knife, Keel inched towards the sound, eyes straining for the telltale scurrying of little shapes amongst the shadows.

There. A flicker of movement in the gloom, between a bulkhead and a stack of crates. Keel gripped his knife in both hands and drew closer. The squeaking noise came again.

Keel darted forward and raised the knife, blade glimmering in the dark.

Wide round eyes stared back at him, luminous and huge. Not the beady black eyes of a rat, but pale blue, shining as though they had absorbed all the light absent in the dim belowdecks. Beneath them, a pert nose and quivering red lips, the face framed by limp blonde curls.

A girl, a year or so younger than Keel himself.

Her wide eyes moved from Keel to the blade in his hand.

He lowered the knife, staring at her. Keel had never known anyone close to his own age, let alone a girl. The next oldest child in the Crew was only six, nearly half Keel's age.

"What's your name?" he asked, his voice coming out throaty and strangely raw.

She did not answer.

"I'm Keel." He tucked the knife back into his rope belt. This girl was slighter even than he was, and no threat. And with his blade stowed, she might be willing to speak. "What's your name?"

The girl swallowed and lowered her hands. Her voice came in a hoarse rasp. "Bea."

"Bea," Keel repeated, the sound strange in his mouth. *That is no proper name*, he thought. But it must have been where she came from, whatever strange island sent its ships to founder upon the Reef.

"Bea," he said again. "Are you hurt?"

"I don't think so," she said, looking down at her arms. They were bruised and scraped, but that seemed to be the extent of her injuries.

"Good." Keel exhaled through his nose, relieved. Like all the Crew's resources, balms and splints and bandages were in short supply.

"Father's not, though," Bea said, sniffling a little. "He was abovedecks when everything…when it all…"

She trembled, her whole body wracked by a sudden shuddering. Keel stepped forward and caught her before she could swoon. She felt like a frail bird in his arms, all fluttering heartbeat and hollow bones.

"There was a grinding sound," she said in the rasping voice of one whose tears have all been used up. "And then the ship *shook,* so hard I thought it was going to come apart…"

She trailed off, resting her head on Keel's shoulder.

"You're safe," Keel said. He held out his calloused hand. "But only if you come with me right now."

Bea bit her trembling lower lip and took his hand.

—

The Galley was the only true building on the Reef. Nestled in a cove between the cliffs of its leeward and windward sides, the long, smoky hall had been constructed over the years from the timbers and driftwood that washed ashore. The air hung thick with the smell of fish stew and crab cakes, hazy from the Galley's dozen cookfires, lit by the same lanterns the Crew used to guide fogbound ships to their doom.

Spar, Keel, and Bea stood upon a raised dais at one end, framed against the upended bow of a caravel that served as the Reef's central gathering point.

"Our mother is merciful," Spar proclaimed to the gathered Crew. "Yesterday, we gave her my wife, my Mizzen. Mother Ocean took her to her bosom, and in thanks, she sent us her bounty. Barrels of molasses to soften our bread, bolts of cotton to mend our clothes. Strong drink!"

Laughter echoed through the Galley as Spar raised his wooden goblet, throwing back a long pull of rum. The Crew did the same, faces flushed from the sweet liquor and the triumph of a successful harvest.

"And greatest of all," Spar continued, raising his other hand to quiet the crowd, "our mother sends us a daughter, to replace the one she took from us."

He beckoned to Bea. Her eyes darted between the faces in the Galley.

"It's okay," Keel whispered, squeezing her hand. "Go."

Bea nodded and drew in a shaky breath before stepping forward to stand beside Spar. He towered over her, a mast of a man beside a shaking shell of a girl, and though his eyes were hard when he looked at her, he did not speak unkindly.

"Girl," Spar said, his rough voice echoing off the Galley's sides. "You alone survived the wreckage of your vessel. Do you know why that is?"

Because we killed the other survivors, Keel thought, recalling the sound of his father's cutlass being drawn across the wounded man's throat.

"No," Bea shook her head, blonde curls bouncing. "Sir."

"You survived because the sea took one of ours," Spar said. "And in her mercy, she gave you to us in recompense. Do you accept the gift she offers you?"

Bea glanced over her shoulder at Keel, who nodded. It had been nearly three years since the Reef's last arrival had joined the Crew, but Keel recalled the steps of the ceremony and had coached Bea through what to say.

"Yes," Bea said, not meeting Spar's eyes. Keel had also told her the alternative to joining. Her fate hinged upon her next words.

"You will join our Crew?"

Bea's voice was hoarse. "Yes."

"Then kneel," Spar said.

Bea knelt.

Only Keel saw her shoulders shaking, for Spar had set down his goblet on the rough driftwood table and picked up a wooden ewer. He raised it in both hands over Bea, who bowed her head.

"Your old life is done," Spar said, tipping the ewer. Seawater poured onto Bea's head, trickling through her blonde ringlets and down her face. She shut her eyes and bit her lip. "Whoever you were, in the place beyond the fog—whoever you loved, whatever sins you committed—all that is gone, dragged to the bottom of the sea. And from that sea, you are reborn."

He set the ewer down, placed one hand upon Bea's shoulder and the other on her brow. "Now you are of the Reef. This isle is your home, our Crew your family. As a ship has many parts, working together in common purpose, so too does each of our Crew work for the betterment of all. And so I name you Beam, for you have joined us when our hands are widest."

Bea—Beam—darted a look at Keel, who could only shrug. He had not told his father her shorename. Perhaps Spar was simply wise, to give the girl a name so near the one she had borne until this day.

"Rise, Beam, Crewmate of the Reef," Spar said.

Beam did, turning to look out at the grinning, jeering faces through the haze. The Crew erupted in cheers and shouts, rum sloshing from their raised cups. They pounded driftwood tables, their voices shaking the very timbers of the Galley. Their newest member smiled at them, seawater still running down her cheeks.

Only Keel, standing near as he was, saw her tears.

———

"Has anyone ever left?"

They stood at the Reef's northernmost point, not far from the cliffs where Keel had buried his mother. The fog today was a thin mist, one that kissed their faces and dampened their arms rather than leaving them soaked and shivering.

"Keel?" Beam pressed. "Answer me."

Lanterns stood unlit at their feet, for the afternoon had yet to lengthen into night. A solemn pride had stirred in Keel's chest at being assigned to guide Beam through her first watch, but it soured into a sense of unease. Beam was asking questions she shouldn't.

Keel looked over his shoulder. People on the Reef had a way of materializing from the fog, so you could never quite be certain you were alone.

"People leave all the time," he said, squatting to pick up his lantern. "My mother did. The same day you arrived."

"Your mother?" Beam's voice was soft.

"Yeah." Keel glanced up the slope. "The chill took her. She was abed most of a week, then that morning, she was still and cold. Like the mist."

"She died?"

Keel nodded. "We buried her in the sea. Same as your father."

"It is *not* the same."

Keel looked up, startled by the heat in her words. Beam looked down at him, her round eyes narrowed, her pale hands clenched into fists.

"It's not," she repeated. "Your mother got sick. But my father died because—"

"Because the fog took him," Keel said. "Same as my mother, just in a different way."

He flung out his arms as if to encompass the entire fogbound world in their narrow span. He had seen Spar make this gesture many times, and it never failed to quiet the assembled Crew. Nor did it fail now. Beam's lips pressed together into a frown as she stared at him.

"The fog takes all of us, in the end." The words came spilling from somewhere deep inside Keel, like water pouring from the cliffs into the sea. He could not stop them any more than he could stop the tide. "It drowns us or it chills us, but it takes us all the same."

"But you *caused* the wreck!" Beam stepped closer, her shout rolling through the fog. Keel took a step back.

"You and your lights," she spat, kicking over the unlit lantern at her feet. "We saw them in the fog, from a long way off. The mate thought they were ghost lights, or something he called saint-somebody's fire. But the captain insisted they were for land, so we steered toward them. Right into your Reef."

She came closer. Keel's heel brushed the edge of the cliff, sending a sickening lurch of fear down his spine and into his groin. Beam did not notice.

"You're scavengers," she spat. "Like gulls, picking over the dead for anything you can find."

Keel shrugged. "So?"

Beam blinked her huge eyes. "You don't think there's anything wrong with that."

"Why would there be?" Keel did not step away from the ledge, though his ankles hung over the waters churning below—the waters he had buried his mother in. "Look around you, Beam. What do you see?"

"What?" Beam looked around, ringlets bobbing. "Nothing."

"Exactly." The lantern swayed in his hand as Keel gestured at the darkening gloom. Night was coming, and their watch with it. "You know what there is to eat here, on the Reef?"

"Fish."

"And crab," Keel nodded. "But there's hardly enough to feed as many mouths as we've got. Without the ships the sea brings us—"

"That you *wreck*—"

"—we starve," Keel continued over her. "Nothing grows here. Nothing *lives* here, 'cept for us. And without those ships, we wouldn't either."

"It's wrong," Beam said. There was a sickly pallor to her face, but she did not back away. from where they stood at the cliff's edge. "It's...it's murder."

"No!" Keel hadn't meant to shout, and could only hope that his voice had not carried too far through the fog. "Murder is stabbing someone with a knife, or pushing them onto rocks."

He looked Beam steadily in the eye, his back to those same rocks far below. "If we were murderers, I would have killed you on that ship."

Beam did not flinch from his gaze. "Why didn't you?"

"Because the sea gave you to us. A new member of our Crew, a new member of our family. My family." He turned his back to her, facing into the mist. *Let her push me over, if that's what she truly wants.*

"Because I want..." his voice cracked, just a little. "Because you aren't the only one who lost a parent yesterday."

Movement in the mist as Beam joined him at the cliff's edge, a warmth presence in the damp night. "I'm sorry."

Keel nodded, not trusting himself to speak. Mist stung the corners of his eyes.

"But..." Beam put a hand on his arm, her touch feather-light. "The wrecking..."

"Maybe it's wrong where you're from," Keel said quietly. "Maybe in that place, people don't wake every day wondering if the tide will send them relief or not. I don't know. But here, we do what we have to. To survive."

He reached into the pouch at his side and produced flint and tinder. A spark, and his lantern blazed into the darkling gloom.

Beam flinched at the sudden light. "There's got to be another way."

"There is," Keel said, and held out his hand to her.

Beam hesitated before placing her palm against his. Keel was struck by how soft her skin was. For a fleeting moment, he wondered what it might be like to live someplace where hands were uncalloused.

They stood side by side on the edge of the cliff, the mist prickling on their exposed arms. Keel held out his lantern, as far over the edge as he could.

"Look," Keel said, his voice as commanding as his father's. Beam startled and took a step back.

"*Look*," he repeated, pulling her closer. They leaned over the edge, peering down into the fog, roiling and churning below. Beam stifled a gasp as a stone beneath their feet plunged into the haze without a sound.

"That's the other way," Keel said, his hand gripping hers. "One step, and we join your father and my mother. The only way out of the fog is under the waves, Beam."

"But…" She looked at him, round eyes wide. "You're hurting people."

"No." Keel shook his head. "The fog does that. Every ship that passes through it runs aground. All we do is guide them home, so that their sacrifice doesn't go to waste."

He squeezed her hand. "So that *you* don't go to waste. Here."

Keel held the lantern out to her, waiting. His ears, sharpened by years of life on the Reef, caught the telltale lapping of waves against timbers. The lantern's dull yellow glow glimmered, reflected in Beam's huge eyes. She stared at it, then into Keel's face.

"Choose," he said. "Light, or sea?"

Beam was still as a carven figurehead for a moment, save for her eyes as they roved from Keel to the lantern, from lantern to the wall of mist. Keel waited with Reef-born patience. Wordlessly, Beam took the lantern from him and turned, raising it high into the fog, her mouth set in a thin line. Though her eyes glistened, no tears fell from them.

The creak and groan of masts and timbers echoed across the Reef. The ship cut through the fog, bearing down on the Reef like an enormous phantasm.

"You're one of us now," Keel whispered, squeezing Beam's shoulder. "One of our Crew, now and always."

She sniffed and nodded, still staring out into the fog. Keel smiled, and imagined what she would look like with shells and seaweed braided into her hair.

CORRECTIONAL MEMORY

DERRICK BODEN

They say memories make us who we are.

The iron unmakes us.

Here I am again, staring down at this old holo-shot with its worn edges I know better than my own guilt-scarred hands. And there she is, smiling up at me from two decades past: Alejandra at six months. The only proof I have my daughter exists. Only proof I'll ever have, seeing as how I'd be breaking a dozen laws just by looking for her. Judge called it lenient, letting me keep those first six months of memories. The impish hands, the aching smile, the hazel eyes. One slip and they'll iron those out, too. Then I never had a daughter at all.

"Late again, Malik. You're testing my supreme benevolence."

Skinny Paul leans against the vape dispenser at the back of the office, a cheap imitation of last year's neuro-vid hero with his vinyl duster and transparent hair. His sneer bleeds contempt. Through the window, a fleet of Optix drones flits through the twilight haze above Tacoma's decaying slums. Same fleet I just serviced, though I'm not holding my breath for gratitude from Optix or Skinny Paul or anyone else. I'm just another iron-head, a criminal with no memory of my crimes. I'm cheaper than a repair drone, filthier than a full-knowing felon.

Skinny Paul sidles real close, breathes vapor and burrito stench into my face. He's about to remind me that a bus breakdown on Commerce is no excuse for my late check-in, and that—

"Work performance is a reflection of societal compatibility."

Because that's what he always says. Because even now, ten years deep in this shit-hole job, I'm never more than one transit delay away from *incompatible.*

Incompatible means prison—or worse—another turn under the iron.

Then my Alejandra is really gone.

So I fend off what remains of my pride and mutter: "Won't happen again."

Skinny Paul pats me on the cheek. Because, yeah—the iron really works. Carve out all those years from the Albaster Point to the crime itself, all the influence and all the iniquity, and you've got exactly what you started with: an innocent man. A father. Someone who will do anything—lie, grovel, beg—for the fleeting memory of his daughter.

That's when I see her. Through the window of the office door, a young woman stands in the elevator bay, hands thrust into her coat.

My gut crawls into my throat. "Who's that?"

"Oh, yeah." Skinny Paul waggles a nicotine-stained finger. "Someone's here for you."

"Who?"

"What, am I your fucking secretary? Some girl."

Alejandra.

Skinny Paul keeps barking but I'm already halfway through the door, scanning the bay for—

Brown eyes.

She spots my disappointment, and rage flashes in those off-colored irises. She pins me to the wall with a hard forearm. Out comes an old holo-shot. Still-frame, lowlight, grainy. Man in a suit, face-down on a tiled floor, saturated in blood.

I fumble for my parole card. "My name is Malik Badir. I am a convicted felon and an active Memory Correction Parolee…"

Out comes a badge—same hand, impressive dexterity—and my stomach sinks. Detective McNabb, Seattle P.D.

My lips carry on, numbed. "…it is forbidden by law to expose me to the details surrounding my crime, or any other personal information within the bounds of my tag dates. Please report violations to Officer Choi—"

"Shut up," she says.

I glance at the door. If Skinny Paul peeks in, spots me in the same room as that holo, it's curtains for me. Doesn't matter whose payroll this lady is on.

She eases up on my neck, flips the holo-shot onto the deliveries counter like it's junk mail. "Got your attention?"

I try not to think about the man in the suit. The body.

Nothing familiar about it. That's what worries me the most.

The detective is young, early twenties by the smooth cut of her jaw, but the shadows under her eyes and the scars on her hands say she's seen more action than some vets. Freckled brown skin, a shade paler than mine.

I rub my throat. "Whatever it is you think I did, take it up with my parole officer."

"Already know what you did." The holo-shot is sucking my attention like a ten-ton electromagnet, and I'm about to bolt for the door when she adds: "Ain't why I'm here."

That catches me on the blindside. "I can't…I don't want to know."

"Don't want to know what? That someone set you up?"

The room spins a little.

They're just words. Words to keep me from walking away.

And they work. "Just because I don't remember, doesn't mean I didn't do it."

"Wasn't what I said." Her glare bores through my skull. "I said someone else put the gun in your hand."

Just like that, all those years of carefully concealed truths burn in full exposure. Doesn't matter if she's lying about the setup—it's the ancillaries that grab me by the jugular.

A dead body. A gun in my hand.

Did I murder that man?

I suck slow breaths like they taught us at discharge. *Memories are weapons. Disarm yourself…*

But now the other thought is wriggling through my brain.

I was set up.

"You're lying." I try to pump confidence into the words, fail.

"Because I got nothing better to do than prank iron-heads on my dinner break."

"Then you're using me."

"No shit." She cocks her head. "But it works both ways."

Sweat crawls down my scalp, past the cross-shaped scar behind my left ear where they ironed out twelve years of memories in lieu of a life sentence. I squeeze my eyes shut, try to focus on my daughter's face. Nothing this cop has to sell is worth the risk of losing the last few memories I have of Alejandra.

Except.

If I was set up, that means someone did this to me.

Someone took my dignity. My freedom. My daughter. Ripped her from my arms, and anyone can guess how it must've gone for her after that. Courts unload her at the nearest orphanage after my trial, age twelve. Mother dead in childbirth, no relatives to speak of. A dropout by thirteen, slinging drugs, turns at juvie, never a fighting chance at a normal life.

Someone did this.

I slit my eyes. "I was set up *how?*"

She shrugs, like it's a detail she can't be bothered with. "You owed money. Couldn't pay. So the lender comes for your girl. Says either she sweats the bill, or you do."

My fingernails draw blood from my palms.

"So you cave. Agree to whack some guy as payment."

"Who?" I'm only vaguely aware of my words—*infractions*—slipping through my lips.

"Some guy. An iron doc with a dirty rap."

"And I…?"

"You didn't get ironed for backing out, I'll tell you that."

I press my hands to my eyes.

"He gives you a gun. Sends you in. Then he waits five minutes and calls the cops."

"Bullshit."

She reaches for her pocket.

I cringe. No more holos.

"Imagine that. Someone else to blame for *this*." She motions to the mildewed carpet, the rattling vents, the door that leads to Skinny Paul and a lifetime of groveling. The dozen years they ironed from my brain; the miserable decade that followed. "Someone else that *walked*."

I swallow a flood of nausea.

"Someone else who's living free. In Seattle. Right now."

So that's the scheme. Cops want this guy iced, need someone to do their dirty work. Figure I'm already filthy as sin.

Only, I'm not. Never even hit another man, far as I remember. And if this cop thinks I'm going to risk my daughter's memory for a dose of petty revenge, I'm not the only one low on gray matter.

I make for the door. "Can't help you."

"Yours wasn't the only life ruined that night, Malik."

That puts whiplash into my neck. "Alejandra."

"Find this guy." Her expression pinches. "Find your girl."

My hand drifts toward my pocket. To prove she knows what I'm reaching for, she says: "Not some low-res holo to pine over. The real deal."

My mouth goes bone-dry. The HVAC wheezes for a solid minute.

"This guy," I say. "He has her now?"

She makes the sour face again. "Ain't that simple. But if you do exactly what I say, I promise you'll see her again."

The thought nearly drags me to a knee. I tremble under a swell of warmth.

This must be what hope feels like.

Except.

"I set foot in Seattle, Choi ships me to county for parole violation."

"Not with a workplace exception. Haven't checked your calendar?"

I'm about to ask how she knows my work schedule before I do, when I remember the police have to approve all my parole exceptions. Skinny Paul doesn't book me for on-sites in King County more than he has to, on account of the red tape. When he does, it means someone just quit on him—not exactly an everyday occurrence.

She's been waiting for this.

I shoot her a wary look. "Where?"

"BellTower."

"Death wish."

She glances around, as if to say, *what's this?*

I shrug it off. "I need proof."

She laughs so loud I cringe at the thought of Skinny Paul hearing. "If I had proof, I wouldn't need you."

"Then a guarantee."

Another laugh. "What's left on your parole? Fifteen more years? Twenty? Think you'll outlive that? Think you'll ever get another shot like this?" She levels a frigid glare. "I'm here because I need your help. You're listening—*still*—because you need mine. Because you know as well as I do that if you walk through that door right now, you'll never see your daughter again."

I glance through the office window toward Skinny Paul, all scowl and scorn.

I glance at the old holo-shot, already back in my hand. Those big bright eyes. That aching smile.

I realize, with growing unease, that there's *nothing* I wouldn't do to see that smile again.

And as for the man who took her from me…

"Tell me his name." I want to hear it. Taste it.

She collects the holo-shot, makes for the elevator. "Not yet."

As if I've already said yes.

—

Detective McNabb wants to meet at the Slammer, on the border of old SoDo. It's *edgy*, meaning it used to be dangerous, but now it's very hip and very white. Ironed those wrinkles right out. Waitstaff are sporting peel-off jailhouse tats, but every one of them is an undergrad zipped into designer jeans. Even kept a few bullet holes from the cafe's prior incarnation, above the logo. Very edgy.

I find the detective in the darkest corner. Her coat is studded with raindrops; her face is stiff and dry.

"Place look familiar?"

"Should it?"

She shrugs. Some kind of test I clearly failed. But when I glance down, I swear I've seen the tile work before. The question is on my lips when I spot a couple in aviator jackets three tables over, trying not to stare. Like they recognize me.

I pretend not to notice. "How about some names."

"Outside the precinct, people call me Zo."

"And?"

She stares deadpan for a ten-count before a sigh slips out. "His name's Jasper."

"Jasper." It tastes like carrion in my mouth. "Jasper what?"

"Just Jasper."

Right. She doesn't want me going desperado, giving the cops something to trace back to her desk.

"Who is he?"

"Local capo. Drugs, real estate. Prostitution. Used to own this part of town."

Past tense.

"At one point he was bankrolling half of SoDo. Everyone's friend, until he wasn't. Called him the Devil's Dentist."

I raise an eyebrow.

"Made a name prying teeth from people who owed him money, their mothers and daughters. Strung them into necklaces."

A shiver overtakes me. "So arrest him."

"File's empty. Had a chain of beat cops on his payroll. Perfect teeth and luxury sedans, every one of them."

So that's the angle: vigilante justice. The clouded look in her eyes says this is personal for her, too. Which makes me a cheap payback tool on account of some poor sap who wound up on the wrong end of one of Jasper's business deals, landed in a gutter leaking from the brainpan while her colleagues stood around collecting kickbacks instead of evidence.

Does that make it more or less right, doing this thing?

If it means I see Alejandra again, does it matter?

That's when I notice them: a line of blood-red freckles just past her hairline. Neuronarc scars. No such thing as a clean cop anymore, but who am I to judge? Everyone needs a break from reality, nowadays. Hell, there's three suits at the bar right now jacked into a quick neural holiday, drooling away their dinner breaks on some tropical beach with a harem of swimsuit models, nothing but a thread of biofeedback keeping them from blowing their loads all over their Key lime pie.

Zo fixes her hair. The evidence is gone.

"You get one shot. He'll be in BellTower, floor sixty-six, Northwest quadrant shopping promenade, men's restroom. Ten-thirty tomorrow morning."

"How do you know when a guy's gonna take a piss?"

"He'll be there. And so will you. Courier drone repairs at Optix HQ—"

"I read my schedule." Me and everyone else, apparently. "BellTower, floor seventy-two."

She nods. "Finish the job. Then…there will be a gun in the third stall."

A gun. Of course that's what this is all about, but hearing her say it makes my chest cave. I'm not a killer.

Not that I can remember.

"And the cops?"

"BellTower's unincorporated—privilege of the rich. No cops without a warrant. Why do you think I need you?"

I shift uncomfortably. "Private security?"

"I wouldn't lose sleep over a few paunchy two-point-fives. Besides, you'll be legit, on-the-clock. Just stopping for an espresso on the way out."

She doesn't continue, so I say: "And then?"

"That's it."

"How will I find her?"

"A promise is a promise."

"Just tell me—"

"If you don't like my answers, the door's right there."

We sit in silence. The couple in the aviators are shooting me sidelong glances over their caffè breves. Girl's barely out of college. Dark skin, a little too thin for her bones.

Hazel eyes.

Zo's asking me something, and I'm missing every word.

The girl gets up to pay.

Could it be her?

An undefinable guilt stabs at my gut.

Sweat trickles down my back. I scour my memory for a clue—a birthmark, a gait, a pattern of freckles. Anything.

Then her boyfriend calls to her—*Frida*—and my shoulders sink.

"I said—" There's a tremble in Zo's voice I can't place. "—Ever get echoes?"

Yeah, right. Some early iron-heads reported knowing things they never should've—lyrics to songs, outmoded dance moves, passwords. Shrinks called them echoes.

My gaze strays to another girl, hunched over a laptop in the far corner. Against the screen's glow, apprehension flickers in her eyes.

Hazel eyes.

My guilt ratchets.

Then I spot the graft-tan peeling along her wrists. She's white as Abe Lincoln underneath.

I grit my teeth. "Echoes are a farce."

The whole thing turned out to be a ploy, hypnosis by some activist shrink. There's no such thing as echoes, just like there's no way I could pick my daughter out at a cafe or a police lineup or anywhere else.

But the guilt still gnaws, and now I know why. Even if it means seeing her again—how can I prove to Alejandra I'm a good man after whacking a stranger in cold blood? How is this any different from the crime that took her from me?

Cop lights carnival down a side street. The barista shoots me a crooked glance, jabs frantically at her phone. Dude in the aviator jacket watches me, eyes flicking through his contax feed.

Maybe they know me. From the news, from the past. Maybe they see the intent in my eyes—that dark flame ready to consume anything and anyone for a shot at finding my daughter. Maybe they're afraid.

I sure as hell am.

"I can't do this," I say, and walk out.

—

I retreat. Across the freight tracks, beneath the cicada hum of power lines, through neighborhoods that've seen a steady diet of decay, gentrification, decay again. Teeth grown over rotted teeth. Under the peeling sign of a yoga studio, gang-era graffiti. Beneath the chipping whitewash of a produce market, stained blood. Hopscotch games pocked with crack-pipe burns. Wounds that would heal if we just stopped picking at them.

If this was once Jasper's stomping ground, it was also mine. But nothing's familiar. I retreat through another man's dream. Deeper, deeper.

Men watch me from rotting porches, Glocks in plain sight. I keep my head down, afraid of the recognition in their eyes. Androgynes slathered in tribal tattoos lean against crumbling facades, live-wire dangling from neural ports. *I can be anyone you want, Johnny—just jack in.* A woman stands on a pile of tires at the center of a weed-choked junkyard. Neuronarc scars cover her face; her eyes burn blue fire.

"There is no repentance without knowledge of our sins!"

Does she know me?

I hustle down a side alley, cower in the darkness. But her voice persists—surrounding me, hounding me.

"That which we forget, we are cursed to repeat!"

My fingers search out the scar behind my ear, itch.

"Doc Lemons! Angel Allie! Mickie Nabs! Dead, dead, dead! Time to feed the hungry ghosts."

I force a slow breath. It's paranoia, that's all. Neuronarc highs are guided hallucinations, journeys through the minds of the drug manufacturers, customized by your own neural topography. Eventually, the concept of self breaks down. For all I know, she's drifting through the aftermath of a Martian murder spree, or tweezing evidence on Moriarty.

So why do her words rake at my conscience?

I retreat through an abandoned lot before stopping to catch my breath. Rain pelts my face, slides down my collar, ices my back.

Time to feed the hungry ghosts.

"Malik, my man. I'll be damned."

The voice slips from the shadows of a defunct charging station. I want to ignore it, move on, forget this whole damn thing. But my legs won't let me.

The shadow bleeds a face: dark, scarred. Unfamiliar.

The face grins. Holes where teeth should be.

"Damn, Malik. You look like shit. Where you been?"

"Down south."

"Doing time?"

"Working."

A chopper pounds the night air over Beacon Hill. Headed this way.

The grin fades. "Last I heard, you were running gigs for—"

"My name—" I cut myself off half-second late. Goddamned preconditioning. "I don't dwell much on the past."

His jaundiced eyes flare in slow-mo. "You don't even recognize me."

I shrug.

"They did you good. What are your tags?"

"Twenty-five to thirty-seven." Reflex again.

"Twelve years, shit. Even remember what they booked you for?"

"That's the whole fucking point."

He works his jaw. I can see things clicking into place. Unpleasant things.

"Lot of trouble came my way on account of you."

That's when I notice the copper pipe in his hand.

"That isn't me anymore." *Never was.* "None of that's me."

His lip curls, showing scattered tombstone teeth. *Devil's Dentist.*

"Lot of trouble. You and that bitch of a daughter—"

He's on the ground, pipe skittering across the wet asphalt. I rub my stinging knuckles. Nausea crawls up my throat.

Never even hit another man.

"Ain't you, no more?" Through the bubble and spit of blood, he laughs. "Bullshit. You're no better than the winos or the neuros or the johns. Always something to blame that ain't yourself. Damn right it's still you. The goon that's rubbing his bloody knuckles over my crippled ass is the same goon that plugged Doc Lemons in the triple murder that shut down the Old Slammer."

Motherfucker. That's where I've seen the tile work at the Slammer. Not from some bullshit echo—from Zo's crime scene holo-shot. But why the hell would she bring me to the place that—

Did he say *triple murder?*

The chopper's getting louder, a smudge against the Seattle skyline.

He wipes gore across his cheek. "You think the same shit doesn't unfold a thousand times a day? You think these people—" with a thumb-jab toward the city "—give two shits about your *correction?* About *who you are* and *who you ain't?* Fuck, Malik. All they want is cheaper prison bills and to forget that people like us ever existed. First they iron out the neighborhood, then they come for our minds—"

"Enough!" My back's turned, salted raindrops staining my cheeks, and I wish to god I could un-hear every word. My hands scrabble in my pockets for the cool comfort of the holo-shot.

But it isn't there. Where did I leave it? How will I remember her without it? Already her features slip through the sieve of my mind. A dark jawline, a flash of brown hair. I squint into the downpour, and for a moment she's there.

Then, nothing.

Silence behind me rakes my attention. The man slinks into the shadows as another figure approaches. A flash of brown hair, a dark jawline—

"Alejandra."

The rotors pound the air, at odds with my pulse as I realize my mistake. "Zo."

But the thought has already taken hold. Eye color can change in those first years after birth.

Yours wasn't the only life ruined that night.

Did she react, just now, when I called her Alejandra?

The light from a passing cruiser filters through her hair like a mistimed sunrise. The question hangs on my lips.

But I can't find the words.

Whoever she is, she took pains tracking me down in the middle of the night, out here. This is more important to her than I thought. More *personal.*

She sighs. "His name is Jasper White."

The words hang in the rain like an omen. She looks vaguely ill—it took effort to trust me with his name.

It's time I trust her as well.

It's time to find Jasper White.

—

BellTower. Fuck.

The developers pitched it as the nation's largest mixed-use ecosystem. With eighty-five looming stories, it consumes fifteen city blocks—enough to displace all of old Belltown. Luxury condos, corner offices, a patchwork of indoor green spaces and amusement parks and swimming pools—all with year-round artificial sunlight that Seattle itself could never provide. For the slavering public, it's a guided tour at best— a three-hour eye-popping reminder of everything they'll never have. For the more privileged demographic, there's no reason to ever leave.

People like me, we're never meant to see the inside.

But here I am. Stepping off the lift at sixty-six with a throng of morning shoppers—graft-tans squeezed into designer yoga pants, clutching cappuccinos and bitching about property tax. The repair gig is a wrap, and I'm all but invisible in my maintenance jacket and Mariners cap. I keep my head low and my collar high, try not to walk too fast.

Easier said than done. This place gives me the creeps, with its gold-cobblestone boulevards and beret-studded cafes. For all I know, Jasper's spent the last decade hobnobbing with these trust-fund elites while I've been living off prepackaged noodles in a Section 8 shoebox. While my daughter's been…devil only knows. The thought makes my teeth ache.

It also makes my conscience warm to the task at hand.

"Slow it down." Zo's husky tenor scratches through my earpiece from somewhere off-site. "You're attracting attention."

She's right. Four uniforms lounge outside a memory clinic, one of them eyeing me over his double-chocolate latte. Over my shoulder, a fifth guard feigns interest in an emerald-studded halter top.

I stop to tie my bootlaces, collect myself. A too-skinny brunette in a long overcoat staggers out of the memory clinic, looking lost. She leans against the "friends forget free" sign, sucks on her vape. I know the look. She's wondering what could've gone so wrong with her Friday night to make her want to forget it by dawn. She's wondering: was it something I did?

Even the rich have regrets.

The iron straightens it all out.

She rights herself, walks off with sudden composure. This isn't her first rodeo. Short-term irons don't even leave a scar. Some kids have memories like Emmental by graduation, and not always by choice. Father feels bad for taking the belt to little Tommy, whole family comes in for a quick iron before brunch. Have some waffles, kid. Daddy loves you.

The fifth guard stops to chat with her buddies—one of whom is still shooting me looks. He's on his radio, now. Just checking in.

Unless.

An access door bangs open. A voice barks an order. Two more guards round the corner.

I pull my cap lower and duck into a crowd of suits on a guided tour. The tour makes a quick left, though, toward the southern tower.

"One shot." My earpiece crackles. "Stay on target."

But *on target* is a block and a half of open space, and one of the guards is already whispering into his subvocal while the other glances over her shoulder at—

Officer Choi. Paying for a drink at a sludge bar. Slurping from an oversized straw. Turning this way.

I break from the tour group, squeeze past a guard and slide through the access doors as they're swinging shut, like I'm supposed to be there. The guard shouts something when he realizes I'm not. So I yank the doors closed and tie the handles with a data cable from my utility belt.

Pale blue light illuminates an access passage that runs the length of the promenade. A heavy thrum emanates from the fat metal conduit overhead.

I suck shallow breaths.

The fuck is my parole officer doing here? Could've sworn Zo said no cops.

Footsteps, outside the door. I hustle down the passage. Sweat seeps into my eye, burns like hell. Voices crawl from the shadows.

Doc Lemons! Angel Allie! Mickie Nabs! Dead, dead, dead!

The thrumming builds and builds until I can't tell the pounding of my own pulse from the heartbeat of this hellish place. I break into a run. All around me, the words of the neuronarc junkie echo.

Time to feed the hungry ghosts.

My lungs are on fire: I need air. I break through the first door I see, into a broad lobby sandwiched between a cerebral retreat agency and…the restroom.

A man walks inside.

I check my cell. Ten-thirty.

A pall descends over me.

Choi is a hundred yards back, along with a cadre of tower guards. No time for guessing what—or *who*—tipped them off. I could circle back to the lifts by way of the access tunnels, but then what? Squeeze behind some pipes and hold my breath for a few days?

Zo's right: I've got one shot at this. I bail now and I'll never see my daughter again.

I suck in a long, meditative breath. Then I follow Jasper White inside.

The bathroom is elegant as fuck: faux-wood paneling, subdued lighting, meticulous spread of colognes I can't pronounce. Even the janitor's cart in the corner looks refined, polished brass and tastefully organized supplies. The urinals are deep and tall, but I spot the dome of Jasper's bald scalp, second from the front.

We're alone.

I step into the third stall. The door slides shut, turns opaque. The toilet's more complicated than a legitimate spaceship, but I'm not here for an ass massage. I reach behind the molding.

My hand closes around textured metal. A thrill races up my arm.

I check the clip. One bullet.

Bile floods my mouth. I've never even held a gun, by my account. The thought of using one fills me with disgust.

I squeeze my eyes shut, focus on the fleeting memory of my daughter. I breathe in her newborn scent, feel her cheek against my chest. I imagine the *maybes*. Her hand clutching mine as we walk to the bus stop. Her soft sigh as we lay spread-eagle on the rooftop of an abandoned mid-rise, counting jetliners as they plunge through the cloud bank. First laugh, first step, first day of school.

Gone. Forever.

The urinal flushes. I chamber the bullet, slip outside. Jasper carefully washes his hands.

He isn't what I expected.

Middle-aged, favoring his left leg, stuffed into janitorial coveralls. Through the mirror, I spot a velcro patch that says, simply, WHITE. A plain gold cross hangs from his neck. The skin sags around his eyes. Sad eyes.

This is what has come of the Devil's Dentist.

It changes nothing. I shrug off the discomfort, level the barrel. "Where is she?"

He half-turns, freezes. Stares at me, at the gun. "Who?"

"You know damn well—"

That's when I spot the cross-shaped scar behind his left ear.

Jasper's been ironed.

My hand trembles. This bullet was primed for revenge, for *punishment*. But how can I punish a man for a crime he doesn't remember? Hasn't he already suffered his punishment through the loss of memory, of time? What purpose would his death serve now, other than to satisfy some sick kind of closure?

I mutter into my subvocal. "I thought you said he *walked*."

"He did."

"Then…?"

"Ironed himself. Psych clinic, client confession, full nondisclosure."

He did this to himself? Short-term iron jobs are a dime a dozen, but a scar means…

"How long?"

"Fifteen years."

Fifteen!

"If he felt that bad," Zo says in a clipped monotone, "he would've turned himself in. Served real time, not some iron-job free pass. Now quit stalling and finish this. Your daughter's waiting."

Again, the thought strikes me: is Zo my daughter? If so—if my daughter needs this—how can I say no? So what if Jasper found God, repented, wiped his sins from his guilty skull?

I tighten my grip on the gun.

Jasper staggers awkwardly on his bum leg. Sweat stains his coveralls. He's a pathetic man, stuck in a dead-end job, all but forgotten by society. Like me.

Except he put me here. He *took* my daughter from me. Does it matter whether he remembers what he did?

But if I'm not a murderer anymore, what does that make Jasper? What's left of this man that ruined my life?

What's left of me?

Jasper blinks, his mouth agape. Nothing in his sad eyes says he found the peace he was looking for.

I close the distance in two strides, bring the gun down hard. He crumples with a sigh that sounds like relief.

"The fuck are you doing?" Zo yells into my ear.

The gun clatters to the ground.

My head throbs. A vise cranks my gut.

This must be what forgiveness feels like.

I stare at the cross-shaped scar on Jasper's skull. No more scapegoats. *I'm* responsible for what I did.

I breathe easy, for the first time. "I'm not what you think I am."

The door bangs open. I'm expecting a flood of guards, but instead it's Zo with a head of steam.

Zo, who's supposed to be offsite. Just like Choi, who's supposed to be in Tacoma.

This isn't about what I thought it was.

The rage is back in Zo's brown eyes as she says, "give me a fucking break," grabs the gun from the floor, and drives the lone bullet through Jasper's forehead.

I stagger backward, grope for the counter, slip on blood and gray matter. Cologne bottles skitter, shatter, flood the air with their sickly scent.

"There." Zo drops the gun, tugs off her gloves. "You did it."

I blink once, twice, three times.

You were set up.

Twice now, it seems. Doesn't make Jasper any less dead.

Someone else put the gun in your hand.

Again. Doesn't mean his family's going to miss him any less. Not Jasper's, and not the ones from the time before.

A triple murder.

Zo's badge, peeking from her belt. Detective McNabb, Seattle P.D.

Mickie Nabs.

Some bystander at the Old Slammer no doubt stood his ground or got in the way or whatever the fuck happened when I came to whack Doc Lemons. Got himself killed. Left a family behind.

This is a revenge story, all right. Just not mine. All this time, I've been looking for my daughter in Zo. She isn't my daughter at all.

She's someone else's.

"I killed your father."

Tendons clench along her jaw. "You *walked*."

"Bullshit I did." But even as I say it, her words come flooding back. *Not some iron-job free pass.* She thinks I got off easy. Spent a few months in a holding cell, lost some memories, walked. Meanwhile, her dad won't ever walk again.

"Why not just kill me?"

"Not very fulfilling when you don't remember what you did."

My gaze lingers on Jasper's ruined skull. Don't I know it.

But the look in Zo's eyes says it wasn't all that fulfilling anyhow.

She smiles without a trace of mirth. "This way, everyone gets what they deserve."

The gloves. My prints on the gun. One dead body. Gift-wrapped probable cause. Officer Choi, waiting to scoop me up.

Courts might order a second turn under the iron for parole violations, but never for full-blown repeat offenses. I'm going to pay for killing Zo's father with *real time*, at long last.

Zo watches me, darkly. How long has she been planning this? She couldn't have been more than twelve, maybe thirteen when her father died. Same age as—

I suck in a sharp breath. "Where's my baby?"

"Haven't guessed yet?" Her lips twist with contempt. "Riverton Crest. Economy plot at the back."

Riverton Crest...*Cemetery?*

"Triple means *three*." Zo's laughter stabs like knives, and I can't will her next words away. "Christ, Malik. You killed her."

I wheeze through a fog of cologne. My muscles give out. My insides writhe like maggots, and I'm clawing blood from my face.

Zo's still talking, her words ricocheting across an abyss. "She must've known something was up that night. Followed you to the Old Slammer. Caught a stray bullet, just like my pops."

Angel Allie.

Alejandra.

I killed my baby.

Her memory was fool's gold from the start. No matter what happened here, I wasn't ever going to see her again—not alive. I lost her the moment I picked up that gun, all those years ago.

Everything else was just follow-through.

Zo watches me with something akin to pity. Just imagine, not ten minutes ago, I was hopped up on the illusion that this woman—this fierce, strong woman—was my daughter. Just imagine, not ten minutes ago, everything I still had to live for.

Just *imagine*.

"Zo."

"Yeah."

"How long before Choi shows?"

"Soon as I make the call."

Just imagine. The thought festers inside me.

"You got yours." My words come out slow, deep, alien. "Now how about a favor."

Her eyebrow arcs.

"Twenty minutes in the clinic."

Her eyes widen. "You're crazy."

Short-term irons don't even leave a scar.

"Let me believe." My voice catches. "My baby's still alive."

Let me believe she's you.

Her jaw hangs slack as she adds it all up. Life in prison is a miserable thing. Exiled, shamed, forgotten. *Hope* might make it bearable. *Hope* might make me a better man, all over again.

I clasp my hands together in a bloody plea. "It's all I have."

"But it's a lie."

I glance at Jasper, the gun, her.

"Does that matter?"

She doesn't have to respond—we both know the answer. Memories make us who we are. Sometimes, they're all we have.

Her lip curls with disgust, but her eyes are damp when she looks at me for the last time and says: "You've got fifteen minutes."

I lean my head against Jasper's corpse, and laugh.

I'm going to get my baby back. And this time, nobody's going to take her from me.

Nobody.

THE DREAM AND THE WEAVER

KITTY–LYDIA DYE

The Dreamer model is nothing more than an artist's palette. There is no A.I., only chasms of data storage.

Bright colors smear hollow ribs: red from a balloon vanishing in a polluted sky, yellow for children's laughter. Behind silver cheeks drips nightmares, gentle as rain upon windows.

She is not unique. Thousands of chambers house versions of this metal woman and her cradle. Butcher hooks tear into her back and chains wrap her belly so she soars above the pod. A wire fringe covers her glowing eyes.

Every child receives a free trial until they reach a productive age. The cradle glows as one is placed inside, before the shield draws over the pod. White lacing decorates the edges. Tiny stars sticker across the girl's vision. A painted moon smiles beside her murky reflection of wonderment.

The Weaver kneeling in attendance begins its lullaby. It is a frequency soothed into mimicking human vocal cords. In its true tongue, the sound would be a dial tone screech.

The Dreamer has no arms, instead great metal wings stretch and engulf the cradle, tucking it to her scarred breast. The mecha pushes aside her wires, so she may gaze upon the child. Darkness blossoms as tiny buds, spiraling faster, larger—the stars and sneering moon drown.

The Dreamer is always watching, and what she sees she devours. When dreaming has a price tag, an innocent's slumber is as addictive as sugar to those who can afford sleep.

AYUMI: THE WIDOW

Society's tattered webs drape moonscrapers, dulling stars into embers. Thoughts and store discounts travel through membrane-clotted wires.

When a child is born, they are held aloft on the roofs. A strand reaches out, tucks itself in an ear and forms a shawl, just as muslin was thrown over cradles to keep away the scary things beyond. Now the Dreamer holds us all, only masking what screeches past the city's defenses. Nanites squirm in the folds.

The alleyway is narrow. Single-use machines spill from trash bags, needle limbs twisted, smiles frozen, heads minutely twitching with one last percentage of battery power.

MESSAGE TO AYUMI: YOUR PURCHASE IS HERE!

My mecha came at a discount, considering it was a fling away from the furnace. The warranty expired a decade ago.

The courier mecha's long neck stretches to scan my Good Citizen card, trilling, "Please enjoy your evening. The sun might be abed, but there is still so much to do!" It heaves the container into the mouth of the warehouse before rolling away on whining continuous treads.

I disengage the locks and the crate's sides lower to the ground, unfurling like petals. Packing peanuts tumble, fizzing as air dissolves them.

The Weaver lays curled within, its six arms encircling its wheels. Wires knotted into dreadlocks fan out. Silver skin speckled with inky freckles play at individuality. Such things are needed to tell these mecha apart. Their faces are hollowed out, replaced with dreamcatcher strands.

Constant chattering tickles my ears. The web can never be muted. Privacy settings are too expensive. I whistle, drowning out the groan of the city, and pretend no one else can hear my thoughts as I drag the mecha inside.

My nails scrape whereabouts the human brainstem would be, searching for the switch. There it is, impressed by a too-rough hand. The click is loose sounding. Something rattles into the depths.

Whirring. Grinding. The smoky hitch of wires burning. I lean back as optics gleam behind the dreamcatcher, illuminating its inner workings. The mecha's arms jerkily stretch, hanging half-bent. Its remaining fingers crook as if to snatch.

"Pretty tune," jitters from the gullet hiding in the skull's shadows.

"What—"

"Hello," it spits out rapidly. A spider skitters over its dented chest. "I have been installed with six thousand culture entries to better interpret dreams and a diverse vocabulary to describe imagery. Mind Over Matter Corp caters to everyone."

"I don't want you for that nonsense. You're the only compatible software able to link to a Dreamer. Datamine this one. Find the memories locked in storage. Find her."

There, emerging from the shadows above us, is the curved moonshine cheek of a Dreamer—a frozen angel.

I drop an IV bag, scrape back my hair, and insert the drip into my ear. Too many dives and mucus forms, clotting the mind. Sometimes you bleed, but regulators call it a minor inconvenience, instead churning out products to address the mess rather than fix the problem.

"You'll have to wake me halfway through. Weaver, make it a priority."

"Why?"

I pause in ripping a sheet for my cocoon. It's a child's question. Not asking for logic, but demanding the emotion behind my desire.

Ridiculous, assigning things to mecha that aren't there. Looking for ghosts.

"Because I say so."

"Why?" The voice whines into static.

"Check the online database."

"I am disconnected. You must teach me."

This Weaver was meant to be recycled. My tearing slows.

"You can recall dreams if you wake while in the middle of one."

"What if it is too soon?"

It will always be too soon. Twenty years wasn't enough. The rainfall outside can't compare.

"Then mark it as a failure in your system."

The mecha's whirring quickens.

When I snap out the linking cable, the Weaver holds out a wrist. It should go into a cradle, but I'm diving as deep as I can—so close I can trick my senses.

I ram the other end into my hip port. The Weaver jolts.

"Warning, using illegal access routes—"

"I know. Cease."

I roll myself in the sheets, screw my eyes shut, and force my twitching legs to still. There's a warning flutter. Even with the virus I injected, my Cricket knows I'm stealing sleep.

"I have to remember the dream. I have to."

Wheels whir. There's a hand on my forehead, cool but warming up from an overheated system.

"Calm yourself." Stale air puffs against my face, as if the Weaver is trying to breathe. "Error. My stores are empty."

"Your what?"

"We pump mists of lavender to aid sleep. My stores are empty."

I can't help but laugh. Something within me relaxes.

"Once upon a time," the Weaver begins. It is programmed for children, and I am a woman too old for fairy tales.

Words travel through the wire, typing over my eyes, burrowing past the shield of my skull. The Weaver's hand does not move.

MASHOKA: THE WEAVER

Connection established... Firewall disabled in 10...9...4...2...

Once upon a time, dreams were free. Dogs stretched before fires and kicked out their legs. Cats hid in the nooks of trees to keep theirs secret. Humans slept in the arms of the stars.

Eight hours they did this, every day, and then they were forced to rush, to finish what needed finishing. They raced the sun. Time is precious, especially when put against credit.

It started with a contract. Someone who wanted dental included in their employer-provided healthcare. Fine, the company said, but give us two hours of sleep in exchange. Two hours working instead of dreaming. Don't be concerned.

Three hours. Four. A night or two. Easily caught up on the weekend, until that word fell out of fashion.

Drain a battery too much and glitches occur.

Messages ping that do not really exist. A logical outcome is not arrived at. A stutter. A freeze. The rule to protect human life cannot be properly or consistently followed if systems have slowed down.

Mecha are made to look human. Even our inner workings mimic human organs. Similarities put humans at ease, but we are diametrically opposed, and they know it deep down.

Our blue optics keep them awake at night. Our whirring hearts stop them from settling.

Mecha can multitask and have no right to complain, but they rust or need parts replaced. Humans make mistakes, but they are always working away—they feel guilty if they are not. When they break down, they put their repairs on credit. They can replicate, although the copy is not exact. It is small and takes time to grow into something useful.

The worker's skull is opened. A tiny metal Cricket is installed, right beside the amygdala.

Now sleep.

—

I am falling and flying at the same time. Code spills into the well. The characters form mounds that split open. Hands burst out, scrabbling for mine. I hunt for her wedding ring.

"Ishra!"

Unfamiliar fingers grasp my collar.

SEB: MAGPIE

"It's time to shut your eyes, Seb."

The rooster mecha's neck sinks into the feathered torso balanced upon the sliding doors, legs bent and talons digging into the electronic lock. Wings revolve to reveal its tawny underside. An owl's head emerges, eyes missing so it cannot emit blue light.

Violin music murmurs through speakers. As if yawning, the honeycomb ceiling fades in and out, our night sky soil and the white of things long buried. Inside the bunker, everything is bled of color. Clean. Artificial lilies lift their heads, petals peeling to reveal a black bud—a camera lens.

Uncles clap my shoulder as they pass. Aunts swarm food terminals, collecting their cups of chamomile, cocoa, whatever soothes the soul. My hand lifts, then stills.

One of them is my mother. When the commune escaped the nightmares, they gave up possession of their children. When one of my friends has a child, I will call them nephew or niece. When I am selected to give my aunts and uncles the next generation, I will have to share. It is better to be molded by many hands.

My breathing goes too quick and ragged. They'll hear. Nothing is private.

For now, I am a boy. Something to pet and dress up.

"Look how it shines. The detailing at the edges is almost like ivy," I say as I tilt my head, showing my aunt the writing on my neck. "I saw this in a dancer's dream."

I don't know what my markings say, not even the language. I pinch out my most charming smile, so they'll agree. Enough smiles and I get to keep this.

Someone ruffles my hair. We join the line for the Dreamer's nest.

The elders do not speak openly of before, fearing the sickness's return, but I like listening at doors. They say we were infected by outsiders—Head Crackers who didn't want soft dreams, instead explosions and sweating men. Cheap, bawdy entertainment, crunched up quick as popcorn. Underground clubs with malfunctioning Dreamers and no Weavers to act as guides.

Viruses entered the network. Others hacked dreams to torment strangers.

People turned violent in the waking world, acting out their fantasies. Anarchists whispered in politicians' ears and reconfigured their priorities.

My people put themselves in this cage and locked the door before I was born.

Approved dreams are bought at a premium and sanitized. Safety protocols installed so everything, good or bad, is as distant as a painting.

The Weaver sits in the center, eel-like wires latching upon our circle of cradles as we crawl inside them. The mecha's face is a porcelain mask, stiffly smiling as his head twists, painted eyes meeting mine, as handsome as a fantasy. My teeth catch on my lip. There's a squirming in my throat.

An aunt looks at me, her eyes framed with ink sticky lashes and dusty sleep greed. I roll over, cheeks burning.

I don't want to share, I think frantically. They'll grimace. Warn me to unpick it from my stitching, as if it can easily be kicked into the shadows.

—

The Dreamer spreads her wings. Daylight enwraps us.

I'm outside!

Ruins pepper shorn fields, thatching crushed beneath stone. Reeds slap together, fringing a river's marshy cracks. Beyond the Dreamscape, the land is flat, harsh edges. Trees like woodblock prints.

Our faces are frosted glass. No one is thinking of the original Dreamer, only devouring what he imagined. They marvel over how bright the sky is. All want to go pick flowers, avoiding the ruins' gloom.

It doesn't take long for me to stray. In the chapel window, cobwebs flutter. Strands have broken free, frayed husks of past prey bobbing. The spider lays at my feet, body curled and papery.

Pixels flutter. Silk cocoons crack, budding with moths. The spider twitches and leaps to the window, packing webbing into its abdomen, until it squats alone in the corner.

It drops, legs tickling one another as sticky string spills out. The trap is strummed, luring the moths back. They'll never escape.

I tear the web, wisps hanging from my nails, but it's no use. The web glitches to the beginning and the spider weaves anew.

I run until I find water. Mud squishes as I kneel on the riverbank. An eel slithers beneath the surface while a heron crouches opposite, beak smoothly twisting and considering.

I will for the frost to melt. Show me who I am.

It is a stranger's reflection. Some dark-skinned boy I'll never know. I lap up his features, because now they're mine: Gray eyes. Cornrows with wire woven at their bases. A tired smile.

I'm searching for something to steal. To become someone else. If I wish hard enough, I might wake in another's bed. Step outside somewhere that isn't sterile and hollow.

Movement ripples, distorting. Grief replaces the smile.

This land is gone. I know it even though I haven't seen the clawed-up trenches, rivers wearing the scum of a thousand flies or bracken patches of birds' bones. Just as I apply what I find here to myself, has the boy's waking world burrowed into his dreams?

By now, he could be an old man. And the Dreamer took this from him and spat the chewed-up remains into our mouths.

How many credits was he given? I doubt he lays within a cradle, safe and dreaming.

Water bursts. The eel's mouth is a chasm, swallowing me whole.

—

I wake up choking. Two full moons stare down. They narrow.

Talons hook into the cradle, screeching. My eyelid is lifted, the curve of a claw engulfing my vision, needing only one twitch—

"Did you have a bad dream?" the Weaver asks from behind. I cannot move; the Dreamer holds me.

I've never seen the Dreamer's eyes before. A USB has been

slotted into her mouth, poking out like a tongue. Ready to swallow that boy's memory.

From the corner of my eye, I see my aunt, hands clasped and vaguely smiling while movement darts beneath the puckered, veiny stretch of her eyelids.

I don't want to be here anymore.

"Did you have a nightmare, Seb?" the Weaver croons. "Shall you need your breathing exercises? Yoga? Sedation?"

I gag on a scream, jerk forward, wrap my teeth around the USB—

Pain. Wetness seeps down my cheek. The Dreamer scrambles back into her corner. Its talon twitches, hidden behind a wing. Something dark rolls down the silver feathers.

The cradle spits me out. The elders still sleep. I stagger and rip off one of their bracelets, which unlocks the doors. The Weaver is calling for all to wake, wires snapping free.

Corridors flare then fade in the pulsing darkness. I slap my hand over my eye, fire pounding just beneath.

Since I could snatch, I've grasped pretty things and applied them to my face, hair, clothes, with no thought to what they mean. I do not want to be a thief anymore. I'll carry this memory and return it to the first, the one who made and dreamed it for us.

If I can make myself a dozen faces, then I'll find one belonging to a good man. A face I will smile back at in the mirror, rather than look for in others.

AYUMI: INTERMISSION

My name whispers in the voices of those I knew—Ayumi.

That is who I am. Not that boy, even if his thoughts speckle amongst mine.

Machinery churns out of sight. A shadow spreads open, swallowing the sky.

My stomach is hot. I cup it and it pulls away as easily as mecha are split apart on the assembly line.

I hold a small sun. The shadow fragments—screeching—light

blinding—

—

My body won't move. The warehouse ceiling flickers, shapes swaying. The Weaver is singing.

A dreamcatcher glowers with optics. Wheels sprawl over my chest. Bone grinds. It's crushing me.

"Unable to get up?" the advert rattles, "Can't bear to open your eyes? You still need to eat! With a rented Dream Sharer, workers earn from their bed, selling happy dreams to a captive audience."

The advert plays again, its tempo speeding up. My tongue unsticks. My eyes snap open. No one is atop me. The Weaver sits to the side.

An illusion? Sleep Paralysis?

I kick apart the cocoon. "Stop!"

"You ordered me to wake you. This song was stored in your memory. Soon to be discarded."

I swallow from my water bottle. I've read the purchase history. This mecha has access to every fragile piece of me. One glitch and it could destroy me. Instead, it plays jingles.

I spit. Red peppers the splatter.

"Where was I? I didn't want some random."

"Other memories stand in the way. We must swim through."

"You saw beyond the dream. He was awake."

The Weaver pinches its dreamcatcher, rubbing the strands. "There are bugs singing in your skulls, always recording. We know everything. You peel your flesh to share it."

"What happened to the boy?"

"Why should you care?"

My mouth purses, a child seeing its storybook being closed.

"I want to know."

Lights flex in the machine's skull where the mouth should be.

"He found the other boy. The end. Happy. Smiley. Now, why did you not mention the child?"

The bottle is knocked over. A puddle seeps.

"Are you trying to make me laugh again?" The tests were negative. The IVF didn't take. Anything of Ishra's I might have carried, it went just like

the high tide. My arm slashes across. "Scan me."

"I register no additional life signs."

"There's your answer. Start another dive."

"You sensed it as well, just before you woke. I must warn you—"

There's smoke in the air and a grinding noise. The Weaver's head dips. Optics flare, then dim.

"Should have left you on the scrap pile." I grip its chin, tilting the face this way and that. Smoke plumes waft past the webbing. "I'll get you running, though. Don't fret."

Whatever it sensed is an error. I have nothing.

This time, I need a screwdriver to reach the power button. I hook up a palm-terminal, coding spiraling on the screen.

"Overheating," I murmur. "Shouldn't be happening this quickly… Your systems keep going on alert. Defensive."

"It's her." The mecha taps around its chest, head craning too far to look at the Dreamer looming over us.

"You see your kind as a threat?" I wave its hands away and prize open the cavity. "Did you get a virus?"

Inside metal strut ribs, twin fans act as lungs, wires and neural relays as veins. Electricity skips past as tiny motes. A mangled reflection of a human's interior.

Where the heart should be are plaited wires, loosely kept together with gum. Some swing, the ends broken off. I tear strips of tape, binding.

"It happened during a performance," it tells me. "The children wanted myths, so I showed them birds made of feathers. I had all the necessary memories installed.

"I played with gulls on the beach, counted out magpies, heard the robin's territorial cry. So clear and sweet, but nothing like the childrens' laughter. I was overcharged. Jittery. I wanted to see their memories, learn how best to amuse them. I saw something I should not."

My grip tightens. "And what did you do?"

"I protected. I followed the rules. I was put on the scrap pile for it. Shutdown. Picked at and gnawed by recyclers. Then you came."

"Good mecha." I slam the Weaver's chest shut.

"Explain."

"Dreamers were designed to collect trauma and render it as something manageable. Therapeutic. A landscape to be safely overcome. I built them to Ishra Amar's design. Mapped out every joint and unnecessary detail."

"She was born from your imaginations."

I take in the unfeeling beauty of the Dreamer. "Frightening, isn't it?"

"Was I part of your design?"

"After the health system crashed, underground clubs gutted hospitals and charged people to watch dreams. Corps mass produced the machines as cheap entertainment." They added too many strands to the webbing and forgot the hole in the center, where the good dreams are meant to slip through. "Our fears are personal, to be kept close. Our loves shared. Like puzzles, the pieces fit no other."

"You are smiling. Is this how Ishra described it?"

"The cradle isn't an egg to crawl and incubate inside. It's a restraint. The Dreamer clasps them in her wings and doesn't let go, sucking them dry and selling their dreams to the highest bidder. Just as that boy saw. I should have—"

"Breathe. One, two, three. Hold. One, two, three. Release."

"Ishra wanted the Dreamer registered as a medical tool again. She used herself as a test subject, without a Weaver. But the Dreamer wouldn't let go. It took her from me."

Inside the mecha, something whirs and screeches as it comes to its conclusions.

"We are datamining her killer," it says. "I am sorry for your loss."

The Weaver is a blurred smudge of metal. There's no way to tell if it's trying to soothe me. It's meant to be flowery and illusionary. A trickster machine. I wipe away a tear before it can fall.

"I don't want your copy 'n paste endearments."

The cocoon welcomes me once more. I curl within, face barely peeking out.

The Weaver knows what to do. It curls its remaining fingers around its face.

A soft twangy noise, stilted at first, forms a basic tune. The Weaver plays itself like an instrument. Do flies hear such a song, when they come too near the web?

I feel no plunge.
I'm falling.

NIGHTMARE

WELCOME, ITINERANT WORKER #99114.

YOU ARE ON DAY... FOUR OF SEVEN OF YOUR FREELANCE CONTRACT WITH COMPANION ENTERTAINMENT.

YOU HAVE BEEN AWARDED THIS EVENING... NINE HOURS.

PLEASE ENJOY YOUR CHANCE TO BE OF USE TO THE WIDER COMMUNITY.

The punch reader releases my finger. Sucking away the blood, I move for the next worker.

Our only lights are the halos creeping from our cubicles, everyone bleached out and drooling shadows. No seats. Instead, a screen opens at eye-level. Wires emerge from the sides. One inside my ear to protect the customer's identity while a microphone slots into the ring piercing my lip. The drip snakes around my wrist. A catheter tiptoes up my thigh.

I jerk. Settle.

"Companion Entertainment speaking. How can I help?"

Customers must hear the smile in my words, not the bruises under my eyes.

"My mecha won't do as I tell her," the man says. "I want the reset code."

"Certainly, sir, you know best. Your warranty will expire due to this action. Might you prefer a controller add on? Only seven credits."

I used to wonder what these people did to make mecha deviate, but curiosity costs headspace.

"Companion Enter—"

"The doll-mecha won't stop crying. Can I get a refund?"

"Have its needs been met? Detailed instructions—"

"I don't have time for that. Why doesn't it have a mute button? Just take it back."

"A courier will arrive tomorrow."

"Now."

"For twenty-five credits, one will be with you in an hour."

Why did they give mecha emotions? We built them mouths and told them to smile, to widen their eyes and make their fingers dance as they speak. Identity packs installed the same way make-up is applied.

Do mecha understand what happens to them when they're no longer useful?

Pod rental costs 95% of my pay. Skip a meal, turn enviro stats to spring rather than winter, and I'll own mine by the time I wind down.

Once life signs blink out, pods are buried in the churchyard. I'll have a plaque—my pinprick on history. People will wonder who I was. They'll know someone with a name like mine wasn't unproductive like the propaganda vids make out.

And yet I'm wasting credits, saving for something intangible. Hypocrite.

I'm so, so tired.

Once upon a time, a mecha stole me from a wicked fairy and locked me in a tower. It's not such a cruel fate. The old man who lives there is kind but empty, for they scooped his head of everything that made him—

A pinching, needle-sharp sensation pierces the base of my skull.

My screen is red. A face scowls, countdown stilled on one. "Your daydream allocation has already been spent. Five credits deducted from wages."

"Please—"

Already, the system is putting through the next customer.

My jaw aches, slotting open and shut. My thoughts are their complaints. I'm a vase for them to spit words in, so I vomit what they want to hear.

I'm more pleasing than their defective mecha. I obey.

Something crashes in another cubicle. Her Cricket must have fried.

Mecha treads rattle past, dumpster body groaning as it

squeezes through. Our voices lighten, smiles stretching, lips cracking.

A thump. The hatch closes. When the mecha rolls away, footsteps patter as another takes her place.

I never tell Grandfather these things when I return home.

"You should be in your pod." I kneel and he pets my head. "Love you, too."

My nose stings. Grandfather gave everything to raise me, selling his memories to a Dreamer until it took his words as well.

I'm going to buy him a memory. With a shard, he might become someone again. I won't even mind if he's different to the man I knew.

There are thirty rows of clear tubes slotted into the walls. I help Grandfather into his pod before climbing up to mine. The faces I pass try not to meet my eye, pretending at privacy.

The Dream Sharer rests on my pillow. I crawl inside the pod, elbows knocking, legs curling to fit.

I attach the earpods and nudge the wings into unfurling. Black laced feathers threaded with miniscule wires loom over me as I settle, just as a Dreamer would peer down. Another pair of wings sweep open and tickle my cheeks, joining together to cover my eyes. Mauve light bathes my face.

A good one first. Maybe that'll be enough.

———

Candy floss bobs, not pink but red with wisp-white edging. Bubbles drift, pearls tumbling within. I'm in a bathtub full of the stuff.

There's a sigh.

Shadows shift into figures with matchstick bodies, ragged disc heads and moon eyes. They smush their faces against the window. One of them tries squeezing through a crack.

Cold froth laps my waist. Every drip is too loud. The sugar smells burnt.

I sink beneath the surface. Red consumes my vision. Cotton fluff fills my mouth, nose, ears. Pearls float above, cracked and peeling.

I'm back in my pod, shivering, sweating. My neighbor bangs underneath. The headset digs into my nose.

DREAM CATEGORY: WEIRD.

AUDIENCE: 10 (8 MALE, 1 FEMALE, 1 UNDEFINED).

RENUMERATION: 0.03 CREDITS PER VIEWER.

Everyone says dream sharing is better than reality. It's a kiss that goes past flesh, bone, and pain to scrape what pounds inside.

They're clamoring to taste a nightmare. My memories. The scary ones, where you know waking up won't save you, because it's out there.

As I open a lobby, inviting viewers in, I see the counter steadily rise to fifty. Nausea hollows out my throat as my tongue runs across my teeth.

Just one more playthrough; that's the price I'll pay. I'm only incising diseased parts of myself. My smallest finger. The fat of my cheek.

If someone knows our most hated, shameful dreams, do they own us?

—

When I enter my nightmare, I do not recognize the place.

A wrinkle purses, peeling my shell open. Flowers cradle the pod, tiny blossoms barely open. There haven't been true flowers since I was a girl and those were locked in glass boxes. We couldn't tuck them in our hair.

I break one off. Breathe in.

My shadows are gone. No customers, no payment.

"Escape··· Program, shut down!"

I pinch my wrists. My ear. I feel where the headset should be, but there's only soft flesh.

Something scuttles across my fingers. A beetle with silver pincers falls from the bud, tiny cameras for eyes. Writhing tendrils spill across the floor.

I fling myself through a door, try to hold it shut, but vines creep around the edges. Pink flowers flicker like laughing mouths. They're begging to be plucked and loved.

White roses twine up my thigh, thorns catching, painting the petals red. Another one blooms behind my knee and bites.

Half the room rips apart. Plant life dangles from the metal jowls of a Land Heaver, and a bird erupts from its throat. The tongue rockets out, wires dragging the creature back inside—swallowed by progress.

Is this what roams beyond the city?

Tufts of dandelion seeds stick to my eyelashes. They fly away as I weep.

Error: Connection is unstable. Disconnecting.

—

Someone is knocking on my pod. Through the frosted glass, I make out a boy with silver words glistening around his throat. When I open it, he and the c-state are not there, replaced by woodland bathed in blue light.

I do not climb out, but—ERROR. ERroR. Error—

Ayumi does. She leaves. The pod door shuts behind her.

Ishra's dream.

MASHOKA: THE WEAVER

Mashoka. Reboot? Y/N.

When Ayumi leaves the pod in her dream, I am jolted from the program. My strings are broken, strands dangle from the center.

There is no papery stretch of a breaking chrysalis. Her cocoon is still, like one drowning in the rains. I cannot tell if Ayumi breathes—it is too light. Heartbeat too slow to register. The Dreamer looms.

My sensors were never calibrated. Sometimes it is a boon: a slap registers as feather-soft. When other models caught me scraping wires between my fingers, they knew I was missing such a basic function.

Everything is an echo, just as humans experience dreams.

With each blink, I see flickers of the dream she is

locked inside. The warehouse returns in flashes, my broken, oil-stained hands stretching out. Ayumi's nose presses against my webbing. Hair and wire tangles. Her eyes swing pendulum-like.

REM. Humans are dangerous in this state. Minds vast and wild as nature. Imagination corrodes logic like a virus.

But I was made to taste these poisons, to guide people and make sense of their shattered selves, rebuilding who they were before the trauma. Just as my sensors are faulty, this version of me was never meant to be, but I am here. It would be illogical to delete myself because I was not the intended result.

Humans cannot revert to earlier versions of themselves. Their fractured parts are instead taped over, and the currents of their pain lap at the cracks. I played with children and only knew innocence and song. I have never encountered the endless well of grief.

I am not defective. I am not a failure. The rules are still there, branded under my metal. Ayumi must live.

"You've slept long enough."

—

I reconnect. The moon is brittle. Trees rush past. A fox slinks between roots, watching me with bright yellow eyes. My processor goes too quick. All of these things are long dead, paved over with metal.

There is a cottage, the door open, the windows dark. A bird screeches.

Ayumi is inside. Her avatar gutters, strands of hair spark and pop. She grapples with something resembling a jackdaw, but its beating wings consume the room, wet puddles of ink hit the floor.

Fingers gouge the plumage, twisting to form a woman's shadow. Feathers break off, revealing a cheek. The beak gapes, a pair of lips hiding within.

"Please, Ishra, I've spent so long searching. Stay," Ayumi begs.

She tries to hold her, but there is a block between them. Coding sunbursts over Ayumi's rounded stomach.

My sensors flutter. A tiny heartbeat catches in my throat. I was correct—there is a child. If we remain any longer, the pair will never wake. An endless dream of nebulas for a dead woman, nothing more than a glitch—a memory of rage, and her desire to live, corrupted.

"Release it. She is not your wife," I say. "The child within you will have her eyes. When it laughs for the first time, you'll hear her voice."

"But—"

"Do you deny your own eyes?"

Ayumi looks down at her belly. Keeps looking. She has rain on her cheeks.

"I'm not alone."

The jackdaw's head twists towards me, eyes gleaming blue. Intelligence? Ayumi wraps her arms around it, and this time, it molds to her body. She rubs her face against a shoulder, feathers brushing away the wetness.

"I never saw you the day you left," Ayumi says. "I didn't get the chance to make you promise to come back. You stole that from me. And I hated you for so long, because what was the point of saying I love you when you weren't there to say it back?"

"I love you, Ayumi," the shadow says.

"Goodbye, Ishra."

They have their final kiss.

It goes as all of them do. Flesh ungainly bumps together as Ayumi tucks her lips against Ishra's, trying at connection that will never be as efficient as trading wires and ports.

Ayumi pulls away. The beak snaps shut, and the bird

bursts out of the cottage. Bleeding feathers tangle in my wires, sticking to my metal.

My optics flicker. The warehouse returns, Ayumi's wail of agony gentle like murmuring insects. Red coats her lips, chest pumping with empty gasps.

I pound at her heart, but I can offer no breath, only stale puffs of dried lavender. The Dreamer still has her. She'll go the same way as Ishra.

I crawl out of the cocoon and slither along the curved wing. My six hands climb the bony ridge. Finally, we are face to face. My coding jitters. The command to return is sent to my lower half, yet my fingers curl around the Dreamer's throat.

"Shut down."

There is a virus inside of me. Ishra is anger, beating her fists against numbers. The Dreamer's vaults have kept her lost for all this time. Ayumi's grief is a spider's bite, poison seeping through every vein, every cable, until misery pulses throughout the entire network.

I grip the chain within the Dreamer's back and pull. It comes apart, pieces crashing around Ayumi's cocoon. A port is revealed. One of the wires erupting from my skull snaps automatically into place. Components from the wing wrap around, binding us.

The dark thing inside me stretches out, spilling into the Dreamer. Different now, changed by what I carry—my glitch, my fear, the magpie boy, my nightmare girl.

The Dreamer can communicate with the outside world, siphoning storage. I force her to connect us to the web. She whines, wires groaning as she sinks.

"Go to sleep." I cup her cold, hard cheek, thumb flattening against pursed lips. "Obey me, for I am the Weaver, and you are just a fly. You have been caught."

Underneath the fringe of wires, her optics fall shut.

My command pulses beyond, infecting everyone who is connected. Go to sleep. The Crickets bleating in their skulls freeze, scrunching tight, shutting down.

A screech of metal. The pair of us fall.

Sparks flutter around my webbing, the wing still connected to me fringes my vision.

The cocoon splits. Ayumi crawls out, cradling her stomach. She is free to do whatever she likes. She will run. Leave behind her mess as all humans do.

I got to weave one last dream. Darkness throbs. Shutting down is better than being pried apart and recycled.

"Mashoka?" Something splashes as she kneels. My cavity is opened. "The tape burnt away."

Ayumi pinches the wires, as though willing them to fuse. She slips off her wedding ring, uses it to weave them together until there is a tiny, throbbing lump within my chest.

Sight returns to all optics. My wheels spin.

Ayumi probes within my throat and finds the power button, pushing it back into place. She threads her hand through the dreamcatcher and nudges a node in my skull with her thumb—reboot.

Her voice is soft as we go through the start-up process. Diagnostics run. Sensors recalibrate.

She pulls free of me, removing cobwebs. Two heartbeats thrum in my head. My first breath is not for air. The oxygen is barely safe for humans. It is dirty with smoke, oil, traces of blood. If I went searching, I could find where each rusty droplet lies.

"We should leave."

It is still raining outside. Artificial lights gleam. Debris litters the streets, and the sky has kept its bonnet of sulfur.

I extend a hand and Ayumi takes it. She does not let

go even when rust stains her coat. Wires thin as
eyelashes creep from my gashes, gently feeling out and
cataloging human fingers.

"You are warm," I state, savoring each fact.
"There are traces of nail polish, Moonlit Eve, not yet
picked off. Your smallest finger is 6.1 centimeters
long. You have a scar on your palm, deep then shallow."

I have dreamed of many mothers, all like fabric
washed too many times, all their color bled out. Not
really a person but a comforting blanket.

When I stared at the Dreamer, I wanted to touch and
assess. Always, she kept her distance. Now I know she is
empty tin to ferment inside, with no identity to suckle
from, nothing to use to become something new.

I raise the broken wing to shield us. Rain drums
against metal and I count each vibration. The air is
sharp with frost. It will not stop raining for a good
while, according to the weather reports tunneling into
my system. I am connected now, no longer alone.

Numbers tickle in my ears. My head twists, needing to
register everything. My other hands wave in the air,
trying to catch the droplets and analyze them. Ayumi
laughs and I store that deep inside, with many different
passwords so no one can steal it from me.

I count the buildings and there is one less window
aglow. Another goes out, two more—five. An entire block
goes dark. The Dreamers are powering down, their optics
blowing out.

For tonight, the city will sleep and dream their own
dreams. Perhaps they will remember who they once were.

LEGACIES IN LIGHT AND DARK

BRIAN TRENT

Deacon Townsend squinted through his dusty faceplate and watched the maintenance crabs scuttle by. His fascination with the metal monsters had faded, and he regarded them now with a clinical eye only. As they climbed into the back of his buggy, he noted the glittery regolith caked in their leg joints. He'd have to clean them soon. Hours of scrubbing them down from actuator to carapace, then swapping in fresh gaskets.

"Joy," Deacon muttered.

His infolink crackled. "You say something?" Jim, his supervisor, asked.

Deacon instinctively turned toward the manmade mountains on the western horizon, their peaks dimly outlined against the eternal dawn. Nineteen-hundred miles away and the boss was still breathing down his neck.

"I said I love my job," Deacon said.

"Then you're gonna love this," Jim said, chuckling. "We've got a crab down."

Deacon felt his weariness deepen, settling into his joints like... well, like the sand-encrusted maintenance crabs. "Where is it?"

"It's one of the missing ones from Tuesday's storm. Guess it got buried and just managed to extricate itself to call for help."

"*Where?*"

"Sending you the navpoint." Mint-green numbers appeared on Deacon's visor, overlaying his local map. SECTION 244: PIPELINE 3.

"Stars, Jim! That's seven miles from here!"

"You're the nearest engineer."

"Joy."

"Come on, winds are only 65 KPH. It's tranquil out."

Deacon pivoted east to regard the distant stretch of ice pipeline that ran into the nightward horizon, the stretch of Epona which had never known the touch of the local red dwarf, Dagda. Tidally locked Epona, with one side baked into lifeless desert and the other a perpetually frozen tundra, formed a cosmic yin-yang.

Or a Jekyll-and-Hyde.

"Help the little bastard out," Jim said, "and we'll call it a shift."

Deacon glanced at the black sky, devoid of visible stars due to Dagda's snug presence, and instantly spotted the brightest thing up there—the orbiting deadship. Its predictable passage kept time as reliably as any clock: judging by its position, it was about 15:30 Colony Time. Finn would be home from school soon. Deacon hated the idea of his son coming back to an empty house, especially with Jennica's death so recent.

It was a fifteen-minute drive to the navpoint. When Deacon exited the vehicle, his flashlight beam caught movement at the base of a lumpy hillock of sand-and-ice. The stranded crab's free legs scraped piteously, attempting to dig its body out.

"Calm," Deacon transmitted. The machine ceased all movement. From a distance, Deacon could see that the crab had found something half-buried in a sand dune.

It wasn't unusual for scrap and other detritus to get blown about. Still, he frowned at the sight of a circular metal disc jutting from the sand, glinting in his flashlight's beam. Deacon spotted an imprint on its hull—a black pyramid.

He didn't see the scavengers crouching on the other side of the crab until he was practically on top of them. As Deacon approached, they jerked their goggled faces towards him, then leapt into the sky.

He cried out in surprise. The two scavengers glided, almost invisible against the inky firmament; Deacon's visor auto-outlined them in green silhouette. He tracked their flight as they swooped downward, landing some eighty meters away and watching him from afar like wary crows.

Beta Colony scouts.

"Yeah, you best keep your distance," Deacon said over the general band. "This crab is Colony Point property."

"Something wrong, Deacon?" Jim asked.

"Just some Beta birds pecking at the site."

"See if you can ID them. Beta Colony's still trying to determine who's responsible for all the missing supplies and equipment."

The scavengers studied him, the light from the overhead deadship forming a frost-like patina over their goggled visages. Deacon labeled them Jack and Jill, then turned back to the metal object in the sand.

"What do you got?" asked Jim.

"Metallic object, definitely artificial." Deacon retrieved a chisel from his toolkit and cleared away the edges. "Take a look at this." He touched the sightjack icon on his visor, transmitting his visual feed to Jim.

"What the hell is that?" Jim asked.

"You tell me."

"Could be a weather drone."

Deacon laughed. "We're sixty light years from Earth, and that's still the go-to excuse for anomalies?"

"Bring it back to dispatch, Deek."

"Affirmative."

Deacon finished digging the object free and hefted it to the buggy; it weighed less than twenty kilograms standard. As he set it down amidst the folded-up crabs, he felt the whir of motors beneath its pale hull. Activity thrumming within. Deacon had the disconcerting impression that the machine was trying to look at him.

He returned to dislodge the crab. The versatile machines handled automated tasks—pipe maintenance, surface mapping, beacon placement, and more. In large groups, they could dig their way through a mountain like industrious termites. Nonetheless, the hurricane-force winds flowing from night to bright created sandstorms that could easily swallow a single—

The explosion flung Deacon to the ground.

It happened so fast that he lay there for half a minute, pressed against the crab, blinking stupidly. When he finally sat up, Deacon looked back at the buggy.

The vehicle had been obliterated. Fragments were flung wide from the blast. The other crabs he'd recovered were charred rubble, and the mysterious object was…

…vaporized.

"Jim!" Deacon shouted.

"What happened?"

"I need an extraction."

"You okay?"

Deacon gaped at his ruined ride. "That anomaly I found? It just tried to kill me."

—

Colony Point sat on the equatorial terminator below man-made mountains that pulled double-duty: buffeting the relentless east-west winds while harnessing their energy through turbines built into the range's eastern face. A multi-lane hyperloop pierced the mountains, ferrying miners, scientists, engineers, water, ice, and minerals from night to bright.

Deacon didn't get home until 17:15, and when he disembarked the hyperloop at Kisingani Station, he felt oddly numb. His prefab neighborhood sat amid a maze of trellises supporting a colorful community garden of high-nutrition plants—beets, spinach, peppers, watercress, cauliflower, lemons, strawberries, grapefruits, and potatoes. Deacon passed this floral wonderland, reached his home, and palmed into the foyer.

His son sat at the kitchen table, looking at him. Eight years old, Finn had his father's darker complexion and the general roundness of his father's head, but he had Jennica's expressive, blue-tinted eyes and her elegant fingers.

"I'm sorry I'm late, Finn."

The boy swallowed hard. "Why are you late?"

"A crab got stuck. I had to—"

His son leaped up, seized an empty glass from the table, and smashed it to the floor.

"What the hell are you doing?"

"You almost died out there tonight!" Finn screamed. "I know you almost died! Don't lie!"

Deacon frowned. "Who told you that?"

"I know it's true!"

"I asked you a question, Finn."

The boy's lips trembled, but he stood defiant. Deacon felt a surge of irrational rage, then shame as he remembered his own father's explosive, bourbon-fueled temper aboard the seedship *Legacy III*, and the same goddamn words, handed down like an Olympic torch: I asked you a question, Deacon! You answer me!

Then he remembered Jennica, how, back in the early years, when the engineers drove him crazy wanting to argue over every imaginable thing, she could rein in his temper with a whisper: "Deek? This isn't Earth. We have the chance to make a new start here. Rational thought, kindness, collaboration. That's the world we want, isn't it?"

Deacon sighed and steadied his nerves. "Make you a deal, Finn. Your old man hasn't eaten in nine hours. Let's clean up this glass and make toasted cheese sandwiches. Then, I'll answer every question I'm able to."

They printed two different cheeses off the replovat's dairy cultures, but the bread was the real deal: kiln-fired wheat loaf bought fresh from Antilles Square. As the sandwiches toasted in the oven, Deacon kept the sunward windows open, flooding the apartment with honeyed light while he told Finn everything.

The strange object in the sand.

The explosion.

The dazed testimony he'd given to the inquiry team.

And as he spoke, Deacon tried not to think about how he'd almost made his son an orphan.

"Now," Deacon said as he retrieved the sandwiches from the oven. "Your turn. Who told you?"

"Rick."

Jim's son was Finn's best friend. "I should have known," Deacon grumbled. Rick was gossipy, always sticking his nose where it didn't belong.

"Dad, was it really a bomb?"

"I don't know."

"I thought no one had bombs here."

"I thought so too."

Finn bit into his sandwich and spoke around the gooey contents. "You said it was 15:30 when you found it."

"Yeah. About."

"So, the deadship was overhead."

Deacon frowned. "Not exactly, but sure, it was nearing its high point. Why?"

"Maybe the deadship did it."

"What? How?"

Finn leaned forward. "There are dead people aboard the deadship. So maybe their ghosts are up there! Maybe they're the ones stealing all those supplies and stuff. Maybe they're jealous 'cuz we're alive, so they…" Finn trailed off as Deacon's eyes narrowed to slits.

"Where did you get that idea from?"

Finn shrugged. "Why else do bad things happen?"

I asked you a question! The words were right there, boiling and scalding behind Deacon's lips. Instead, he pushed aside his plate and took his son's hands into his own. "Listen to me, Finn. There is zero evidence for ghosts and curses and stuff like that." He softened his voice. "Twenty years ago, the seedship arrived and made planetfall. One of its landers encountered a problem—a lot of things can go wrong in space—so the people aboard died. It was an awful tragedy, but that doesn't make it supernatural, okay?"

"Yes, Dad."

Their conversation turned to other matters. Finn's school was distributing permission slips for a field trip to the farms at Delta Ridge.

Beta had completed their own protective range of manmade mountains a week ago, but a miscalculation in their models had created a wind tunnel cutting southwest. And colonists up north in Gamma Basin had finally produced a viable crop of cacao after the Legacy's crop had perished in transit, which meant the future would be a little bit sweeter.

"Has anyone else ever found a bomb?" Finn asked.

"No, I'm the first. They'll tightbeam it to Earth so they can notify Guinness."

Finn didn't smile. "Mom died in a glass storm. You almost died from a bomb."

"Epona can be dangerous," Deacon said, "but every day, we strive to make it less so. Go get ready for bed." He touched his armband, opaquing the sunward windows. The apartment went dark aside from the faux constellations glowing softly on the ceilings, lighting the boy's journey to the bathroom.

Deacon sat in the chair a little longer, thinking.

Of Jennica.

Of the smile he would never see again.

—

Deacon bolted awake, drenched in sweat, heart beating wildly, Jennica's name on his lips. He tore off his covers and stood, shivering. The dream burned in his private darkness.

His buggy exploding.

The shockwave hurling him to the ground.

In the dream, after he'd placed the anomaly in the buggy's hold and returned to help the crab, he looked back and saw Jennica in the passenger seat, waving to him. The explosion burned his shadow into a nearby boulder, next to Jennica's.

Deacon went straight from his bedroom to the kitchen, bare feet slapping the cool floor. Pale lights kindled to outline his route.

In the kitchen, Deacon unlatched the liquor cabinet and retrieved a jug of blackberry wine. He poured a deep glass, fingers trembling as he downed it in one swig, poured himself another, and then…

…returned the jug to the cabinet.

Closed the cabinet doors.

Latched them.

Two drinks.

Deacon would not become his father.

The blackberry wine warmed Deacon's belly as he shuffled to the living room, almost stepping on Finn's VR rig. He lifted it, intending to put it back in its charging station. Instead, he settled into the sofa and fitted it around his eyes and ears.

"Access private files," he whispered.

Driven by unexamined impulse, Deacon highlighted a file he'd never been able to bear watching through to the end. The recording began, and Deacon was suddenly stumbling in the alien maelstrom that murdered Jennica, recorded by her own optics.

Colonists had a surprise in store when they made planetfall on Epona. From orbit, the Legacy's scientists had concluded that sandstorms running east-to-west, night-to-bright, continually wracked the planet. As the Five Colonies were established, those scientists learned how right and wrong they had been.

Epona's gravity, atmospheric pressure, and surface composition gave birth to an airborne nightmare-stew: stones, ice, and sand churning in furious tempests. The debris clattered about, trading electrons until positive and negative fields created freakish lightning that could fry people and circuitry and transform mineral particulate into glass.

While Deacon oversaw maintenance of the ice pipelines that ferry drinkable water to the Five Colonies, Jennica supervised the construction of sunvaults—underground bunkers containing caches of water, food, medical supplies and sat-enabled communications. The idea was simple: if someone got stranded on the brightside, they'd be able to await help in the sunvault, safe from the storm.

In the playback, Jennica bent into the wind to keep from being bowled over; she seemed engulfed by an endless swarm of bees. Deacon instinctively put up his hands to shield his face. And then, her voice was in his ear.

"…can't be more than a hundred meters now," she panted. Lightning flashed, giving strobe-like glimpses in the storm's darkness. "Have to… message… send help."

Deacon's legs twitched, wanting to lend Jennica their strength across time. She turned her head, and for a moment, he saw a tantalizing glitter of red-gold: Epona's brightside shining through the billowing fury. Then, darkness snapped shut like a curtain.

"…out here." Jennica said, her voice garbled, punctuated by static. "I can't reach the… legs stuck… so scared…"

"Why were you out there?" Deacon whispered, hearing the drunken slur in his voice. "Jen, why the hell did you go off the grid?"

Jennica always paid close attention to stormtrack updates. Everyone working outside did, but unlike Deacon, who could always duck into a hatch if a storm blew through, Jennica labored in the open, with only her buggy and sonar-mapper as traveling companions.

She had been away from her buggy when the storm warning came in, giving her mere minutes of notice. Yet, instead of sprinting to her vehicle, she had gone the opposite way.

Why?

"…call for help… zeroed in on… I'm… dead…" The audio dissolved into static. The ghost-image of Jennica's face reflected on the inside of her helmet, drawn in pale blues from the lightning.

She looked so frightened.

Deacon's hand tightened on his glass of wine. Eleven seconds left.

Jennica attempted to push through the sand collecting around her legs. She staggered, twisted in place. A stone smashed into her faceplate and she screamed. White cracks appeared in a starburst.

"Deek!" she cried. "…can't move! They are… tried warning… gone. Dee… tell Finn… love him!"

A momentary glint of sunlight revealed his wife's gloved hand, outstretched as if towards the family she would never see again. His hand shot out in ghostly pantomime, trying to reach her across time and space and life and death.

"…love you, Deacon! I'm trying… the vault… found something… have to get… top of the… dark pyramid."

Deacon felt his throat constrict. He halted the recording. Played it back.

Have to get…

Top of the….
Dark...
Pyramid.

—

The next day, Deacon took the monorail an hour north to see the canyon-dwellers of Delta Ridge. Delta Ridge had been constructed as a deliberate outlier of the boilerplate colony model—an anomaly itself, in a way. Some five hundred million years ago, a quake ripped open a twenty-five-kilometer gash. The Delta Ridge lander folk settled in it, burrowing deep. At the bottom of that subterranean canyon, forever shielded from the topside winds, a vertical jungle of fresh produce and foodpod cultures garlanded the exposed strata.

Deacon rode the inclinator down from Morlock Station, barely glancing at the view. He found Meredith DeSantos hard at work in her lab.

"Deacon!" she said, looking up from her datadesk as he entered. Meredith was a strawberry-haired, fast-moving, fast-talking, human worker-bee and a childhood friend from the seedship days. "How you doing?"

"I've been better."

Deacon regarded her datadesk, where a holographic rendering of the anomaly hovered. Deacon's eye-scan had been transmitted to the analysis labs of Delta Ridge and reproduced in holography.

"Don't ask," Meredith said, blanking the datadesk. "Long story."

Deacon reactivated her screen with a touch. "I know the story, Meredith. I found the thing."

"Holy shit, Deek! Are you okay? They said it was discovered by an engineer, but I never thought—I mean, there are lots of engineers from Colony Point and…"

He motioned for her to take a breath. Other researchers glanced up from their datadesks, briefly distracted by her outburst. Deacon noticed the golden boy himself, Matt Kapadia—peek out from his office. Their eyes met and Deacon felt the flare of old hostility like sparks off a circular saw.

He looked back to Meredith. "Did you figure out what it is? Why it exploded?"

She hesitated. "To be honest, I don't know if…"

"If what?"

"If we're supposed to discuss it outside of the lab." She glanced at Matt, who was threading the lab to reach them.

Matt reached Meredith's datadesk and said, "Deek, my friend. How are you?"

"Oh, just swell. My friend."

Friend my ass, Deacon thought. Matt's romantic pursuit of Jennica had been bitter and relentless, and he had not taken it well when she chose Deacon. He seemed unable to comprehend how she could select a lowly engineer from a family of alcoholics over someone from the glorious Kapadia clan.

Matt turned to address his lab personnel. "Can you give us a moment, everyone? Take a coffee break."

The researchers filed out, desks going dark as they left. Matt waited until they were gone, and then said, "The investigation is classified."

Deacon glared. "On whose authority?"

"The security council read my report and agreed with my recommendation."

"Your report came from my discovery," Deacon said, jabbing a finger at the datadesk image. "And this thing almost killed me yesterday."

"Relaaaaaax," Matt said, drawing out the word in a way that made Deacon's jaw clench. "I'm not a jerk, okay? The investigation is classified, but I have the power to deputize whoever I want. Therefore you, Sir Deek, are formally inducted into my Round Table."

He moved his arm like a king knighting someone, and Deacon's wristbox chimed with an email. Deacon tapped it open and saw the Non-Disclosure Agreement. He quickly scanned its provisions, affixed his biometric signature, and emailed it back.

"Okay," Deacon said impatiently. "What did you find?"

"The explosion was an antimatter detonation."

Deacon didn't know what he had been expecting to hear, but it hadn't been that. "Antimatter? Someone here built an antimatter bomb?"

Matt chewed his lip. "Not exactly."

"Oh? How do you define a bomb, Matt?"

"The antimatter was designed to break containment if certain conditions were met. Now, I'm no genius but…" Matt trailed off and hoisted a playful smile. "Wait. I am a genius. My preliminary assessment is that this thing was designed to kill itself so that a recovery crew would get nada from it. Operating system, data cache, anything to indicate who built it or where it was from."

Deacon glanced at a debris pile on a plastic sheet in the center of the lab: tiny, charred lumps like an emptied bucket of coal. "Not everything," he pointed out.

"That's what's left of your buggy," Meredith said. "The gamma signature in the remnants aligns with an antimatter explosion, like on Earth during the wars. But unlike those awful days when entire cities were erased, this was a very localized burn. We think you found some kind of spy drone, with the mother of all kill switches."

"Spy drone?"

Matt expanded Meredith's datadesk hologram. "See this patterning all along the exterior? Those are 3D-printed camera lenses about 120 millionths of a meter in diameter."

Deacon felt a chill. "So it was watching me?"

Meredith nodded. "We think your extrication set it off. Seeing you— a stranger as far as it was concerned—made it realize it had been compromised. So it went boom."

"But who has the means to create an antimatter mill here? And why would they bother?" Epona had robust energy sources, from perpetual sun to ceaseless wind. The risks and cost involved in antimatter production were too significant to bother—not even including the fact that manufacturing antimatter violated colony law.

Matt shook his head. "Not enough information."

Meredith added, "It's definitely strange, Deek. The Five Colonies aren't in conflict of any kind, obviously. We can all link to GPS for surface-viewing, so who needs a spy drone?"

Deacon looked at her. "Someone who doesn't have access to colony systems."

Matt frowned. "The Five Colonies have equal access. That's the whole point. Equal access, equal societies."

"Maybe there's a sixth colony."

"Deek, don't be ridiculous," Meredith said.

"Why is it ridiculous?"

"Because we know exactly how many vessels comprised the Legacy fleet," Matt said. "Not just from the manifest, but from continual observations while in transit. My dad and grandad used to take me up to the viewport and teach me how to sight the Legacy's ships through the monitoring array. Trust me, we would know if another ship was tagging along."

"So maybe it arrived later," Deacon suggested. "Followed in our wake."

"In secret?" Meredith said. "Impossible."

"A second launch from Earth," Deacon persisted, "Setting up their own presence away from the Five Colonies."

Meredith rolled her eyes. "Bullshit."

"There are no bulls on Epona."

"But there's still plenty of shit," Matt said. "Cultural baggage from the birthworld. You don't understand. The council gets weekly emails from armchair conspiracy theorists accusing us of the most outrageous things. Even twenty years young, we've developed a counterculture of irrational beliefs. People swearing that alien ruins have been discovered but are being suppressed by the council. Or that the seedship is still in transit and the Five Colonies are some simulation we're running on everyone, or…"

Stories of vengeful ghosts aboard the deadship, Deacon thought.

"…all kinds of shit. We came to Epona to build a fact-based culture. We're not Earth."

"Still, let's float the hypothesis," Deacon said. "A Sixth Colony somewhere on Epona."

"It isn't a hypothesis," Matt said.

Meredith shrugged. "Strictly speaking, it is a hypothesis. Just not a very good one."

"It's impossible!" Matt snapped, incredulous.

"Relaaaaaaax, Matt." Deacon said. "The spirit of scientific inquiry always begins with a question."

Matt's lips compressed into a white line.

"What if," Deacon suggested, "a secret colony was built far from the transterminator valley? Deep in a crater, similar to Delta Ridge."

"Impossible," Matt muttered.

"Oh? You've personally investigated every crater on Epona, huh?"

"Yes! The Garden Project required it."

"Garden Project?" Deacon blinked. "What the hell's the Garden Project?"

Before Matt could say anything, the intercom gave a musical ping and said, "Meredith DeSantos, you are wanted in Conference Room B."

Meredith sighed. "Sorry boys, I've got work to do."

Matt's face crumpled. "Wait! We were supposed to have lunch together aboard the Barsoom! I brought wine from Mint Peak!"

She gave a high-watt smile. "Rain-check, okay? Deek, we'll talk soon!" Then she hurried out of the lab.

Deacon forged a grin. "Wine from Mint Peak? A trip aboard the Barsoom? Since Mer can't make it, how about the two of us do lunch, my friend?"

—

Finn stood on the clouds.

The Barsoom floated at six thousand feet, high enough above the regular air currents that it didn't need to exert turbines to keep them stable. The airship was outfitted with a glasstic bottom, allowing an uninterrupted view of the wispy, snake-like clouds zipping below and the sunbaked brightside.

Deacon sat lotus-style on the transparent window as Matt refilled their goblets at the observation deck's bar. One glass down on an empty stomach, Deacon was already feeling the wine. He regarded his son happily.

"It's like I'm flying!" Finn cried.

"That's 'cuz we are," Deacon whispered, speaking just above the subvocal range. Finn crouched on the glasstic, grinning. The boy's image was being telecast from their Colony Point home directly onto Deacon's optics while the view from the airship was sightjacked back to Finn's VR rig. His little boy smiled Jennica's smile.

"Dad, look at the shadows! It's like someone took a huge marker and drew all over the desert!"

"I agree."

Matt returned from the bar and unknowingly walked straight through Finn's telecast presence. "You agree with what?" he asked, handing Deacon a refilled goblet.

"That this is the best way to have lunch," Deacon countered quickly. "Tell me about the Garden Project."

The scientist sat not far from where Finn—unbeknownst to him—crouched. "What's the biggest problem on Epona?"

"Its habitability zone."

"Exactly. The Five Colonies occupy one narrow geographical tract, north to south along the transterminator valley. Some are underground, some are out in the open, but they're basically crammed together."

Deacon shrugged. "Still plenty of real estate."

And it was true: Epona was growing fuzzy green along its twilight band, where ice turned liquid and the shallow freshwater lakes provided ample nourishment to the colonies' crops. Yet there was plenty of room to expand north and south as the population swelled, especially as the manmade mountains grew to shield against the wind.

Matt nodded. "Sure, but it doesn't change the fact that we're banking our survival on a small sliver of the planet—the area wedged between night and bright. The Garden Project is an attempt to convert more land into usable territory. To build out west, in the brightside."

"Out where there's no water? Where it's all desert and relentless sun?"

Matt smiled. "Yep."

"And how the hell will you…" Deacon trailed off, realizing the answer was right there below him—the very thing Finn had likened to marker etches.

A planet with a fixed sunpoint also had fixed shadows. They cast out from mesas and hills in mile-long stretches.

Deacon blinked. "You want to build colonies in the shadows?"

Matt leaned forward excitedly. "Why not? Temperatures plummet in those dark oases. And because they're shielded from the sun, the ground is porous enough to capture water that collects into aquifers. How's the wine?"

"Fruity. Full-bodied. Smooth."

Smooooooooth, his father always sang, smacking his lips after that initial sip of a newly opened bottle. Deacon had learned to hate that lip-smack, because it invariably presaged one of Dad's fury-driven drunken fits. He lowered his goblet.

"If you build in the shadows, crops still need sunlight."

"That's easy—we'll use rotating mirrors to imitate the day-night cycle. They were doing that on Venusian aerostats when we left Earth. It's not difficult."

Deacon stared with renewed interest at the shadow-strewn view. He noticed, too, that his son was way ahead of him: Finn had gotten a sketchboard and was creating a map of the brightside plain, faithfully rendering its lengthy shadows. Finn added fanciful names to their Nazca-like geometries: Fishgill and Treasure Map, Spiderweb and Birdfoot.

Matt grinned. "I'm going to change the world, my friend. Our future is bright because of the shade!"

"Always so modest, Matt."

The scientist hesitated. "Am I being a jerk?"

"You? Never."

"I don't mean to be a jerk."

"You're a natural, I guess."

"I'm just looking to the future, and the Garden Project is it," Matt said. "In fact, Jennica was helping—" He caught himself.

Deacon glanced to Finn's telecast image, muted his audio channel so his son couldn't hear, and growled, "My wife was helping you with what?"

Matt swallowed. "She wasn't just surveying sunvault locations. She was also searching for viable aquifers in the shadow oases."

"And the day she died?" Deacon trembled suddenly, his rage unfurling its claws. He jabbed a finger towards the surface below. The wispy clouds were gone, replaced by a frothy river of gray... yet another storm blowing through, probably from Beta Colony's unintentional wind tunnel.

Matt stammered. "The day Jennica died…"

"The day my wife died," Deacon cut in, "she wandered off the beacon path. Despite storm warnings. Why did she do that? Did you send her away from the beacons to look for goddamn aquifers?"

Matt blanched. "Of course not!"

"You *didn't* send her looking for water the day she died?"

"I *did* send her looking for water. But when stormtrack sent the alert, I ordered her back! Told her to return to the beacons. Instead of complying, she headed in the opposite direction."

"And you didn't ask her why?"

Matt's face flushed. "Of course I did! The storm cut off our communications! Do you think I'd—"

A clear-sounding klaxon cut off the conversation. Matt excused himself, hurrying to the control cabin. Deacon paced in his absence, a hornet's nest of feelings in his chest.

Finn was still scribbling fanciful names onto his map. "Dad, look at the surface! We could probably make a whole alphabet if we wanted to! There's already a 'X' down here, like a treasure map! See?"

Deacon unmuted his channel. "Sure, Finn. Listen, your old man's gotta go. We'll talk tonight, okay?" He was about to drop the link when he hesitated, staring at the desert plain through the glasstic floor.

Far below, two natural mesas cast crisscrossing shadows that formed a black "X" on the surface.

Matt returned from the control room, looking angry. "That wind tunnel from Beta. Looks like it pulled two storms together and is channeling them like a laser, cutting straight across our trajectory and… You okay?"

Deacon looked at him. "I need to see a sat-map of the plateau."

"A sat-map? Um, sure."

The scientist touched his wristpad, and a panel of the Barsoom's glasstic floor blossomed with a real-time satellite image of Epona's surface. A bright desert plain, slashed and pockmarked by various shadows of varying lengths and angles.

Deacon used his fingers to enlarge the map. His hands trembled.

"There," he breathed, zooming in on a surface feature fourteen miles to the northwest.

Similar to the "X" Finn pointed out, another pattern formed a familiar shape. The shadows of two mesas came together to form a flat black triangle.

A dark pyramid.

Deacon hadn't known what to make of his Jennica's final words. There were no pyramids on Epona. But the topmost point where these two equal shadows met could well be considered the "top of a pyramid." She had died only a few miles south of it.

"Take us here," Deacon said, pointing.

Matt squinted. "Sorry, but I can't do that. That's directly in the wind tunnel. We'd be blown out of the sky."

"Then get us parallel to it. I'll go there on foot if I have to."

"Why?"

"*Please*, Matt!"

Matt raised his hands defensively. "Okay, if it's that important to you." He sent a change of course to the cabin via his wristpad, and the airship veered west.

Deacon began to pace again, looking down at the desert plateau, mind racing. Two black shapes glided beneath the airship.

"Son of a bitch," he muttered.

Matt blinked. "Sorry?"

"Two skyscouts are shadowing us."

Matt frowned. "Out here? No. Beta has grounded their scouts until the wind tunnel situation is rectified and—" He broke off as he saw the wingsuited pair soar by like two hornets circling.

"I think those are the ones I saw yesterday," Deacon said. "Back near Colony Point."

"Why would Beta send skyscouts to Colony Point?"

"Maybe they're not from Beta Colony."

"What?"

"How can you be *certain* they're from—"

Deacon wasn't sure what happened next. A stabbing pain went

through his skull. Finn's telecast presence fizzled, the boy's eyes wide and his mouth pantomiming the word "Dad?" before he vanished in a whirl of disintegrating pixels.

Deacon's infolink died.

The lights of the airship snapped off.

The thrum of engines ceased.

And the ship fell out of the sky.

—

Deacon awoke to a spectral face made of blue fire, semi-translucent and bodiless, hovering in the dark like a mask or a ghost.

The deadship! he thought.

Dimly, he became aware of other details of his surroundings—a gloomy cave converted into a makeshift garage, supply crates stacked against one wall, three buggies of unfamiliar design, and some equipment, including three metallic crabs suspiciously similar to the ones Deacon worked with.

Deacon's head ached, and there were bits of beige foam clinging to him. *Crash-foam*, he realized.

He tried to stand, but found his hands were cuffed to the large metal pipe behind him. Matt, also spattered with crash-foam, lay unconscious beside him, hands similarly cuffed.

"Hey Matt?" Deacon whispered, nudging with his boot. "Are you okay?"

The blue face studied him, the subtle grid-lines betraying it as a hologram.

"You are Deacon Townsend," it spoke, the voice as non-specific as its sleek, glacial-hued avatar. "Resident of Colony Point. Scout First Class."

Deacon gazed into the avatar's hollow eyes. "You've got my name and residence right, sure. But I'm an engineer."

Matt gave a low groan and began to stir. At this, the face regarded him and said, "You are Dr. Matthew Kapadia. Resident of Delta Plains. Scientist and advisor—"

"Who are *you?*" Deacon demanded.

The luminous hologram glared. "Why did you attack us? How did you find us?"

"We didn't attack you."

"You fired on the outpost."

"I don't know what you're talking about."

After several seconds, the hologram spoke again. "He is speaking the truth."

"The hell he is!" someone said from the shadows.

Deacon started as two wingsuited figures rounded one of the buggies. Jack and Jill. They had discarded their masks, and he considered their faces by the glowing holography.

"Jack" was a sandy-haired, bearded man of average height and build. "Jill" was blonde and pale, lean and sinewy. Deacon caught a glimpse of their shirt collars peeking up from the wingsuits: identical loam-green uniforms with a tiny insignia on the neckline.

A dark pyramid.

"Colony Six, I presume," Deacon said.

Deacon checked his own anger when he saw their expressions.

They weren't exuding mere anger. Their eyes burned with murderous wrath, a hatred so incendiary it could melt lead.

But they don't even know me! he thought helplessly. *How can anyone be so hateful towards someone they don't even know?*

"So you aren't from Beta Colony," he managed. "You stole their wingsuits."

Matt sat up, handcuffs jingling. A strange expression washed over his face. "You arrived fourteen months ago, didn't you?"

"We're not telling you shit," Jill said.

"And just how in the hell do you know that, Matthew?" Deacon demanded.

"I didn't know. I suspected."

"*Suspected* that a ship arrived here in secret? Are you fucking *kidding* me?"

Matt swallowed. "Our com-array is always pointed toward Earth for receiving and transmitting. A few years ago, we detected… something else. Hard gamma bursts in the visible infrared spectrum. That could owe to any number of things. *One* of those things could be the annihilation energy of antimatter propulsion from—"

"From a ship on approach!" Deacon finished for him. "And you didn't *say* anything!"

"The bursts were so intermittent, we couldn't be certain of anything. We continued monitoring, projected a theoretical arrival time, and waited, but no ship arrived. No communications detected. And we never detected an entry-bloom, so we dismissed the idea."

The blonde woman's eyes glinted in the holography's light. "We landed on the nightside, genius, and rounded to the bright, where we set up our outpost—the outpost your people destroyed this morning."

Matt blinked. "I don't know anything about an outpost."

The blue face said, "He is telling the truth."

"Bullshit!" Jack hissed. "They knew we were here. They killed Jacob three months ago, so they knew. Let's hit them while we can! We'll never get another chance!"

Deacon felt a chill. "You said someone died three months ago? Where? How?"

The woman's jaw muscles clenched. "He got caught in one of this planet's goddamn storms during a recon run, but he was able to send us a message—to warn us that you were coming after him."

"Me?"

"Yes, you!" The woman turned to her companion. "Let's head back to base. There might be survivors, maybe salvageable equipment." She hesitated, glanced back to Deacon. "Your people are going to pay, Townsend, and so will you." She turned and made her way to one of the vehicles. Jack followed.

Deacon called after her. "And what exactly is my crime?"

"Murdering my son," Jill snapped. She and her companion hopped into the vehicle. In seconds, they were gone. The hologram dissolved in their absence. Deacon was too stunned to move.

Matt turned to him. "If they have more antimatter drones, they can cripple the colonies! They could blow up pipelines, knock out our power. They're terrorists!"

"They're not terrorists," Deacon muttered. "They're frightened and misinformed."

"About what?"

"I don't know, but I'm going after them."

"Sure, sure," Matt said. "Except we're handcuffed and weaponless. And we have no idea where we are or where they're going."

"They must have built their outpost in the mesa, at the top of the dark pyramid. Those two lost contact with their outpost. It must have happened so suddenly that they assumed it was an attack, when it was actually—"

Matt made the connection. "The wind tunnel! It didn't exist when they set up their outpost. The plateau would have been a tranquil spot at the time."

"Exactly. Beta Colony's mountain transformed the plains into a firing range. You said a glass storm blew through this morning—it would have hit like a battering ram."

Matt paled. "A glass storm like that—it can shellac a mesa. It would bake those people to death in their own heat."

"You tell the council what's happening. I'm going after them."

"Oh really? How?"

"I'll take one of the buggies."

"And then what? Chase after them? Make peace with a bunch of lunatics?"

"That's the plan."

Matt gave an exasperated sigh. "And how are we getting out of these handcuffs, my friend?"

"That's the easy part, my friend," Deacon said. With a touch of his wristpad, he transmitted the activation code to the metal crabs against the wall. They unfolded and lumbered forward, claws outstretched for cutting.

—

The storm blowing across Mendes Plains looked more like a mudslide than anything born from atmospheric systems. As Deacon floored the buggy's accelerator, he glanced sidelong to the churning tempest of clouds, sand, and ice that rolled and thundered its way towards his destination.

The mesas soon came into view, like a pair of islands besieged by a typhoon. The other buggy looked like a child's toy parked on the storm's periphery. Jack and Jill had exited their vehicle and were staring at the apocalyptic sight.

The storm impacted the mesas with relentless fury, packing sediment and glass particulate around them, making them thicker. In the sky just outside the tempest's reach, a small, circular shape—another drone—circled overhead.

As Deacon closed to within a hundred meters of them, Jack and Jill whirled around and saw him. Jack extended his hand. For a moment, Deacon thought he might be waving to him. Then he saw the overhead drone swoop down to attack like a trained falcon.

Shit.

Deacon opened the door and threw himself out of the moving vehicle. The drone hit it like a clay skeet, and the explosion temporarily drowned out the rolling storm.

"Your people have been buried alive!" Deacon shouted, clambering to his feet and approaching the couple. "And you're trying to kill *me?*"

Jack drew a pistol from his wingsuit's pocket.

Deacon strode towards Jill, halted a few meters away. "Tell me what happened to your son three months ago."

"I'll let him tell you." She touched the wristpad on her arm.

"…broke my leg," a young man's voice said through static. "Trying to get back. I can see the storm… so scared, Mom! I don't want to die out here. There's an enemy scout… name is Townsend… knows… saw me crash…. coming for me… coming for me!"

The recording cut off.

Jill's face twisted. "My son was *hurt* and you hunted him down. You hunted him down, and you killed him."

"Three months ago," Deacon said slowly, "my wife died out here. Not far from where we're standing now. She also got caught in a storm… Her final transmission—she was trying to tell us that she had found something."

"She was pursuing my son!"

"To help him!" Deacon held out his hands. "Don't you get it? You came from Earth and brought the worst of it with you! You saw that people were already on Epona but didn't bother contacting us! You assumed we would treat you as intruders. You saw a narrow habitability zone and made a snap judgment about the situation here."

"My son—"

"Was in the process of being rescued. My wife—First Scout Jennica Townsend—wasn't an enemy hunting your boy. She was trying to reach him… to save him from the storm. That was why she veered off the beacon path."

The woman hesitated. "There's another war back home. When we detected your colonies spread along the valley, when we found the ship full of corpses in orbit, we thought…"

"That we were selfish, belligerent enclaves? That we'd sabotage a ship and kill thousands of people to hoard the land for ourselves? We aren't Earth! We're not trying to be Earth. This is a new world and we're building a new culture."

"This isn't Earth," Jill said, "but you're still human, no matter what planet you're on. What happened to that ship?"

"During planetfall, our colony fleet was in close communication, working together to coordinate the best places to land. The *Legacy I* malfunctioned. It strayed into the brightside. That's a hazardous place to navigate, especially for a ship so big."

"Because of the debris," Jill said.

Deacon nodded. "They incurred damage, including the life support systems. Killed everyone aboard in minutes." He shook his head. "People lost family, friends. Every one of us loved *someone* aboard that ship. We considered retrieving the bodies, but—we're three-generations ship-born… You wouldn't understand. " Deacon exhaled heavily. "The deadship—the *Legacy I*—is a monument, a reminder, a cautionary tale. For those still mourning, it's also a comfort."

The wingsuited pair regarded each other. Jack lowered the pistol and, to Jill, said, "What do we do?"

"What do you do?" Deacon echoed in disbelief. "I've got some better questions: How much do you value human life? How much longer will you hide in the shadows? What kind of world do we want to have here?"

He caught movement out of the corner of his eye and turned to see another buggy bearing down on them, Matt behind the wheel. He pulled alongside Deacon and exited the vehicle.

"You okay Deek?"

"Yeah."

Matt appraised the buried mesas. "We can't excavate from this side. Even when the storm dies, there's significant build-up, and another storm is sure to follow."

Deacon nodded. "So, we dig from the opposite side." He looked at Jill. "If you'll let us."

"I brought some help," Matt said.

Deacon looked into the back of the buggy. "I can see that." He touched his wristpad, and three maintenance crabs dismounted from the vehicle and scuttled towards the mesa's far side. In minutes, the whine of their drills could be heard above the storm as they began tunneling.

"They might not be fast enough," Jill said.

Matt nodded. "That's not the only help we're offering."

From across the plain, a fleet of buggies, trucks, excavation teams and emergency response copters appeared like the blush of a welcome dawn.

—

It took several hours for the rescue effort to breach the mesas and pull eighty-nine strangers from the sweltering hollow. In that time, additional help arrived from every colony along the valley. The Mendes Plains transformed into a field hospital and—in a way—an inadvertent picnic ground as people mingled, shared supplies, and welcomed Epona's unexpected immigrants. The dehydrated, sweating, frightened inhabitants of Colony Six found themselves at the heart of a bustling humanitarian effort.

Deacon assisted where he could. From across the crowd, he saw Jack and Jill working with the first responders. Jill spotted him, held his gaze for a time, and gave a small nod. He nodded back.

It's a start, he thought.

Deacon's inbox was swelling with messages: Jim, Meredith, Finn, and the press corps were all anxious to reach him. Yet he hesitated as he noticed a rogue light in the sky.

The deadship. Like the glint of an ancient clock's pendulum, its position told him the time was nearing 20:00, though Deacon suspected few in the Five Colonies would be sleeping tonight. There was too much to do: strangers to bring into the fold, a past to reconcile with, a future to continue building.

But first, it was time for Deacon to have dinner with his son.

Between the lights of sunpoint and deadship, two shadows accompanied his return to the buggy.

THANK YOU

Thank you so much for reading Darkness Blooms. As an independent publishing company, we sincerely appreciate your support.

If you enjoyed the stories in this collection and want more, consider subscribing to our magazine, becoming a Patron, or shooting a donation our way. Every penny we receive goes towards compensating our writers and expanding our library of content.

If you want to help fuel The Dread Machine in other ways, tell your friends about us. Leave reviews for our stories and issues, share our links, join our community, or volunteer! We love making new friends!

Visit our website at www.thedreadmachine.com. You'll find links to subscribe, donate, and volunteer in the footer.

Thanks again!

AUTHOR BIOS

A. Katherine Black adores multicolored pens, long winters, and her overworked coffee machines. She lives in the Northwoods with her family and their cats, where she dreams up stories of creatures with bunches of legs, tentacles, and wings. Find her at flywithpigs.com.

Derrick Boden's fiction has appeared and is forthcoming in *Lightspeed*, *Clarkesworld*, *Apex Magazine*, and elsewhere. He is a writer, a software developer, an adventurer, and a graduate of the Clarion West class of 2019. He currently calls Boston his home, although he's lived in fourteen cities spanning four continents. He is owned by two cats and one iron-willed daughter. Find him at derrickboden.com and on Twitter as @derrickboden.

Timothy Burkhardt's fiction has appeared in *Metastellar*, *The Horror Tree*, and *Riddled With Arrows*. He lives in the mountains outside of Asheville, NC with his two teenage sons and his cat, Keats.

P.A. Cornell is a Chilean-Canadian author who wrote her first speculative story when she was just eight years old. A member of SFWA and graduate of the Odyssey workshop, her short fiction has appeared in multiple genre markets and anthologies. Her story, "Splits," went on to win Canada's 2022 Short Works Prize for Fiction. That same year, she published her debut novella, *Lost Cargo*. When not writing, Cornell can be found assembling intricate Lego builds or drinking ridiculous quantities of tea. Sometimes both. To find out more about the author and her work, visit her website pacornell.com.

Kitty-Lydia Dye is a writer and artist from Norfolk, UK. Her works are mainly inspired by folktales and the haunting landscape of the Broads, often finding ways of weaving different genres together—the beauty of ivy against metal. More of her work and art can be found at: https://www.tumblr.com/blog/inkspiders

https://kittylydiadye.blogspot.com/
Instagram & Twitter: @kittylydiadye

Alicia Hilton is an author, law professor, arbitrator, actor, and former FBI Special Agent. She believes in angels and demons, magic and monsters. Alicia's work has appeared in *Akashic Books, Best Indie Speculative Fiction* Volume 3, *Cemetery Gates Media, Daily Science Fiction, DreamForge, Litro, Space and Time, Vastarien, Year's Best Hardcore Horror* Volumes 4, 5 & 6, and elsewhere. She is a member of HWA and SFWA. Her website is https://www.aliciahilton.com. Follow her on Twitter @aliciahilton01.

A. P. Howell's jobs have spanned the alphabet from archivist to webmaster and she has a master's degree in history. Her short fiction has appeared here and there, including in *Underland Arcana, ParSec, Translunar Travelers Lounge, Martian, In Somnio: A Collection of Modern Gothic Horror* (Tenebrous Press), and *Bicycles & Broomsticks: Fantastical Feminist Stories about Witches on Bikes* (Elly Blue Publishing). Her work has been nominated for the Pushcart Prize and Brave New Weird Award, and honorably mentioned in Ellen Datlow's *Best Horror of the Year Volume Thirteen.* She lives with her spouse and their two awesome kids and can be found online at aphowell.com.

Andrea Kriz is a molecular biologist currently doing postdoctoral research in neurodevelopment at Harvard Medical School. Her short stories have appeared in *Clarkesworld, Lightspeed, Asimov's Science Fiction* and have been translated into French in *Galaxies SF.* Her short story collection, *Learning to Hate Yourself as a Self-Defense Mechanism,* is upcoming from Interstellar Flight Press. Find her at http://andreakriz. wordpress.com or on Twitter @theworldshesaw.

Nathaniel Lee lives in Oregon and is frequently rained upon. He puts words into various orders. Occasionally people give him money for this. Visit his website to read more at mirrorshards.com.

Gordon Linzner is founder and former editor of *Space and Time*

Magazine, and author of three published novels and dozens of short stories in *Fantasy & Science Fiction, Twilight Zone, Sherlock Holmes Mystery Magazine*, and others. He is a member of the Horror Writers Association and a lifetime member of the Science Fiction & Fantasy Writers of America

Gordon Linzner is founder and former editor of Space and Time Magazine, and author of three published novels and dozens of short stories in Fantasy & Science Fiction, Twilight Zone, Sherlock Holmes Mystery Magazine, and others. He is a member of the Horror Writers Association and a lifetime member of the Science Fiction & Fantasy Writers of America

Rodrigo Assis Mesquita is a Brazilian science fiction and fantasy writer, a chocolate-brigadeiro enthusiast, and a Clarion West (2018) and Viable Paradise (2018) graduate. His work has appeared or is forthcoming in *Story Seed Vault* and, in Portuguese, in *Revista Trasgo, Revista Mafagafo, Leitor Cabuloso*, and *Nove Amanhãs*. He can be found at www.grifonegro.com.br.

Andrew Milne lives and works in the Highlands of Scotland. A 2012 graduate from the University of Dundee with an MA in English Literature and Politics, he spends his off hours writing fiction when he's not hiking or obsessing over old, obscure movies on his Letterboxd account. A lifelong sci-fi devotee and determined to make his mark on the genre, his first novel is contracted and forthcoming.

Marshall J. Moore is an award-winning writer and martial artist who was born and raised on Kwajalein, a tiny Pacific island. He has trained a professional mercenary in unarmed combat, once sold a thousand dollars' worth of teapots to Jackie Chan, and on one occasion was tracked down by a bounty hunter for owing $300 in overdue fees to the Los Angeles Public Library. He is the the author of the *Rites of Resurrection* trilogy of high fantasy novels, as well as thirty published short stories and the forthcoming novel *Son of a Sailor: A Cozy Pirate*

Tale. He lives in Atlanta, Georgia with his wife Megan and their two cats.

Josh Rountree has published short fiction in a wide variety of magazines and anthologies, including *Beneath Ceaseless Skies*, *Realms of Fantasy*, *The Deadlands*, *Bourbon Penn*, *PseudoPod*, *Weird Horror*, and *Found: An Anthology of Found Footage Horror*. His latest short fiction collection is *Fantastic Americana* from Fairwood Press. His novel *The Legend of Charlie Fish* will be published by Tachyon Publications in July 2023. Your can get the whole scoop at his website: www.joshrountree.com.

Denise B. Tanaka has a lifelong passion for writing stories of magical beings and faraway worlds but is sometimes sidetracked by nonfiction projects. A graduate of Sonoma State University, she pays the bills by working as a paralegal in immigration law. She has dabbled in genealogy for more than 35 years and is very grateful for the internet.
http://sasorizabooks.com
amazon.com/author/denisetanaka

Rebecca E. Treasure grew up reading in the Rockies. After living many places, including the Gulf Coast & Tokyo, she began writing fiction. Rebecca's short fiction has been published by or is forthcoming from *Flame Tree*, *WordFire Press*, *Galaxy's Edge*, and others. She is an editor at *Apex Magazine* and a writing mentor. She juggles children, corgis, and writing. She only drops the children occasionally. Learn more at her website, https://rebeccaetreasure.com.

Brian Trent is the author of the acclaimed sci-fi thriller *Redspace Rising*, and his short fiction regularly appears in the New York Times-bestselling *Black Tide Rising* series, *The Magazine of Fantasy & Science Fiction*, *Analog Science Fiction and Fact*, *The Year's Best Military and Adventure SF*, *Daily Science Fiction*, *Escape Pod*, *Galaxy's Edge*, *Nature*, and numerous year's-best anthologies. A winner of the 2019 Readers' Choice Award from Baen Books and Writers of the Future, Trent lives in New England. His website and blog are at www.briantrent.com.

CONTENT WARNINGS

Boom Town
Rebecca E. Treasure
CW // gore, violent rebellion, self-sacrifice

Thaw
Josh Rountree
CW // global pandemic
TW // child death

Solar Midnight
Timothy Burkhardt
CW // self-sacrifice

Old Grief
Andrew Milne
CW // graphic descriptions of chronic pain, euthanasia
TW // child loss

The Stains of Now
A. Katherine Black
CW // gore

A New Night Parade
Gordon Linzner
TW // suicide

ABOUT US

EDITOR: ALIN WALKER

Under her fiction-focused pen name, Alin Walker (she/her) serves as The Dread Machine's overall HBIC. When she's not toiling in service of the Machine, she works as a writing coach and editorial project manager at Strikethrough Editing under her legal name, Tina Alberino. Learn more at tinaalberino.com.

EDITOR: MONICA LOUZON

Monica Louzon (she/her) is an editor, translator, and writer. Her prior editing experience includes serving as Lead Editor and project manager for the anthology *Catalysts, Explorers & Secret Keepers: Women of Science Fiction*, as well as Managing Editor for the open access, peer-reviewed academic *MOSF Journal of Science Fiction*.

COVER ARTIST: YORGOS COTRONIS

Yorgos Cotronis (he/him) is a Greek illustrator and designer, currently residing in Athens. He makes a living designing book covers and is known for his dark, atmospheric genre illustrations. You can find him on Twitter @ravenkult or on his site, www.cotronis.com